EXTRADITION

MOBSTERS + BILLIONAIRES: BOOK 1

KELLY FOX

ALSO BY KELLY FOX

SERIES

Wrecked

Guardians

Rebel Sky Ranch

Mobsters+Billionaires

Wild Heart Ranch

Orpheum Avenue

STAND-ALONE NOVELLAS

Summer Makeover

Bee Cave Magic

Texas Detour

Roots and Sky

Liar's Gambit

-

FREEBIES

https://www.authorkellyfox.com/freebies

BEFORE WE BEGIN

Story time: I was plot-bunnied hardcore by a TikTok video that mentioned the wolf study referenced in chapter one. I wasn't planning on writing a #murderswoon story, let alone an entire mobsters-with-hearts-of-gold series, but here we are.

As with all of my series, we end up with a found family. However, instead of starting off with dozens of characters, we start off with a solitary guy standing up for the right thing, something he's been trying to do his whole life.

While this is in many ways a uniquely American story, I think the theme of standing up to the wealthy and demanding equity is universal. We are more powerful than we think.

1

JOE

I UNDERSTAND that the purpose of these all-hands-on-deck meetings is to shake up our day, maybe even pump us up a little, but somebody forgot to tell the CEO that. Jesus Christ, this pompous asshole hasn't taken a breath in over thirty minutes. At this point, he just wants to hear himself talk.

"And that is why we have been successful. Each of us is willing to go above and beyond, work the fourteen-hour days, work the weekends, miss the soccer games...because what we are doing is important. I would dare say it's the most important thing you've done in your entire life."

Is he fucking serious?

"*Bullshit*," I bark out, shaking my head.

The entire ballroom, over a thousand people, goes silent as frozen air. I realize, belatedly, that I am the reason for the lack of oxygen in the room.

Ah, jeez.

"Who said that?" he asks, scanning the audience.

Garza, my buddy, elbows me. "Shit, dude. I can't believe you said that. Make it better," he hisses.

I can't though. His entire speech has been a nightmare from top to bottom, and I'm sick of it. Expecting free labor just because everybody is salaried is preposterous. Fuck, even my horrible father, an actual mobster, pays people for the work they do.

I think about all the money and time I spent getting my MBA, and I want to vomit. I can't believe I worked so hard to leave mob life behind, only to end up working for another crook.

I thought the advantage of working for a millennial CEO is that he'd be more ethical. Thoughtful, even. I certainly hadn't expected him to sound like some eighties throwback, *greed-is-good* motherfucker.

I think about my student loans and...*fuck it.*

"Not gonna do that, Garza. Not gonna make it better. I can do poor. I can't do whatever the fuck this is," I whisper back.

Rand Wolfe, our illustrious CEO, puts his hands on his hips. "I'll ask again—who said that?" He looks flushed, like he's about to jump into the audience and interrogate people.

Might as well go out with a bang.

I raise my hand. "I did. Because it is, in fact, *bullshit.*"

Wolfe's eyes finally land on me, and I stuff down the nerves threatening to run riot.

Squinting at me, he asks, "How can working for a common goal over something so essential be bullshit?"

Essential, my hairy Italian ass.

"We're not feeding the hungry here. We're making expensive cross-training shoes for elite athletes. Our entry point is three hundred dollars a pair. There is nothing noble about three-hundred-dollar shoes. Certainly not something so important as to put aside family responsibilities. Certainly not so important as giving a billionaire our precious hours in exchange for shitty coffee and an early grave with no extra money to show for it."

The guy in the four-thousand-dollar suit sneers at me. "Only someone with so little vision could think of it that way. When this company does better, we all do better. And we do care. We have excellent insurance, a coffee bar on every floor, and a gym with a pool on the top floor. Proof of our commitment to our employees."

I snort. "Your insurance is shit, and you put in the coffee bars to prevent people from leaving the building for their coffee breaks. As for the gym and the pool...quick show of hands. How many of you have time to use the gym? How many of you have actually put on a pair of trunks or a swimsuit, gotten into the water, and enjoyed the goddamn pool?"

I look around at the vast conference room, and not a single hand goes up. Not surprising. I gesture to the lack of response in the room, making sure our esteemed robber-baron CEO can see the point.

"That's not proof of commitment if people are so overrun and overworked they can't use it."

Garza smacks me. "Shut. Up."

Yeah, not gonna happen.

Wolfe stands to his full height as though being marginally taller than most people is some grand achievement. "Only small minds think of limitations. Great minds, the alpha wolves of the pack, think beyond their limitations."

Jesus, Mary, and Joseph, not this shit again.

Swear to the Holy Mother, this man cannot get over the fact that his last name is Wolfe. He's made it an entire personality. He loves talking about the alpha-wolf mentality, how everyone who's ever succeeded displays the same raw virility.

I read his book on the subject and eye-rolled my way through the entire thing. *This is what happens when you don't have enough people willing to say no to your face.*

My Psych 101 professor would've had a field day with the fake-posturing-parading-as-masculinity in those pages. Hell, I should just mulch the fucking thing—at least then the book could do something useful, like grow a garden.

"You know that concept is bullshit too, right?" I ask, standing up. "That there is *no such thing* as an alpha wolf, just like there is *no such thing* as an ethical billionaire."

The way he's grinning, I can tell he thinks he's got one over on me.

"You could not be more wrong," he says, smug as shit. "There was a scientific study done, and the wolves who got it done, the ones who led the pack, were the alpha wolves. But maybe you're just content to be a lonely little beta. And by the way, I lead the industry in manufacturing ethics, and I've shut down factories with problematic practices."

I snort, shaking my head. Motherfucker. This is why all those fucking night classes were worth it. This moment right here.

"That study you're misquoting is from the *seventies*. Are you aware that the original scientist later recanted the study?"

"What are you talking about?" Wolfe walks to the edge of the stage, shielding his eyes. "Stand in the middle so I can see you."

I comply, if only because it'll make my exit easier. I make my way out to the aisle, excusing myself past the twenty people, and face him.

He's my age and looks like the gods themselves bestowed leadership upon him as a birthright. He's refined: a sharp dresser with a full head of wheat-colored hair and cheekbones sharp enough to slice through the opinions of those less than him.

Meanwhile, I'm wearing a wrinkled button-down that I borrowed from the guy I fucked last night.

I go in before he can open his trap again. "Much to the chagrin of you and the online neckbeards spouting this shit from their mother's basement, the scientist recanted that study. Turns out, he was studying wolves in captivity. Wolves in captivity take on alpha and beta roles because the resources are restricted to nearly nothing, and they have to fight for every scrap. You might be on to something, actually. Because it sounds exactly like working for a company owned by a multi-mega-billionaire who can somehow only afford to pay entry-level wages."

Looking like he swallowed something sour, Wolfe starts pacing the stage. "I own the company. That's how it works. I pay you a salary, and you do the work. I get an average of four hours of sleep a night. I bet you can't even function with less than eight."

"Well, you've got me there. I guess that means you're better than me. But back to the bad science you keep going on about. When that man looked at those wolves in the wild, when he saw how wolf packs actually work? He retracted everything he had to say. You know why? Because wolves in the wild don't have to compete for scraps. The pack is structured around a family dynamic, and the hierarchy you talk about doesn't exist."

"Well, guess what? In the business world, it does exist, and it works just fine."

He's so fucking right and so fucking wrong at the same time that it makes me want to scream. I wish I'd known what a racket this corporate life would be before I started college. *I should have gone into plumbing. Those motherfuckers make a killing.*

The fact of the matter is, I'm about to get escorted out of the building. I'll be blackballed in Manhattan, if not the entire state, and tonight, I'll be calling my father, begging for a job back on the docks. At least until I can figure out what to do next.

But that's tonight's problem.

"The only reason it works in business is because we are, by definition, in captivity. Look at all of us in this room sitting so quietly and paying rapt attention to you as you spew the same bullshit."

"Bullshit, huh? As you pointed out, I'm a billionaire. Who the hell are you?" he asks, puffing his chest out.

"Who am I? Motherfucker, you don't wanna know who I am, but I'll tell you this: if you think that you escaped captivity because you're the top dog, you could not be more wrong. If I'm in captivity, you're in captivity with me. The only thing that alpha bullshit ever got you was a prettier cage."

He opens his mouth to say something, then closes it. He blinks a few times then points at the door. "I don't suppose I need to tell you what your next steps will be."

"Go ahead. Because it's the last fucking order you'll ever give me."

Turning on my heel, I walk out the door, middle finger as high as it'll go. I'm joined by two security guys who walk me to my desk and stand guard as I gather my few sad things and my one dying plant.

One of the guys leans in just as he's about to airlock me. "Sorry that you lost your job, man, but thank you for saying what needed to be said. We ain't cogs in a machine. We're people. We're his human resource, and he keeps forgetting the *human* part."

I give him a quiet fist-bump and make my way to the street. This next part is going to suck salty balls, but lesson fucking learned. At least I'll never have to deal with that asshole again.

2

RAND

I NORMALLY TRY to greet the day with some level of
enthusiasm. Is it manufactured? Occasionally. But I firmly believe
that how you wake up determines how your day will go, and I have
always determined that I'll greet the day with aggressive positivity.

I'm not too proud to say that I am struggling with that this
morning.

Actually, that's a lie. I'm entirely too proud to say it to anyone
but myself. And there's no denying yesterday was a blow. It stirred
up an old set of insecurities I've never quite been able to erase. I
often feel like a poser, like a little boy trying to clomp around in his
father's ill-fitting Oxfords.

It was as if that guy in the rumpled shirt held an interrogation
lamp to my inadequacies, and I couldn't escape it. Unable to shake
his words, I looked up the history of that wolf study last night, and
the guy—Joe Something—is right.

Free wolves don't need to establish dominance. And a pack is
usually just the parents and their pups. A family, just like he said.

He also said something about *neckbeards*, which is a phrase

I've never heard before. When I looked up the meaning, it was exactly what it sounded like and somehow so much worse.

Things did not improve when I combined a search of neck-beards and alphas. I fell down a Reddit rabbit hole that took me far too long to crawl out of. What I found was a bunch of cringe-worthy, gun-flashing men spouting the vilest misogynistic filth about what it means to be an *alpha man* in one's life.

This Joe person was the first in my life to ever note the shared-word association, and I shudder to have any connection to those men. I don't even own camo.

A few hours into it, I was swamped with an uncomfortable moment of recognition. These men and I cling to the alpha mindset because we're fighting against the same deep feelings of disconnection and powerlessness, despite belonging to the most powerful demographic of modern society.

But I wasn't ready for that level of self-awareness, so I kept scrolling.

After making a sizable donation to a women's shelter, I still couldn't sleep, so I started thinking of ways to pivot from the alpha language into something more freedom-related. Unfortunately, *that* Google search led back to the same Reddit articles, and...yeah, no.

I tried brainstorming after that. Maybe there could be some-thing in the wild wolf. The untamed wolf? I didn't get very far before finally passing out in a frustrated heap.

Things only got worse once I was unconscious. Despite his unkempt appearance, Joe is a rough, sexy sort of handsome. Not that I could make out the details from a distance, but his carnality translated across the room. It was in the way he held himself—he's a man who knows his own mind.

While this sort of thing can never be public knowledge, he's exactly my type.

How that leads to me pulling up his employee file is a leap of logic I'd rather not examine too closely. Joseph Portelli, resident of Brooklyn, recent MBA graduate, second in his class. His employee ID picture is frustratingly fuzzy, and a quick check of his social media reveals a mostly desolate wasteland and no photos. Not even a damn gym selfie.

Things get a lot more interesting on Twitter. In addition to dozens of business and self-help gurus, he follows several gay content creators, many of the OnlyFans variety. I close my laptop and set it aside because that little revelation is not helpful. At all.

I pull up the phone app three minutes later, proud of myself for holding out that long. Clicking through the accounts he follows, it's clear his tastes run diverse, and he's not opposed to tall and slender. Or kink, for that matter.

Not that his tastes are of any consequence to me. Though as I think about the animated man prowling the aisle, I can't honestly say I've ever felt as deeply about anything in my life. I bet he's just as passionate in bed. I bet he likes to take charge.

I bet he's good at it.

Anyway. I've got well-paid men on the side for that sort of thing. Even though I was not thinking about *them* when I ejaculated into a handful of tissues at three-thirty in the morning.

While gripping my throat...pretending it was his hand.

I wonder if he smells like sandalwood or pine needles or just good soap.

On the plus side, the shameful—and eye-rollingly intense— orgasm finally allowed me to fall asleep.

Since starting the day on a positive note just isn't in the cards, I check my phone. It's four forty-five a.m., time to run. After getting dressed, I walk into my workout room, with its view of Central Park and the shades of sunrise just starting to color the morning sky. I sigh as I hit the start button on the treadmill and begin jogging, missing the feel of humidity on my skin.

I used to run through the park in the mornings, but then Wolfe

Athletics went global. Being one of the youngest billionaires on the planet comes with a level of notoriety, and I refused to be that jackass jogging with his security detail.

Stuck as I am in the fishbowl, I use visualization to keep me motivated. I normally like to imagine being a wolf on the hunt as I get my six miles in, but that's not particularly useful this morning. Maybe I'm more gazelle-like: elegant, above it all.

I Google gazelles through the first mile, and the only photographs I find feature lions dining on the ones they just mauled to death.

So, perhaps not a gazelle.

I run a few more miles, but my focus is shot to hell and the visualizations range from desperately sexual to violently bloody. Frustrated, I punch the stop button with a little more force than is absolutely necessary.

Maybe I'll try quiet meditation this morning. Maybe not. It lasts all of three minutes before my phone goes off. I check the lock screen and let out a heavy breath.

"Good morning, Father. How are you?"

"Get to the office."

My father is never one for preamble, so this morning's attitude is par for the course. Doesn't mean I don't wish it was different.

"What's going on?" I ask, hoping there's a fire to put out. It'll take my mind off things.

"Have you not seen the news?"

"I don't pull up the news until after my morning run. Was there another...incident? With the new tower?"

Everyone over the age of twenty-five has a story about what they did on 9/11. I'll admit to brief anxiety every time there's a breaking news bulletin.

"What? No. Your exchange with that employee went viral."

I pull back, staring at my phone as if it's lying to me.

"Rand? Answer me."

My father likes to state things without questions then demand answers.

"How? Phones aren't allowed in those meetings."

"There are *always* phones in those meetings. I've called an emergency meeting of the board, and anyone who's in town will be coming in. We need to discuss what the stocks did overnight."

His words send a shiver down my spine. I've seen and prevented too many reversals of fortune because I understand exactly how quickly things can turn around. I pull up my browser to check the local online papers.

Oh.

The headlines immediately create tension in my neck and shoulders.

Billionaire Goliath Taken Down by David in a Rumpled Shirt

Wrinkled Shirt Guy Takes Down Alpha Wolfe

You're Just in a Prettier Cage: Working Class Stiff Annihilates Billionaire Randolph Wolfe, Jr.

"I'll be there in fifteen minutes."

I call my security detail because people take the whole *eat the rich* thing far too seriously for my comfort.

Stripping out of my sweaty workout clothes, I rinse off and thank the gods of engineering for whoever invented multiple showerheads. I take a second to dry myself as I put on the suit Grayson laid out for me the night before.

My phone pings again, and this time it's Mads.

Mads: *Smooth move, Ex-Lax.*

Rand: *Did I wake up in a bad 80s movie?*

Mads: *Funny you should ask.*

Mads: *Did you know that you can be a billionaire without being a dickhead?*

Mads: *Look*

He sends me a selfie of him drinking coffee with a serious case of bedhead, and I have to laugh.

Rand: According to Wrinkled Shirt Guy, there is no such thing as an ethical billionaire, so don't get up on your high horse.

Mads: Horses? How agrarian of you. I prefer to judge from my Maybach.

I send him the middle finger emoji.

Mads: Oh, did the sexy man with a probably valid point hurt your feelings?

Rand: Shut up.

Rand: Also, pretty sure a best friend would have my back.

Mads: Pretty sure a best friend would tell his boy when he's got shit on his overpriced trainers.

Mads sends over both the poop and the shoe emoji, and I feel dread for the first time. Like maybe I really stepped in it.

Rand: Do you know what a neckbeard is?

Mads: Bet you're wishing you'd taken my advice about cutting out your father's alpha bullshit.

Rand: You may have been right about that.

Mads: Drinks after?

Rand: Pretty sure this is about to be my entire life for the next few days. Let's chat next week.

Mads: You got it.

Mads, Dr. Madhuban Laghari, is CEO of Tracker Technologies, the world's leading manufacturer of personal GPS devices. Last year we partnered with him on our Wolfe+ cross-trainers, which track distance, speed, stride, and about fifteen other things, all of which get sent to the Wolfe+ app after a workout.

Elite athletes started praising the combination of high-performance shoes and athletic technology, and the shoes began selling out across the globe. More importantly, to me at least, Mads and I hit it off. He jokes about being my best friend, but the sad truth is that he kind of is.

We sign off with our signature fist-bump emoji because we're actually eleven years old, and I prepare to face my father. This day is going to *suck*.

I make my way through my penthouse, and Edgerton, my very stern head of security, is waiting for me in the foyer by my private elevator. He's a no-nonsense ex-military machine made entirely of scowls and sharp angles. Even his suit is tailored to within an inch of its life. His striking cerulean eyes make him appear approachable, but Mother Nature was lying when she gave him that feature.

When you get close enough, he reads dangerous in that way women and men seem drawn to as much as they are intimidated by. I'm not attracted to him, at least not sexually, but he fascinates me.

He's what people think of when they talk about an alpha male. It's frustratingly effortless for him. The billions of dollars in my various investment accounts across the globe lock in my status, of course. But Edgerton could be homeless, and he'd still have that edge of steel.

As my father would say, born or bought, the result is the same.

Aside from the inconvenient fact that yesterday turned all of that on its head. Anyway, his presence here instead of James, my usual guy, means the threat factor is off the charts.

Great.

"Sir, a little early this morning."

I puff my chest, which feels entirely fraudulent given the circumstances. "Didn't you hear, Edgerton? The sky is falling. We'll be walking. Outside. And before you say anything, yes, I understand the increased risk, but needs must."

"I'm sorry, Mr. Wolfe. Not today."

I roll my eyes because Edgerton says it gives him angina when I walk the whole city block to the office, but this isn't weather-related.

"Dare I ask?"

He removes his phone from his pocket and pulls up the video feed from the building's exterior. There's a group of protestors and reporters right at the entrance, harassing everyone leaving and entering the building.

God, what I wouldn't give for a little fresh air. "Fine, Edgerton. Let's just get going."

"Of course, sir."

He accompanies me on the elevator, pulling out his phone to send a quick text. By the time we hit the basement, we're greeted by two additional members of security provided by the building.

When we had these buildings built, we added a private passageway between the two. With as much as I've been using it these days, I suppose it makes sense, but it feels like walking through a tomb, a macabre parade of suits leading the way.

On the positive side, we reach the offices less than five minutes later, and Edgerton dismisses the two additional security guys as we head up the elevator. I glance over, curious about Edgerton's take on the matter or if he's even aware of what the stock market is doing.

I wouldn't want to play poker with him.

When we arrive at the executive suite, Edgerton insists on doing a sweep of the area first. That feels excessive, but everything about this feels overblown and excessive.

Satisfied that there aren't any bogeys waiting for me under my desk, he accompanies me through the luxe executive lobby into my big corner office. I'm told it's twice the size of the average Manhattan apartment. A fact that used to make me feel proud. Now it makes me wonder about the people who live in apartments half the size of my office.

Sherry, my executive assistant, is waiting for me in the over-abundant space. She looks nervous, which is as unusual as it is worrisome. I hired her because she's a near-retirement battle-ax who cannot be intimidated by me. And yes, I may be an egomaniac, well aware of my strengths, but I do need someone to say no to me every once in a while.

The fact that she's fidgeting with a hangnail is...well, it's not *good*. Even Edgerton looks put off by her demeanor. Silently, she hands me the Times.

Front page, above the fold, is my smug, smiling face under the headline: *The Out of Touch Billionaire.*

Excellent.

"Give me your take on things."

"That one comment is going to hurt us. Badly."

"Was this corporate espionage?"

Sherry shakes her head. "I can't say that for sure, but I've worked with him on several occasions. I genuinely believe he's just an employee. A good one until yesterday."

I'm curious about the kind of work they've done together, but now is not the time. "Pull up the video. I need to see this comment that is giving me so much trouble."

I check myself in the reflection of the floor-to-ceiling windows. I look sharp, clear, good. Strong, dominating. *Just like the alpha I am.*

Yeah, right.

That I still automatically default to that position after everything I read last night makes me queasy.

Meanwhile, Sherry brings up the video, and I'm able to see the details I missed from the stage. Portelli looks slightly rumpled, yes, but that doesn't pull focus from his strong jaw and dark, Italian features. His eyes are a deep brown, set off by thick eyebrows and an enviable fringe of black lashes. His hair and beard are unkempt but rich against his pretty tan skin.

I curse under my breath. I'm describing him like he's some kind of luxury vehicle when there is *nothing* luxurious about him. He's all rough edges and provocative art. Goddammit, he's *gay*. If he was sexy enough to spark last night's solo efforts in the abstract, seeing him in high definition only adds rocket fuel to my humiliating, wayward desires.

Swallowing thickly, I return my focus to the screen.

"You've worked with him before?"

Sherry nods and flicks her fingers across the screen to pause the video and zoom in on him. "What is he *wearing*?"

"Is that not his usual style?"

Shaking her head, she purses her lip. "For one, his clothes usually fit. And I've *never* seen him come to work looking less than put together. Those don't look like his clothes at all."

Edgerton tilts his head, scratching his chin. "They might not be. His social media is a bit thin on the ground, but what he has indicates he's gay and single. Maybe he hooked up the night before and borrowed his lover's clothes."

Edgerton, it seems, did some of the same reconnaissance I did last night. Only, this is his job, and I was just being a creeper. Examining the frozen image, this is exactly the kind of unkempt look one might achieve after fucking someone and maybe borrowing their clothes. I ignore the heat building low in my belly.

Sherry zooms back out, and we watch the rest of the video together. He's careful as he makes his way to the aisle, but when he starts to talk, passion blazes across his face, the tendons and muscles in his forearms flexing as his hands become fists.

He looks like American determination. I could capture that square jaw of his in a marketing piece and sell a million more cross-trainers.

By this point in our interaction, he has to know his job is forfeit, but that's when he starts talking about the wolves. How they act when they are in captivity versus when they are free. His brightness, visible down to his soul, shines out of his warm brown eyes when he talks about the cage we all live in.

I grip the phone, an uncomfortable sensation rippling from the top of my head down to my shoulders, tightening the muscles. More queasiness in my guts.

The only thing that alpha bullshit ever got you was a prettier cage.

Sherry looks up at me when he delivers the line, and Edgerton shakes his head. It was a direct hit. No, scratch that. It was a complete *evisceration*.

Worse, it's the truth.

I can see it on my face as I gawp like a big-mouth bass, casting about for an answer. That line was a perfectly thrown rock, right in the middle of my forehead.

I push the spiraling thoughts aside and go into fix-it mode. "What's your estimate of the damage?"

The grim set of Sherry's jaw is not encouraging in the slightest. "It's a study you've quoted several times. Written a book on. Built your whole personality around. The damage will be significant unless you course-correct hard. Immediately."

To her credit, she doesn't remind me she's also warned me to step back from that language on more than one occasion.

I hand her phone back, shaking my head. "It'll be old news by the end of the week. Just ignore it."

I know as I say it that I'm lying. This has teeth.

"Sir, not to disagree with you—because that is always an unpleasant prospect—but this will not blow over. You need to read the comments."

I remind myself that I hired her to provide counter-arguments. I hate a blind spot, and her job is to illuminate me. I suppose I could ignore her again, but something tells me this is one of those moments where she pays for herself a hundredfold.

Don't take it out on the messenger.

"Fine," I say, gesturing for her to hand me back the phone.

I scroll down to the comments, see that the first several

commenters are making fun of his less-than-stellar attire, and grin to myself. Never mind. This man has no teeth.

"Those comments are from our people. They were ultimately ineffective, even though they got there first. Keep scrolling," she says, touching her finger to the screen and moving it up. At this point, I realize it's not even five-thirty in the morning, less than eight hours since this one video was posted, and there are more than ten thousand comments. And this isn't the only copy of the video out there.

Finally, someone speaks truth to power.

Did you see how he went all shocked emoji at the end there? He knows that the man is telling the truth. He's no alpha. He's just a caged beast.

That man is a multibillionaire, and he has people in this Manhattan economy eking out a living? Eat the rich.

Eat the rich.

He sure looks tasty.

The only language these entitled bastards listen to is that of money. Don't buy those damn shoes.

An auditorium full of lemmings and one man in a wrinkled shirt said the truth. These billionaires get so much of our time and attention already. They don't get the rest of us. They don't get our time with our family. They don't get our weekends. No more.

No more.

No more.

Sherry looks over my shoulder, pointing to the *No More* comments. "Now there's a Facebook group called *No More*. It already has over three thousand members, and that number keeps jumping every minute."

"It's five-twenty in the morning. Eastern."

"You know...they *do* get the internet outside of the United States, Mr. Wolfe. It's mid-morning in London." Sherry's snark is somewhat blunted by the way she's wringing her hands, which makes my stomach drop even farther. "But we're in for a bad time when the rest of the country wakes up."

I scan the empty office space around us and set aside the mantle of CEO for just a few seconds. "Quick, before the rest of the billionaires get here, give me your opinion. Do you really think what he said was right? About this level of wealth being unethical?"

She snorts, shaking her head, her expression a combination of frustrated and amused. "Oh, honey, you don't need my opinion on any of that."

I stare her down.

"Fine. But you asked for it."

I lower my chin. "That I did."

Letting out a big breath, she squares up in front of me. "I believe he's right. There is no such thing as an ethical billionaire."

"How can you say that? You've seen our benefits. Our retirement program."

"There are maybe a handful of billionaires without the words 'slave labor' and 'slave wages' attached to them."

"I stopped doing business with those factories."

"And yet our night janitors make less than fifteen dollars an hour."

"That's double the national minimum wage."

"Yes. And two whole dollars above the Manhattan minimum wage."

"I mean, in the boroughs..."

She blinks at me. "Do you really think that's a livable wage?"

"It's janitorial work!"

Blink. Blink. "If you don't think it's important, try going a week without those folks doing their job. Go ahead."

My jaw drops.

"I said what I said." She makes her way to the door of my office, then stops.

"Yes?"

Still facing the door, her shoulders droop.

"What, Sherry? Out with it."

Slowly, she turns to look at me, disappointment in her sharp gaze. "Do you know why I've tried to walk you back from that alpha language?"

"No."

"Because it's an ill-fitting coat that you keep trying to wear. Put it to you this way—the man on stage in that video sounds *nothing* like the man I work with day in and day out."

Her words hit me square in the solar plexus, but I can't even process it because my office is starting to fill with the apparently unethical executives. As she quietly slips out, unease settles over me.

Edgerton, angling for the door, sends a quick salute my way. "I'll be with your building security much of this morning and must insist you take your lunch here today. I suggest you cut your office hours short, perhaps work from home this afternoon."

"This will take up most of my day, but I'll try to leave by four o'clock."

Edgerton re-squares his jaw and gives me a disapproving nod before turning on his heel to find and intimidate the building's head of security. Glad I'm not that guy.

Dan, our CFO, walks in and takes a seat. "Dan, buddy. What's the good news?"

"There is no good news," he says in his typical Bronx style. He's left over from the old guard, one of the few of my father's men who is willing to move forward with the times.

"What are we talking about?" I say, locking in.

"Our stocks are going to take a hit. A big one. Survivable if we can stop the bleeding now. Your grandchildren's grandchildren will still be living in yachts off the Amalfi coast, but our investors will not be happy."

"This one video is doing that much damage?"

"You haven't heard?"

Gripping the edge of the conference table, I ask, "What haven't I heard?"

"The deal with Weston Eanes is off."

Weston Eanes, the wildly popular forward of the Manchester United Football Club, is a huge cash cow for us and one of my favorite soccer players of all time. And he no longer wants to do business with us.

"He was supposed to sign this morning. We added the inclusive language he wanted. We even worked with distributors to ensure that shoe stores carried all of his styles in the men's and women's departments."

Dan shakes his head and becomes the second of my employees to shove their phone into my hands. He opens Instagram and navigates to Weston's page.

It's a picture of Weston looking straight at the camera, his expression solemn. The post reads: *It is with a heavy heart that I move away from Wolfe Athletics. It's important that the people I work with share my ideals: morally, ethically, financially. These avenues are not exclusive of each other but work well in advancing the betterment of people while making a profit. I refuse to work with people who are stuck in an old way of thinking, one that only serves to benefit themselves.*

Well, shit.

"Old way of thinking? I'm the youngest CEO of a multibillion-dollar company. I'm thirty-five, top of my class at Harvard, head of one of the most successful athletic shoe companies in the world. I've got Nike looking over their shoulders. We even agreed to stop manufacturing our shoes out of those places that had some..."

"Practices that enslaved actual human beings?" Dan says, grimacing.

I'm growing rather tired of discovering everyone's grimace face. It feels a little too close to their sex face if you ask me.

"Yeah, those."

"Then it shouldn't surprise you that one of the things people are bringing up is that while you left those industries, you did nothing for the people involved. Those indentured people you left behind have no way of paying off their debts. Or they do, but you wouldn't like the stories I'm hearing."

Not for the first time this morning, a shameful sensation burbles in my gut.

I hate emotions.

I'm going to need Grayson to book me an appointment with Brock to work out this frustration. Ignoring the heat rising in my cheeks, I refocus on Dan.

"So, what's the move? Do we buy the factory? Do we buy the people out of slavery?"

"I think a good first step is cooperating with the international investigation. We have information that will allow them to find these people."

"We cooperated with the authorities."

Dan shakes his head. "We only gave them what was legally required and not a drop more. We could've given more in the way of names and locations, but it would've made us look bad, so we withheld it."

I pinch the bridge of my nose, remembering the conversation with my father and how he casually threatened to convene the board if I couldn't prioritize the company's financial health. Getting him to cooperate with the bare minimum cost me more than I care to admit.

Jesus Christ. I'm really beginning to hate that man in the rumpled shirt. Just as I'm probably-not-seriously contemplating a hitman, Jackson from Human Resources walks up.

"Yes, Jackson. I've seen it. I know."

"Oh, you *know*. I guess that makes it all worth it then because I'll be lucky to get any sleep this week."

I open my mouth to respond, but he keeps going. "And don't worry. I know that the softball game I'll be missing tonight—my son's first softball game ever—isn't nearly as important as pulling your ass out of the situation you've created."

I recall the framed family picture on Jackson's desk, and more guilt sloshes around in my belly.

"I didn't create this situation in a bubble. Yes, I put the emphasis on forward-thinking, but a lot of this is standard. Why are people complaining about this now?"

Jackson raises his brow. "You know damn well I bring it up every time this board convenes. Other companies are starting to treat their people like humans, and those people are talking. We require college degrees for even the lowliest work, and we don't pay people for their expertise. So now we've got a well-educated group of people calling bullshit on capitalist ideologies. You should read a book every once in a while."

"I read a book a day."

"You should expand your reading past how to make money and maybe include how to work with human beings."

I'm getting censure from all areas. Fantastic.

"I take it you have a suggestion?"

"As a matter of fact, I do. But you're not going to like it," he says, shrugging as though unconcerned with how much I like any of this.

I rub my hands over my face, certain he's telling me the truth. "And?"

More board members are trickling in, so Jackson leans in. "Hire Portelli back. I'll create an HR position for him: VP of Company Culture, or something like that. Have him work with my team to create a series of highly visible events where he helps Wolfe Athletics improve our human face."

"Psychedelics, Jackson? So early in the morning?"

He raises his brows at me, and I lose my temper. "Have you lost your mind? I fired that guy for a reason. I don't question my decisions. He's not what this company is about. He's not the direction in which we are moving. The direction we are moving in is dedicated staff willing to sacrifice for the higher cause."

Sherry walks in with a stack of handouts, and Jackson grabs one, tossing it down in front of me. "If our vision is a willing staff, then we've got a bigger problem."

I grab the printout, flipping through it until I see the numbers. Jesus.

Jackson points to the staffing numbers. "One hundred and fifty-seven employees have tendered their resignations."

"Why wasn't that the *first* thing out of your mouth?"

"Because I wanted to make sure you were paying attention when I said it. Almost all of them are in high-priority positions, and almost all have the same message."

"And what was that message?"

"No more."

Jesus H. Christ.

"So, what is it? Do they want more money? Fine, give them more money. We've gotta stop the bleeding." I stop, knowing my father would *never* do that. "Actually, I take it back. We'll give those one hundred and fifty-seven jobs to people who will come here and work for half the price. Just you wait."

The words feel like a lie as they're leaving my tongue.

Jackson shakes his head. "I don't think you understand the magnitude of what is going on right now. First and foremost, people are no longer willing to work for less than they deserve. There is no reason for them to stay here if they can earn more money and have a better work-life balance somewhere else. Those hundred and fifty-seven were already sharpening their résumés, and you just shoved them out the door. But now, every Wolfe employee is looking at their prospects. You've got CEOs across the city rushing to post on social media about their policies regarding work-life balance. You've got the CEO of Sport-Go playing volley-ball with his team in the park."

"It's six forty-seven in the morning. What the hell is going on?"

Sherry sidles up next to me, whispering in my ear, "You're chumming the water with your arrogance there, bud. Might wanna bring it down a notch."

"I am *so* going to fire you," I furiously whisper back as the last board members fill in the chairs around the conference table.

"You wish." Pointing to Jackson, she says, "Pay attention to what the young guns have to say, not just the moldering leftovers from your father's era. Unless you want to lose everything and become a cautionary tale."

I curse under my breath, and Sherry fixes me with another raised brow. "What is the one thing you've told everybody since the beginning?"

"Evolve or die."

"That's right. It's time to take your own medicine."

My chief operating officer, standing closer than I realize, goggles at Sherry. No one's ever heard anyone speak to me like that. *I've* never heard anyone speak to me like that.

What's worse is that I think she and Jackson might be onto something.

———

AFTER TOO MANY hours in my oppressive office, we reach an agreement. Get Portelli back and start a social media campaign to show we're serious about improving the employee experience.

There was significant pushback on the specifics of improving the employee experience, with the old guard thinking a Christmas party would solve all our ills. When we gently reminded them there's more than one faith tradition at that time of year, some of the answers proved colorful. Not to mention prejudiced.

Unable to sit on this another second, I check the traffic. Getting to Brooklyn is, as usual, a nightmare. I have Sherry arrange for a helicopter to take me to the waterfront, where, according to her, the industrious Mr. Portelli is already hard at work. No matter. I can close a deal on the docks as easily as I close one in the boardroom. The location makes no difference.

As the helicopter lifts off the roof, I pull out my phone and begin to answer the emails Sherry forwarded to me. I ignore the texts from my father and the guy I've arranged to fuck later tonight, but I wince when I see my head of security come across the screen.

Edgerton: Where are you?

Rand: Taking care of our viral problem. We're landing now.

Edgerton: Without a security detail?

Rand: I've got my pilot. He's a veteran.

Edgerton: With all due respect, Desert Storm was a long time ago.

Rand: You may yell at me when I return. I'm just going to throw an obscene amount of money at Portelli and bring him back to the office so we can put this to bed.

Edgerton: Just...don't be yourself.

Rand: I beg your pardon.

Edgerton: I'm talking about Portelli's family. Don't piss anybody off.

Rand: Fine.

3

JOE

AS THE BASTARD son of Salvatore Portelli Sr., I knew that calling to ask for my old job back would leave me open to all manner of insults. But when he simply grunted, told me to call "his real son," and then hung up on me...not gonna lie, it fucking hurt.

I suppose I should be grateful that Sal Jr.—Sally to those of us who grew up with him—lost a couple of guys from his crew and was more than willing to give me the asscrack of dawn shift. I'd complain about the early hour, but given the state of my finances, I don't have much in the way of options. The sad truth is I'll make more doing the illegal shit than I did with a job that required an MBA.

The Portelli crime family is a lesser-known family in the boroughs, which makes them more dangerous, not less. My father's been running it since a dispute between the Portellis and the Stefano crew in Manhattan led to the deaths of both bosses.

He was twenty-one at the time and became ruthless in ways that squashed most territorial disputes or notions of disloyalty. Most families have a scorched earth, kill-every-relative policy when it comes to those things, but my father always reasoned that adult caskets only send a one-time message, whereas a single child-size casket will keep two to three generations of soldiers in line.

He's never killed extravagantly, only with breathtaking brutality.

The more powerful Stefanos, seeing the score, agreed to a truce between families. My father stays out of Manhattan, and nobody messes with him in Brooklyn.

Where my father is measured in his cruelty, my half-brother is impulsive. His penchant for producing bodies is what got him knocked down to the docks in the first place.

Sally isn't complaining though. Working the docks isn't sexy, but it is lucrative, and it keeps him in our father's good graces. He's hoping to make don after our father retires, but I just don't see it.

Anyway, a few texts and the remainder of my dignity later, and here I am, driving a forklift. It's not that I mind good honest work, but that's not what this is. And it feels like I spent all those years slogging through late-night studying and the smirking side glances of people from the neighborhood to end up right back where I started.

I've always been scrappy, what with growing up out and proud on the outer edges of a Mafia family, taking no shade and giving no fucks about anyone's opinion. Still, this morning's soft dew settles over every inch of exposed skin and feels a little too much like humiliation.

I spend the morning unloading boxes and pallets from a ship, then transferring them to shipping containers. And if I'm asked to put certain packages in very specific shipping containers, it's none of my business what's in those packages.

Fuck, I hate this. Even more when I spy Sally making his way toward me, a superior smirk on his stupid face. Almost made it a whole shift without having to deal with his bullshit.

"Hey, Goody Two-shoes. Someone's here to see you."

I got the nickname because I hate hurting other people, another reason I'm back with the crew on the docks. They're not tasked with executions.

Doesn't mean I don't have bodies on me.

I park the forklift and straighten my clothes: a pair of worn jeans, my faded Binghamton College tank top under some coveralls, and a backward baseball cap. Sally waits at the office entrance, which sits at the front of the larger warehouse structure. He's leaning against the doorframe, his arms crossed, smirking as I walk by.

He juts his chin over at the tiny waiting area where *Rand Wolfe* sits in one of his rickety office chairs. "You got some grease on your cheek."

I quickly wipe my face and pray that Sally doesn't know who this guy is.

"What the fuck are you doing here?" I hiss, approaching my visitor.

Wolfe stands, trying to loom over me even though he's only got an inch—two, tops—on my frame. The space is small, and the move is purposeful, which irritates me to no end.

"And a good afternoon to you as well, Mr. Portelli," he says, ignoring my question. "Do you know that you are an exceptionally hard man to track?"

"I was hoping for impossible, so this is rather less than what I was going for. How the fuck did you find me?"

His eyes widen in alarm. I assume people don't talk to him like this very often. Weirdly, he raises his hands in an open gesture. "I had my assistant—"

"Sherry."

"Yes. Um, Sherry." He pauses, shaking his head as he stitches his brows together. "I had her pull your records."

His confused look amuses me. He shakes his head again and asks, "How *did* you come to know Sherry?"

"What, like she's a secret?"

"No. She mentioned something this morning about working with you, but she rarely interacts with...individual contributors."

"Peons, you mean."

"No. Just...she works almost exclusively in the executive environment."

"Seriously, why are you here?"

The repeated question surprises him, and he fidgets with his expensive watch.

"I—" He stops and tilts his head. "I seriously can't tell if you're joking with me or not. Are you not aware of the video?"

"Video? What are you talking about?"

"The viral video of our exchange."

"There's a video of that fucking meeting?"

He opens his mouth, then closes it again. Putting on what I assume is a look of pity, he asks, "Do you not own a phone or some reliable means of accessing the internet?"

Fuck this asshole. I stalk toward him, and he puts his hands up.

"I'm not casting aspersions. I just...this has been my entire day. All of Manhattan is abuzz with the video. I'm...how do you not know?"

Using both hands, I gesture in a broad circle around us. "It may help you to know that we are in Brooklyn, first of all."

"I am aware of where we are. I had to take a helicopter to get here."

The fuck is this guy on about?

"You took a helicopter?"

He sniffs, looking affronted. "Traffic was awful. The owner of the building next door is a friend, and he has a helipad."

Fucking wasteful rich-ass motherfucker.

Growling, I walk over to the lockers and grab my phone. "Been here since five-thirty. They have a no-phone policy for the forklift drivers."

I pull out my phone, wiggling it in his face. Fucking *do-you-not-have-reliable-access-to-the-internet* bullshit.

"Page Six should do the trick."

My fingers fly across the smooth glass and, sure enough, there I am, right in the middle of everything. I let out a low chuckle.

It seems that Wolfe Athletics is having a very bad day.

Well, fuck you very much, Mr. Wolfe.

As I read the article, texts from my friends come pouring in.

Cammy: *Shit, dude. Go you!*

Timothy: *J, you started a revolution.*

SamIAm: *I have an opening, but it's entry-level. Let me know.*

Cairo: *Baby, let me know if you need a good time, okay?*

Glenlivet, neat: *Dare I ask—were you in a rugby match prior to this video?*

Glenlivet, neat: *That shirt was freshly laundered and pressed when I lent it to you yesterday.*

Glenlivet, neat: *I'm here another night if you'd like anything else from my wardrobe.*

A slightly evil grin crosses my lips as I type my response. Sure, my life is in shambles, but that doesn't mean I can't line up a fuck.

"I'm glad this amuses you, Mr. Portelli, but we have a serious problem."

I pocket my phone and square up to this billion-dollar diamond-plated asshole. "No. *You* have a serious problem. I've got an ad executive who'd like me to return his wrinkled shirt before he leaves town."

"Excuse me?"

"That wasn't my shirt. Which is why it didn't fit."

"I don't..." He cuts himself off again, and I take pleasure in the fact that, for the second time in as many days, I've pushed him off balance. Especially since I'm the one in the coveralls unloading fifteen kinds of illegal cargo just so I don't lose my fucking apartment.

"The shirt is immaterial. We must find a solution. A way to work together."

I pull my chin back, smirking at his attempt to tell me what the fuck to do. Asshat.

"There is no *we*. If you think I give a shit that your stocks leapt off the top floor, then let me help you: I don't care. I hope your company goes under. I hope you end up impoverished with no health insurance."

"This could mean hundreds of jobs."

Second shift guys start filtering in, going to their lockers, staring between Wolfe and me.

"Yo, Joe-ee, slummin' wit' us again?"

"Hey, Mikey. You know it, right? Fuckin' corporate America," I say, dropping back into my Brooklyn.

Wolfe's posture shifts as more guys pile in. "So, this is your actual speech? I'm surprised you managed to put together a coherent argument yesterday."

"Look, dick stain," I say, hoping to get this fucking liability out of this fucking warehouse, "I already told you to fuck off."

He startles, his intense eyes narrowing. "I apologize for interrupting your very important pallet loading. Perhaps I should keep my lucrative offer to myself and see my way out."

Thank fucking Christ.

Mikey's heart's in the right place when he answers for me, "Hey, Joe, this asshole giving you a hard time? He's the prick from the video, no?"

Even Mikey knows about the video? I decide not to confirm Wolfe's identity because I don't want to figure out how to get his blood out of my clothes.

"You need me to teach him some manners?"

The rest of the second shift is looking at me funny now that

I'm paying attention. Fuck me sideways. Wolfe blanches as more guys walk in, and I roll my eyes. Weak-ass billionaire asshole.

"Nah, Mikey. You're good people, thanks for that. But I was just showin' this jackoff to the door."

"Hey, Joe, you back on the truck?"

"Who's the suit? Somebody lawyer up?"

"Hey, Joe, ever heard of an iron? If you're gonna rep Brooklyn, maybe fucking don't do it looking like a clueless librarian."

"Took down that bastard billionaire fuck, though, didn't he? Bookies are making bank on how low his stock will go."

"Fuck, is this the douchebag, Joe?"

The guys I never really think of as more than coworkers, crowd around us, curses flying low and furious. All these guys have dreams of becoming made men in my father's army, and how better to do that than to make an example of someone who disrespects the family name? Calgon, take me the fuck away.

Sally, who's been watching this whole time, walks up. "Joe, you still talking to this prick? It's the end of shift, fuckin' clock out if you're havin' a tea party. And the rest of yous fucks get to work. I'm not paying you to fuck around."

He looks at Wolfe with too-sharp eyes and nods to Mikey, who turns to his locker. Ah, jeez. That's Mikey going for whatever weapon he's got stashed in his locker today because my half-brother has exactly two brain cells and no fucks to give.

Christ in a handbasket, this is off the fucking rails.

"Excuse me, who are you?" While directed at Wolfe with a friendly lilt, Sally's words aren't his idea of good manners. He knows exactly who this is. If he's smart, he'll shake him down for cash, but brother dearest is, frankly, a psychopath who loves murder more than he loves money.

Wolfe adjusts his lapel, self-importance right on fucking brand. "I'm Rand Wolfe of Wolfe Athletics. I am happy to wait for Mr. Portelli to clock out. You almost certainly recognize me, and therefore must know that he and I have important business to discuss."

"Aren't you the fuck who fired him in front of all of New York?"

"I believe Mr. Portelli left his employment voluntarily."

Mother Jesus, this man has no clue. Tightening the noose around his own damn neck. *"Shut up,"* I mutter at him through my teeth. Wolfe straightens his shoulders, acting as though he doesn't hear me.

Sally, already jonesing for the smell of gunpowder, riles up the guys. "You hear that, fellas? Lyin' to me with my family's name on his lips."

More grumbling from the assembled—and now locked-in—men.

"I assure you, Mr. Portelli's unemployment status is his doing and his doing alone."

"Jesus fucking Christ, Wolfe. Shut. Up."

He sends a look down his nose at me and cold reality settles in. This asshole is about to ruin my fucking life.

"Oh, now you callin' me a liar with my family's name still in your mouth?" Sally asks, imitating every damn mobster movie he's ever watched.

"I apologize, am I supposed to be familiar with the Portelli family?"

"Put it to you this way. We're not into the stock market."

"Then what, pray tell, are you into?"

Sally looks at me, rolls his eyes, then looks at Mikey and jerks his thumb. Mikey's eyes brighten, and I know exactly what he's thinking: finally, an *in* with the family.

Fuck.

Fuck.

Fuck.

I do *not* want to have to bury this jackass.

I hold up my hand. "I got this one, Mikey." Mikey's expression falls, so I turn to Sally and stage-whisper, "Brother, if you're looking for loyalty, Mikey stepped up in a big way for me. I know he'd do a good job, but I need to take this motherfucker down. These billionaires...this is a different level of heat."

His scowl is loaded with derision as he puts his face in mine, muttering, "You're no brother of mine. You're too squeamish for that. But yeah, I'll let you take out the trash on this one. Fuck it up, though, and you better start running. Or just fucking kill yourself to save me the bullet."

I nod, and Sally points at Wolfe. "You better get him the fuck out of here before he opens his mouth again."

"Excuse you—"

I clamp my hand over Wolfe's mouth and march him out of the building to the shouts and jeers of the first and second shifts. Looking around, I spot the building with the big fucking helicopter on top of it, *Wolfe* emblazoned on the side.

What a fucking prick.

"Mr. Portelli, I am perfectly capable of—"

"You keep talking and you'll be capable of jack shit. My half-brother has a yard full of shipping containers, a loaded .45 in his waistband, and no goddamn impulse control. Keep your feet moving."

That finally seems to shut him up, and he becomes more compliant. Not bothering with the sidewalk, I push him through a hole in the fence to the adjacent building, ignoring his protests of ruined shoes and a snag on his jacket.

The building is a newer structure, and I'm confronted with a locked door and a palm reader.

"What the fuck am I supposed to do with this? How do we get to your helicopter?"

Fucking *helicopter*. What planet is this douche from?

"I...I don't know. We need to go around to the front."

"We don't fucking have time," I grit out, banging on the glass. "And keep your mouth closed."

Luck is on my side for the first time all day, and a trim man with little hair and a military bearing walks into the hallway on the other side of the door. Wolfe raises his hand, signaling him. Mr. Military's expression could melt steel as he swings open the door and pulls us into the building.

"Mr. Wolfe, sir. I've been looking for you. We've got new information on the Portelli family..." he says, his voice drifting off as he notices me. His eyes harden. "And who are you?"

The fuck?

"Who am I? I'm the dumb fuck who just put a fucking target on my back to get this asshole out of here in one fucking piece. Who the fuck are you?"

He blinks, taken aback by the storm of fucks, I'm sure. After a hot second, he straightens and answers my question.

"I'm the pilot, retired Army. And what do you mean, get him out of here in one piece?"

"Yes, what do you mean?" Wolfe says, still no fucking clue.

I turn to him, dumbfounded. "Are you even aware of the world outside of your corner office?"

He opens his mouth to protest, but my phone buzzes right on time. I hold up my finger, and he snaps his mouth shut.

Good boy.

Sally: *Where the fuck are you? This should not be taking that long.*

Sally: *What, are you giving him a blowjob?*

Sally: *Do it and get back here. Babbo wants an update.*

Fuck, fuck, fuck. I hold up my phone so he and Mr. *Be All You Can Be* over here can see where we're sitting.

Retired Army assesses me with a curled lip. "*Babbo?* Who is your father?"

"Salvatore Portelli Senior."

He lets out a low whistle and grabs Wolfe by the arm, walking him toward the interior of the building. I have no choice but to follow. We bypass the elevators and take the stairs.

"Will someone explain what the hell is going on?" Wolfe asks, practically dripping with annoyance and self-importance.

Still dragging him up the stairs, Army grunts out, "You'll get an explanation once we're airborne. Are we taking Portelli with us, or are we leaving him here?"

"We can't kidnap him."

"He stays, he dies. And we can't assume they don't have the weaponry to take out the helo, so we need to take off before they know what's going on." Turning to me, he asks, "How long before he comes out to investigate? Can you stall him?"

"He's impatient but not that smart. How much time do you need to get off the ground?"

"What is going on? Why would he die?" Wolfe asks, clueless as a little lamb.

Helo Guy grimaces, ignoring Wolfe's question as he addresses me. "I had to turn off the engine when Edgerton told me to check on Mr. Wolfe. I try to baby the engines on these luxury sky yachts, but I can get us up in three minutes if I push it." Turning to Wolfe, he says seriously, "Sir, while this isn't particularly unsafe, it is not good for the longevity of your helo. I would suggest a series of diagnostics when we get back, and those are quite expensive."

Wolfe looks at him with alarm and confusion. "I'm sure I can afford it. But you still haven't answered my question. Why would Portelli die if he chooses not to go with us?"

"Sir, this man's father is the head of the Portelli family."

"I don't know what that means."

I roll my eyes for what seems like the hundredth time today. "He's being nice. The people who know call us the Portelli *crime* family."

Wolfe turns to me, mouth agape. "You're Mafia?"

"No. My father is Mafia. I clawed my way out of that life so I could work for a big, shiny, *legal* corporation. Clearly, a brilliant plan that worked in my favor." Turning to Captain America, I answer his question. "I can work with three minutes, but in five, my father will take over and bullets will start flying."

Three more flights of stairs to go, and I start texting.

Joe: *Problem solved.*

Joe: *Fuck, just checked his phone. He's got a helicopter pilot asking when they're taking off again.*

Sally: *What the fuck?*

Joe: *Rich fucking assholes.*

Sally: *Too right.*

Joe: *I answered the text. Told him to take off, that our friend would be taking alternate transportation.*

Sally: *Good, good. Did you fucking clock out? I'm not paying for that shit.*

Joe: *Yeah, I had Mikey clock out for me.*

Joe: *Look, I need to make the final arrangements for this one. Might not be in for a coupla days.*

Sally: *I ain't paying you for shit.*

Sally: *I can send Mikey to help, but you hafta pay for his time.*

Joe: *Understood. I'll let you know.*

What a tool.

We open the door to the roof, where the shiny helicopter sits like a big fucking target. We start running, and I keep an eye on the warehouse. Even if we make it out of here alive, staying alive is about to get real fucking tricky.

4

RAND

HENDRIX PRACTICALLY SHOVES me into my own helicopter and throws a headset at me while Portelli runs to the other side, hopping into the copilot seat. Hendrix hands Portelli a checklist and a headset, instructing him to call out the next steps. To Portelli's credit, he quickly picks up what Hendrix needs, and they get into a rhythm.

I have about a million questions, but clearly, now is not the time. Only a couple of minutes later, with the expensively quiet rotors whirring overhead, the helicopter begins to lift, the takeoff rougher than I've ever experienced. As I consider a complaint to the pilot company, it occurs to me that this is probably an emergency takeoff. Passenger experience is not the top priority here. Right.

Hendrix's gaze is set on the horizon, but Portelli's eyes are glued to the ground.

"Wolfe, keep your ass down," he says, his jaw tightening.

"What's happening?" I ask, wondering when exactly I signed up to be part of some sort of action-adventure plotline.

"It's my brother and Mikey." He swings around, glaring at me.

"I said, keep your fucking ass down. Lie flat." Not missing a beat, he turns to Hendrix. "Hey, *Be All You Can Be*, can they reach us with those guns?"

Guns? I decide that Portelli might have a point and stretch out on the bench, feeling like a kid riding in the back of a station wagon. Not that I've ever been in the back of a station wagon, but I've seen them in movies.

"No, sir. But I'm not exactly hanging around for them to dig out some bigger—"

A distinct pop-pop-pop sound cuts off Hendrix's words, and the helicopter lurches upward as he pulls on a lever of some kind. My stomach is ready to revolt, but I keep that to myself.

"Were they shooting at us?" I'm incredulous, but the facts seem irrefutable. I've been shot at. By the mob.

Well, the helicopter was shot at, but still.

Joe nods, his mouth grim as he looks back at me. "How did you get that cut on your chin?"

My hand goes to my chin, and I pull away to find blood. Not too bad, considering it's a facial wound, but it does lend to the absolute surrealness of the day.

Joe unzips his coveralls, shimmying out of the top and letting it pool around his waist.

Oh.

His arms are *shocking*.

I mean, I know the man has arms, but I didn't realize they'd be quite so...well-formed under all of that. And his tanned olive skin is...inviting.

Reaching back, he grabs a bandanna from his pocket and hands it over to me.

"What am I supposed to do with this?" I ask, looking at the crumpled material.

"You're getting blood down your shirt. Use it to stop the flow."

Ripping my attention away from the prominent veins running

up his arms, I blink at him. *None of that, Wolfe. Reassert your dominance.*

Sitting up, I straighten my shoulders and lift my nose at him, giving him my most imperious look. "You just pulled that thing from your ass. I'm not putting it on an open wound."

I'm wearing the expression I use to intimidate people, and it's usually effective. Joe snorts and rolls his eyes at me.

"I didn't pull it from my ass. I pulled it from my pocket, and it's clean. I've been in coveralls all day long. I didn't get any of the docks on it. There are barely even any poor-people cooties on it, promise."

An uncomfortably warm splash of blood dribbles down past my collar, and I decide this isn't a hill I'm willing to die—or bleed out—on. I pluck the bandanna from his fingers and ignore the amused tilt of his lips. They're unexpectedly plush, which I find mildly annoying.

I pull the fabric up to my nose, sniffing it, anticipating the stench of dirt and oil. I am, however, mistaken. The scent nearly overwhelms me, and it's all rather embarrassing. I'm hoping my cheeks aren't as flushed as they feel. It's Azzaro, of all things, something my first furtive boyfriend wore in high school, something I could have sworn I'd outgrown.

It's combined with an undertone of laundry detergent, and the nostalgia of this smell makes me want to find this man's bed and bury myself in his pillows.

Maintain the upper hand, Wolfe.

He's still looking at me, his eyes assessing. I give him a small nod and gently press the soft, worn material to my chin. I suppose I gained the cut from getting thrown into the back of my own helicopter. Another reminder that this day has gone completely pearshaped.

Looking back at my reluctant savior, I grasp for some level ground.

"You never answered my question. How did you come to know Sherry? What kind of work are you doing with her?"

He shakes his head, his lip curling up in a snarl. It's not an unpleasant look on him, and his voice betrays a hint of amusement.

"Why do you care how I know Sherry? We're friendly. Don't worry though. She wasn't giving away any of your big secrets."

"I didn't think she was. She is loyal above all else. But it is rare for non-executives to interact with her. And I sometimes wonder if we have been too insular."

That's true enough, though I'm shocked to have said it aloud. A real alph—er—*someone in control of themselves* knows to keep such things close to their chest.

"Did you wonder that before or after your stocks began to tank?"

"Mostly after." I wrinkle my nose, hateful of that inconvenient truth and even more bothered that I automatically answered his question.

He scratches his beard, seeming to debate something. With a nearly imperceptible shrug, he finally responds to my original question. "You asked someone to give you a rough sketch of your competition's activities and stock movement every morning. Sherry and I take our coffee breaks at the same time, and I make her laugh. So she assigned the task to me."

My mind immediately goes to the stacks and stacks of print-outs, highlighted to identify points of reading, saving me the time of trying to pick through the relevant data.

"Wait—you're the one responsible for my highlight sheets?"

"Yeah. Not the most fun, but I learned a lot from reading through your competition."

"Your highlights show a lot of sharp observation."

"I'm guessing that comes as a surprise to you."

"Well, no. I mean—"

"Sir, not to interrupt, but I'm assuming that we're landing at the residence, not the office?"

"Yes, thank you." I turn to Joe. "Do you think they'll follow you to Manhattan? What should we tell my security guy?"

Joe shakes his head. "My family avoids Manhattan like the plague. We've got too many rivals on the island, too many ways to step incorrectly in the wrong territory. You didn't witness anything too illegal. I'm hoping they'll decide you're not worth it."

I stitch my brows. "What about you? Are *you* worth it?"

His jaw shifts, though it's hard to get a read on him from the back. "They won't come into Manhattan for me, but my father's gonna create a situation to force me back to Brooklyn. Just a guess."

As he's talking, he reaches for his phone. Reading the screen, he curses to himself.

"What? Did they text you? Do you know what the situation is going to be? The one they're trying to force?"

He shakes his head. "No. It's just my uncle informing me that my father invoked extradition."

"I don't know what that means."

"Means that any family in Manhattan who can put hands on me and return me in one piece gets a reward."

"Family as in...?"

"Mafia."

"Are there many...*families* in Manhattan?"

"None he's friendly with, but a few will do it for the cash."

"Oh."

I look out the window at the astonishing New York skyline. As a kid, it was always my favorite thing to do. Get to the top of a tall building and look at all the possibilities. It occurs to me that there are now fewer possibilities because I couldn't leave well enough alone.

THE LANDING on the rooftop of my building is soft as butter, a complete opposite of the takeoff. I may figure out how much this pilot makes annually and gift that as a bonus. Pretty sure he saved my life.

One look out the window tells me that being shot at from a warehouse on the docks has set off a massive security protocol. Waiting for me is my head of security and six of his guys. No one looks particularly pleased.

Edgerton opens the helicopter door, and before my foot hits the ground, I'm surrounded. I barely catch a glimpse of sunlight as we pass through the stairwell door.

The door slams shut behind me and is immediately opened again. The security team turns, hands on their sidearms. So not just linebacker-guard types. *Armed* guards.

Portelli holds up his hands. "Am I not supposed to be here?"

I push past one of the guards—or attempt to. I give up after a few seconds. "Edgerton, he's with us."

Edgerton nods, and the security detail shuffles him into the middle of the scrum as the sound of the helicopter taking off fills the stairwell.

We go down one flight of stairs and, using the palm reader, Edgerton lets us into my foyer. Awaiting us is my personal physician, Dr. Jensen.

And my father, whose wordless judgment chokes the very oxygen from the air we're breathing.

Edgerton breaks the weighted silence. "We have secured Mr. Wolfe and Mr. Portelli. Mr. Wolfe did sustain an injury to his chin. It appears to be mild..."

The doctor walks up to us, interrupting Edgerton's briefing of the obvious. "Let me take a look." Dr. Jenson has been my doctor since I was very young, and she's more or less retired, save for my annual physicals and the occasional illness. She pulls the bandanna away and nods agreeably. "It's good that you covered it up, but let's wash this out and see what we can do with Steri-Strips. I don't believe you'll need stitches."

I nod and let her lead me to the little half-bath near my entry-way. Using hand soap and hot water, she has me squared away in no time. When I walk back out into the foyer, there's a distinct energy shift.

Portelli is surrounded by guards, and my father is looking at him like a specimen in the zoo.

His coveralls are still half undone, his university tank top is spackled to his chest, and his beard is past due for a grooming. Perhaps it's the contrast of his roughness against the surrounding refinement, but...fuck, he's hot.

Focus, Rand.

My father walks up to me, examines the small bandage on my chin, sniffs, then turns to Dr. Jensen, dismissing her from my care as though I were a small child. It's a classic Randolf Wolfe Sr. move—establish dominance in every interaction, no matter how microscopic.

Addressing me, he gestures at Portelli as though he's a piece of trash that somehow found its way into the middle of my beauti-fully adorned foyer. "Explain."

Drawing myself to my full height, I give a brief rundown of the day's events.

My father shakes his head, his voice cool. "You took a *heli-copter* to *Brooklyn*, where you angered the *Mafia*, forcing your pilot to do a cold takeoff *while being shot at*?"

I glance at Joe, whose hands are in the pockets of his coveralls, unbothered. I spy a faint smirk at the corner of his mouth. My father sees it too.

He narrows his eyes, an indication of his displeasure and a subtle order to fall in line. I've seen this one look work across the dinner table and in boardrooms all over the world. Joe responds with a wink, letting his whisper of a smile bloom into a sharp grin.

I shiver, pushing down an unwanted rush of desire.

Turning back to my father, I seek to answer the question he never got around to. "You're missing some nuance, but yes, you've got the rough sketch of it."

"I still don't understand why Mr. Portelli is *here*."

My eyes flick back to Joe, and he captures my gaze. *Alpha wolf*, he mouths, pointing at my father.

My shoulders drop, as does any of my argument. I know that, save for him being quietly related to one of the most vicious mob families in the history of New York, getting Joe back was a smart move.

Probably.

5

JOE

MAN, wealthy people are a trip and a half. Just yesterday, this guy was standing up on stage, going on about how he was the big alpha wolf. Nothing but smoke and mirrors. He's a little piglet like the rest of us.

I feel sorry for the guy though. Here he is, CEO of a huge corporation, being quietly fileted by his father in front of his own staff. Meanwhile, I don't think the man gives a shit that I just blew up my entire life to save his son from a terrible death. I don't know why it surprises and annoys me, but it does.

My phone buzzes in my pocket. My uncle.

Uncle: *What the fuck were you thinking helping him escape?*

Joe: *Sally was going to put Wolfe's brains all over the inside of his warehouse. That would have brought us all down.*

Uncle: *Ah, Jesus. The only thing faster than that asshole's mouth is his trigger finger, and his brain is a distant third.*

Joe: *Gotta love a no-fucking-win situation.*

Uncle: *Do what you gotta do. Keep your nose clean and stay safe.*

Joe: *Thanks, Zio.*

The Portellis aren't exactly what you'd call emotionally available. *Stay safe* is as close to *I love you* as any of us gets. It sets a cold knot in my stomach.

Wolfe Sr. clears his throat. "I'm sorry. Are we interrupting your social media scrolling?"

Oh, hell no.

I look up from my phone and set him with a glare. To his credit, he reads it quickly and his chin shifts back.

Curbing the Brooklyn, I answer through clenched teeth. "Saving your son's life put me in a bad spot with my family. I'm just trying to see how dead they want me. That okay with you?"

"You would've saved yourself the trouble if you'd known your place yesterday."

There's a flinty, cool edge to everything that comes out of this motherfucker's mouth. Like he's never once been wrong in his entire life. I take a step forward, and so does Wolfe Jr.'s head of security. I don't have any beef with this Edgerton guy, so I hold up my hands.

"You could be planning his funeral," I say, pointing to Wolfe Jr. "All I'm asking is that you not be a dickhead to me. I understand it's your default setting as a rich man. Respect. But not today and not at me, not ever. Don't do it again. Please don't make me show you what happens when you do."

I promise. I'm usually a kitten. But something about this arrogant prick brings out the mob in me.

Wolfe Sr. glares at his son before adjusting his shoulders. "You received the board's communication about the next steps. Do you have any questions?"

Wolfe Jr. shakes his head, looking down. It's a damn shame because the man on the stage, prowling, chest puffed out, was a sight to behold, even if I hated it. This cowed version of him is sad.

Not that I care about his emotional state right now.

Wolfe Sr. heads for the elevator without telling his son

goodbye or even checking to make sure he's okay. He's followed by two of the security guards and the rest disappear. Within seconds, it's just me, Wolfe Jr., and Edgerton, who sets off on a perimeter walk.

Still looking defeated, Wolfe invites me into the rest of his home. If the towering entrance is a museum, his actual living space is surprisingly warm. I expected sectioned-off living areas, uncomfortable seating arrangements, German abstract art, and cold marble flooring.

I'm right about the marble flooring but surprised by the open floor plan, the greenery throughout the space, and the expensively plush Persian rugs that artfully define the space. The couches, a beautiful buttery-warm leather, look like you could get lost in them, and the fireplace, which takes up nearly the entire inside wall, is lit and crackling.

There are several smaller seating areas throughout the space, some perfect for reading, some perfect for...I don't know, doing business. All overlook the magnificent skyline, enhanced by the sweeping wall of windows.

I look outside and laugh. "Guess someone's swimming in a rooftop pool after all."

The weather's been chilly, but the enormous balcony is lush with greenery and cozy gathering spaces set around a turquoise pool with a simple, elegant water feature.

Rolling his eyes, Wolfe answers, "As with the office, you can use any of the amenities here. I'm hardly here to enjoy it."

My grin broadens. "Like I said, you *do* know how to outfit a pretty cage."

Wolfe stares at his feet. "I believe you've sufficiently made your point."

I bite my lip, a little regretful over pouring salt on the wound. Just as I open my mouth to make a peace offering, a short, portly man appears at my side, like some sort of djinn.

"Sir, may I get you something to drink?"

I stifle a surprised shout, but it's a near thing. He's English, or something close to it.

"I don't suppose you have anything decent in an Italian red?" I ask, belatedly fitting my arms back through the sleeves of my coverall, feeling underdressed in such a fancy space. The coveralls, unfortunately, only serve to widen the distinction between me and the extravagant luxury around me.

The man's smile is warm and genuine, not put on for show. Another surprise in the Wolfe's lair. "Sir, I can promise you a beautiful red wine, and Mr. Wolfe's selection from Italy is pure perfection. Is there a particular varietal that you enjoy?"

"I like everything, but I suspect you already have a favorite."

He dips his chin, and I realize I'm expecting a billionaire to have his help dressed in...I don't know, tails? Some kind of suit? This gentleman is wearing nice but practical shoes, sharply pressed jeans, and a soft Henley that gently hugs his round stomach.

"That I do. I'll bring it up right away."

The promise of wine makes me realize exactly how tense I am and how much I'm looking forward to whatever alcohol this man brings me. Hell, it could be Boone's Farm at this point, and I'd take it.

Forgive me, Nonna, for I have sinned.

"Thank you...I seem to have missed your name," I say, embarrassed that thirty seconds into having access to a butler, I've ignored his humanity.

He beams at me as though maybe I've accidentally done something right. Or maybe the stuck-up rich people don't care about his name. "Grayson, sir."

I'm not sure if that's his first or last name, but it's no skin off my nose to call the man by the name he's given me. "Grayson. Thank you."

He grins again then disappears somewhere over in the kitchen, which I can only partially see from the main living area. I turn and nearly startle again as I run into Wolfe. He's looking at me through wide navy-blue eyes, his head tilted.

"What?" I ask, zipping up my coverall.

"Grayson likes you."

"And?"

"He doesn't like anybody I bring here."

"Are they all like the assholes who were just in your apartment five minutes ago?"

"Yes."

"Well, then, that's why. I'm not an asshole."

"I'd contest that, but you did save my life today. Didn't you?"

"Yes."

"At great personal cost." A statement. Not a question.

"It appears that way, yes."

"And I'm guessing it's my fault."

I raise my brows, impressed that he found his way to some semblance of personal responsibility. Shaking my head, I scoff. A sound I'm sure is completely foreign within these carefully crafted walls.

"What? Say it," he demands, a challenge in his eyes. Like maybe he wants me to take him down a notch.

In another context, that would be very enjoyable indeed, but today I'm just a guy wearing dirty coveralls in a fancy place.

"Fine." I shake my head as I get my fill of this beautifully clueless man. "You must be the most privileged, idiotic human I've ever met."

His gaze hits the floor again, and I feel terrible. I want to hate this man, given the way he treated me yesterday, but now I have a frame of reference and, more importantly, I see his mask starting to slip. I don't even have to poke at him very hard.

He's got overstuffed couches, for Christ's sake.

Softening my tone, I ask, "Why treat anybody like shit? And then, especially, why would you treat somebody on the docks like shit? You've got to know what the docks are all about. That was the stupidest goddamn thing I ever saw. It's like you don't know who you were talking to."

"I didn't."

"And now my life is all fucked. My uncle...I don't even know what's going on with him. He risked so much to text me..." I cut myself off, not able to even go there.

His eyes widen. "I can ask Edgerton to send a detail to escort him here."

I stare at him. *He has no fucking clue.* "They'd be dead before they even got to him."

To his credit, he doesn't try to contradict me. "What can I do?"

"I don't know. But I'm gonna drink your fucking expensive wine, and I'm gonna come up with a plan."

"The offer of a job still stands."

I look at him like he's lost his goddamn mind. "A job?"

He nods. "And a place to stay. Because, obviously, I've put you in danger."

"A place to stay, really? You got a Fortress of Solitude around here somewhere?"

He gestures to the space. "I give you one Fortress of Solitude."

"Dude, I am not having a sleepover with you."

"Mr. Portelli, I don't think you have much choice."

The shitty thing is, I'm pretty sure he's right.

6

RAND

"YOU KEEP CALLING THIS AN APARTMENT. It is not an apartment, of that you can be certain."

Joe narrows his eyes, spinning in place as he broadens his arms. "Is this not a dwelling in a building with other dwellings? Is that not an apartment?"

"The people on the floors below are in apartments. Condos, if they're being fancy. But this? This is the penthouse. And you know it's the penthouse because I have a private elevator."

He rolls his eyes so dramatically I'm concerned for his ocular health. With perfect timing, Grayson appears, holding a tray with a bottle of one of my favorite reds, decanted and ready to pour. I notice with a not-small amount of gratitude that he's brought two glasses.

Good man.

He serves the wine, then quietly disappears. I wonder, sometimes, if the act of subtly leaving a room is something they teach to support staff.

"The people in the apartments downstairs don't have a

Grayson," I say, swirling the wine I had flown in from the Piedmont region earlier this month.

Unimpressed, Portelli rolls his eyes and takes a drink—a swig, really—of the wine as if it is some sort of common restaurant offering. He nearly chokes, his eyes going wide as he pulls the glass away from him to study the fine liquid inside.

"Holy Mother of God. What the hell kind of wine is this?"

I take a sip, concerned that maybe it has somehow gone bad. But no, it's perfect, well within season.

"It's from the Nebbiolo Vineyards outside of Turin. Do you not enjoy it?"

He looks at me, scrunching his nose before looking again at the glass of wine and back to me.

"Are you fucking kidding me? I don't think I've ever had anything as delicious in my mouth."

I allow myself a small smile. Joe's approval of Grayson's selection is, sadly, the only good thing that's happened all day. Still gazing at the glass in deference, he slowly brings it to his lips and tips the stem back, taking a much more respectful sip this time.

I watch as his Adam's apple bobs up and down and the way his pink tongue clears the wine from his lips. Which don't quite match his mechanic chic attire. He's got a strong nose and thick angled brows, but his lips are not quite masculine. As I noted before, they're plush. Annoyingly so.

The room is quiet, and I shift my eyes up, meeting his. He tilts his head, grinning at me. Seemingly aware that I'm looking, he makes more of a show of it. This time he slowly tilts the wine into his pretty mouth then licks his lips in a way that can only be described as flirty.

I take a deep breath and a step back. The warning klaxon in the back of my mind reminds me that stepping back is the opposite of what my father would do.

Despite years of training and grooming at my father's feet, I can't hold a candle to this guy. He has more presence and control of a room than I ever did. And today—in coveralls, no less—he spotted my father's various power moves and didn't budge an inch. It triggers every fucking insecurity I've ever had.

I hate it.

But not.

"Anyway, my wing is over here," I say, pointing to the hallway off the living room. "And the guest rooms are just past the kitchen."

The dramatic curve of the building's architecture enables guests to have their own private suite, including a small den and kitchenette, which are out of view of the main living area. I rarely go back there, but I know without having to verify that Grayson's already made arrangements.

"I'm not staying here. This place is way too fancy for me."

"Did you not just indicate that you are in mortal danger?"

"I doubt your apartment rent-a-cops will be happy with this arrangement."

"Again, this is not an apartment, and your living quarters are several hundred feet away from mine. We will not be in each other's way." I pull up my phone and send off a text. "As for the rent-a-cops of which you speak of so sneeringly, perhaps you'd like to talk to my head of security."

Edgerton, who I assume was just out of visual range, steps into the living area. "How can I assist you?"

"We, as I'm sure you have surmised, are in a bit of a pickle. In saving my life, Mr. Portelli very much endangered his own. I offered to let him stay here in the guest quarters, but he has concerns regarding his safety."

Edgerton turns to Joe, his professional demeanor locked in. "What concerns do you have?"

Joe shoots me a narrow-eyed glare, then squares up to Edgerton. "He didn't just piss off some kids with a gun and an idea in their head. He disrespected the son of Salvatore Portelli, head of the Portelli crime family."

Edgerton nods. "I'm aware." Turning to me, grave disapproval evident on his face, he explains, "The only reason you're still alive is that Salvatore Portelli and Luciano Stefano have an arrangement of sorts. The Stefanos do not go into Brooklyn, and the Portellis do not come into Manhattan."

Joe seems surprised. "Do I want to know how you know that?"

Edgerton shakes his head, but I point out the obvious. "You say the Portellis don't come to Manhattan, and yet, there's been a Portelli in Manhattan for several months now."

Edgerton's shoulder twitches. "He is not a member of the Portelli *organization*, as far as I can tell."

Joe, still looking unsettled, starts shaking his head. "That's correct, but going up against mobsters is different. My father's crew enjoys the violence."

I smile, straightening my shoulders and standing a little taller. "Edgerton, perhaps you would like to share your background with Mr. Portelli."

His jaw tightens. "I am unable to share my background, as it is classified. Just understand that keeping this entire building and the people within it safe is well within my skill set, and more specifically, the skill set of the men who I have hired to do this job."

Joe's eyes widen as he takes in Edgerton's no-nonsense stance, which is tightly strung and supremely confident.

Edgerton continues. "I take care of all threats against the Wolfe family: foreign, domestic, and cyber. The security team is on the floor below and accompanies Mr. Wolfe wherever he goes, and we are available twenty-four seven."

Turning to Joe, I find myself grinning triumphantly. "Happy?"

7

JOE

HAPPY? This motherfucker here wants to know if I'm *happy?*

"Sweetheart, I'm a long way from happy. But I'm gonna keep on drinking your wine for now."

Edgerton, I'm assuming despite himself, tries to hide a small grin.

"This amuses you?" I ask, taking another drink of the best fucking wine I've ever tasted.

"You're drinking a thousand-dollar bottle of wine like it's a Two Buck Chuck. That is rather amusing, you have to admit."

I nearly choke again. I turn to Wolfe, incredulous. "You spent a thousand dollars on a bottle of wine? What are the grapes made of? Diamonds?"

"Having toured the winery myself, I can tell you the grapes are not made of diamonds. They are, however, a special varietal that only grows in this one region of Italy."

Addressing the bigger problem at hand, I turn back to Edgerton. "And it is your suggestion that I stay here until you can secure a better place for me?"

"Sir, that is my suggestion and, if I'm honest, I doubt I'll be able to quickly or easily secure a place that comes close to this location. I'm familiar with the Portelli family, and I know as well as you do that if you pissed off one of their capos, you've got a not-small problem on your hands."

I stifle the urge to test his knowledge, see how much he actually knows, but I decide I don't really care. "It's a good thing I'm in the city then, am I right?"

He gives me a slow shake of his head. "I don't know. I'm not sure of your father's next move."

"Do you think I'm endangering anyone at Wolfe Athletics?"

He shakes his head. "No. Wolfe and its employees are under my care, and the Stefano family will not be coming after you."

There was a threat in the way he said that sentence nice and easy. I recognize it because it's the kind of threat my father gives.

"So I shouldn't be in any danger then, correct?"

"As long as you stay here and take Mr. Wolfe's job offer, you should be fine. But if you decide to get stupid and go off on your own, I won't be able to protect you."

"How long before they figure out where I'm at?"

"There's very little chance they don't already know your location."

"So, I don't really have much choice at all."

"That would be my read on the situation."

I run my hand along my jaw, wincing at the unkempt beard.

Turning to Wolfe, I shrug. "All right, then. Show me to my new living quarters and tell me what my job is."

Edgerton gives me another one of his not-friendly smiles and bows his head. "Wise choice."

Yeah, we'll see about that.

I DON'T KNOW how long I've been sitting out here, poolside like one of these rich fuckers. Long enough for night to fall. It's easy to believe this city is a glittering jewel when looking at it from so high up. But I know how gritty it gets at the street view.

I haven't heard anything from my uncle in far too long, and one way or another, that's bad news.

Grayson, who's been kindly keeping me in expensive wine and snacks this whole time, approaches carefully.

"Sir, Edgerton is back with a small box of your things."

I take a deep breath. It's no use putting off the inevitable. I meet Edgerton in the living room, and Grayson wasn't kidding. He is back with a very small box indeed.

"I thought you were at least going to bring me clothes," I say, taking the cardboard box from him.

"The contents of your apartment were destroyed. I believe these things were left untouched as a warning."

Wolfe joins us, holding up a garment bag. "You and I are close enough in size, so I've taken the liberty of lending you a few articles of clothing, along with a suit. Grayson will take your measurements for the alteration, and it should be ready by morning."

I'm about an inch shorter than he is, and my shoulders are slightly broader, but it should work out. "Thank you."

He gives me a shy nod and steps back, then seems to disagree with himself and rocks forward once more.

Edgerton's expression is unreadable as he turns to Wolfe. "You need anything from me?"

Wolfe shakes his head, and Edgerton spins on his heel, disappearing into the foyer.

I sit on one of the comfortable couches, placing the small cardboard box on the large tufted ottoman in front of me. After staring at it for a solid minute, I pick it up and peel back the simple strip of Scotch tape. When I see the contents, I wish I'd kept it closed.

The first item is a framed picture of my nonna. Not a scratch on it. The next object isn't from my apartment at all. It's a Christmas ornament, a round clay imprint of my foot taken when I was a newborn. As far as I know, that's the only memento my father ever had of me. The final item, loose at the bottom of the box, makes my blood run cold.

It's a double-edged razor blade, thin and sharp as fuck. I've seen what my father can do with a razor blade like this one, and the message is clear. I'm no longer part of the family, and if I talk, he'll take my tongue, using this razor blade to do it. Well, that, or he's suggesting I kill myself now.

I have a feeling he doesn't care either way.

I shift and startle at Wolfe's presence in front of me, having forgotten him entirely.

"Sorry," he says, doing the step-back-rock-forward thing again, the defiant tilt of his chin gone.

I lean my forearms on my thighs and rub my hands over my face. "You ever see a rattlesnake in person, Wolfe?"

His Adam's apple bobs. "No, but—"

"I have. I have a cousin in Arizona who owns a lot of property in the desert. Something to do with windmills. Anyway, during a break from college, I spent a month or so with him in the desert. Maintaining these big goddamn windmills."

"I don't—"

I hold up my finger, and he shuts his mouth. "I was walking back to my truck one afternoon, and it was hot as balls. Thought I was gonna die of heatstroke. And there on the little pathway between me and my cousin's work truck was a big fuckin' rattlesnake."

I fit my hands together in a circle. "Motherfucker was over six feet long and his body was this thick. And I tell you, I've never heard a sound more frightening than that fucking rattle. It's not like a kid's rattle at all. It's low. Menacing. And all the while, the snake's tracking you with his body. With that fucking arrow-shaped head. You don't even need to see the damn fangs to know that you're in the presence of death itself."

"What did you do?"

"I backed up and walked the hell around that truck, crawled in from the other side, and I got the fuck outta there. Got myself on a plane the next day and came back to Brooklyn, where shit makes sense."

"What does this—"

I pick up the small box and shake it, careful not to overly disturb its contents. Just enough to approximate that sound that still haunts my dreams. "You stirred up a whole goddamn nest of rattlesnakes. This is just the first shot across the bow. That first low rattle. They don't call my father the Viper of Brooklyn for nothing."

"So, they're trying to warn us off," he says, his shoulders settling out of his ears. "Fine. We'll make a path around them."

I shake my head. "Yeah, that's not gonna work. A real rattlesnake doesn't want anything to do with people, and if a person gives them their space, everyone's cool. Rattlesnakes of the human variety are a different kind of problem altogether."

Wolfe works his jaw, the tendons in his neck straining. After a silent beat, he nods to himself. "Edgerton will do everything in his power to track down any threats. Of that, I am certain."

I let out a deep breath and think about what my uncle would tell me right now. He'd smack me upside the head and tell me to keep my head in the game, not let my imagination run wild.

Think ahead, nipote. *Pick apart their moves and counter moves. Note the areas of weakness and exploit them.*

No bones about it. I've made an enemy of my father. There's no coming back from protecting Wolfe, even if doing so saved my family from the consequences of killing a billionaire.

Rock, meet hard place.

Taking another deep breath, I draw myself up. No more pity parties. "What's next?"

Wolfe's eyebrows go up, and I bite my tongue, waiting for him to respond. "I was going to inquire as to what you wanted for dinner. I can order in, or Grayson has a few lovely recipes up his sleeve."

Pushing myself up from the couch, I shake my head. "I've got to do something with my hands, or I'll go crazy."

Wolfe steps back again, and I roll my eyes. "I'm not taking you out. I just risked everything to get your coddled, overprivileged ass out of there." I scratch the back of my head. "Maybe I can do a simple primavera with some egg noodles. What kinda vegetables you got?"

Grayson pops up outta nowhere. "We have flour and eggs, along with a nice assortment of vegetables, including some cherry tomatoes from my window garden."

"Cherry tomatoes sound amazing. If you've got some fresh basil, I'll be all set."

"I'll have the concierge bring up the basil. Shouldn't take but a few minutes."

I'd complain about the utter ridiculousness of needing a concierge to bring me basil, but it's not like I can just run to the corner market in this neighborhood.

"All right, Grayson. Show me to your kitchen, and then, all due respect, get the fuck outta my way."

Grayson's answering grin is subtle in the extreme, and it feels like a small gift. "Yes, sir."

Having breezed past the kitchen before, I'm impressed by how cozy it feels, despite the modern conveniences. Hell, this place looks like my nonna's dream kitchen, another way in which this Wolfe asshole is playing against type.

It's a bright u-shaped space with dark-gray cabinetry, warm butcher block countertops, and a huge island with plenty of room to spread out. Just past the island is a big rustic dining table, set off by tall green plants and a panoramic view of the city.

A Viking oven gleams under the carefully arranged lighting, reminding me that I wanted to buy one for my nonna with my big, important job. Just as I'm beginning to wonder where the refrigerator is, Grayson opens a pair of cabinet doors to an enormous refrigerator that could almost be a walk-in. He also points me to the pantry, which is fully stocked. It's crazy to me the number of options that Wolfe has at all times. Many of these things won't last more than a week, and I seriously doubt he gets to all of this produce.

"I take it you and yours eat well from the excesses of this pantry."

"We do, Mr. Portelli. I live with my mother. She's getting older, but she appreciates it when Mr. Wolfe is too busy to eat his pineapple."

I laugh, feeling some sort of small victory that I've broken through Grayson's kind but professional exterior.

"Grayson, can you do me a favor?"

"Name it."

"Can you call me Joe? All of this Mr. Portelli stuff makes me feel like I'm not a real person."

"Sir, I can. However, in the presence of Mr. Wolfe and company, I must revert to the more appropriate greeting."

"I'll take it." Smiling, I ask, "How long have you been working for this asshole?"

Grayson's happy expression shutters. "Sir, you have been through something today that I cannot begin to imagine. But I am, first and foremost, loyal to Mr. Wolfe. I've known him since he was a very young boy, and I know that you don't get to see the best of him but believe me when I tell you that he is, at his core, a very good man."

"Then what is it with all of that alpha-wolf bullshit?"

Grayson opens his mouth, then closes it.

I rake my hands through my hair, frustrated. "I'm sorry, Grayson. Of course I'm putting you in an awkward spot, asking you things that are none of my business. I appreciate what you're saying. It's just hard to see him as a good man when I see the results of some of his decisions."

Grayson nods before stepping back. "I would urge you to consider that the CEO of a large corporation with an iron fist of a board has rather less control over the decisions than you might imagine. The things he had to give up just to shut down that slave labor factory..."

"Tell me."

Grayson shakes his head. "I keep Mr. Wolfe's confidences, of course, but I can tell you that he's had to give up pieces of himself for every bit of forward progress he's achieved."

"Okay, okay." I shake my head. "I'm just gonna get to work here, get out of my head, you know?"

"Of course, Joe. I'll be right back with the tomatoes."

"Thank you, Grayson."

I open cabinets until I find a bowl and a sifter, and I hope to hell I made the right decision today.

8

RAND

PORTELLI IS IN MY KITCHEN, making homemade pasta. And apparently, I have a substandard pasta maker, one that his nonna—which I find out means his grandmother—would most certainly scoff at.

I'm fascinated, watching him work. He's since divested himself of the coveralls and is standing in my kitchen barefoot, wearing soft worn jeans and that dangerous tank top, both molded to every beautiful muscle on his body.

If I'd had any idea what he was hiding underneath during our confrontation yesterday, I might have been more intimidated. Though intimidation is not something anyone who carries the Wolfe family name can feel, let alone own up to. If someone makes you feel intimidated, be the bigger asshole.

That, by the way, is the sum of my father's wisdom.

Be the bigger asshole.

Take every penny off the table.

Find the line at which people will leave or stay, and then ride that line as hard as you can and never give so much as an inch.

Grayson disappears for a few moments then comes back with a

bouquet of basil and a small basket of cherry tomatoes, still held together with bits of vine, perfectly orangey-red. From my perch at the window, I surreptitiously watch Portelli as he cooks.

When Portelli spies the tomatoes, his eyes crinkle at the edges with his broad, warm smile. "Oh, these are beauties. Perfect for the primavera. Grayson, you are a miracle worker."

"Happy to help, Joe."

They're on a first-name basis? It's not all that surprising when I think of it—I've already experienced Joseph Portelli struggling under the weight of propriety. Yes, the first thing he would ask is for Grayson to call him by his name.

Some people do that because they want you to think they're friendlier than they really are, but that's not Portelli. Even though he holds himself like a man capable of devastating violence, he's actually being friendly. Human.

How strange.

Also strange is the small curl of jealousy that wraps itself around my rib cage. I wish I could say his name like that. Silly, of course. Portelli doesn't need me to recognize his humanity.

In fact, I doubt the man needs anything from me at all. He's singularly unimpressed with my wealth. If I understand correctly, he's quite disgusted by it.

That thought sends energy zipping through my body, and something dangerously close to a chuckle rattles up from my chest. I don't know why it feels so good to know he thinks so little of me.

My eyes dart back to the kitchen, and I catch Grayson's eye. One eyebrow tastefully arches in my direction. Busted. I glance down, and by the time I look up again, Grayson has gone off to do whatever Grayson does to keep my life in order.

Suddenly, even though Portelli's probably twenty feet away from me, the space with just the two of us in it feels intimate. Another silly notion, of course, because I have no feelings for the man.

Is he attractive? Sure. He's beautiful in that rough working-class kind of way.

If I were to line him up with my typical discreet hookups, would they have a lot in common? Yes, again, but everyone likes ruggedly handsome men. I know my father doesn't like to think of me as delicate, but he would believe differently if he ever saw any of my lovers.

Not that my sex life has anything to do with Portelli.

I shiver and bring myself back to the present.

From a certain angle, Portelli in my kitchen looks like the kind of life I might one day dream about having. Someone comfortable, barefoot in the kitchen, happily zipping about the space, cooking.

I am a modern man, of course, and can well afford to hire a professional cook for me and whoever I end up with. But the idea of someone cooking for me because they enjoy it...

Not because I'm wealthy.

Not because it's just one of their many endless chores.

But because feeding the ones they love gives them satisfaction.

It's clear Portelli is that kind of man. Gruff, though not entirely unrefined, and caring. I suppose he could have easily stepped back and let his brother do whatever he would to me. But he didn't. He jumped into action.

I just wish I wasn't so aware of him in my space. I understand he's cooking to soothe his nerves, but he's making enough pasta to feed a small army or a very large family. And I think he means for me to eat with him.

There is a *sensation*—an emotion, I suppose—of which I am wholly unfamiliar. It's a rough-hewn thing, out of place in my emotional landscape, like a craggy rock in a field of wildflowers.

Without thinking, I pull up my phone, dialing Sherry. Before I can even get a word out, her sass comes through loud and clear. "I see we're trying to get ourselves killed today."

"How is it you didn't know he was related to a mob family? He's been doing my highlight sheets for months."

Sherry pauses before answering, her words careful. "Edgerton did the screening. I'm quite certain he was thorough, but nothing in Joe's background threw up any red flags. And besides, you can't *not* hire someone because of who they're related to."

"Of course you can."

"Well, sure, but how much money have you made on his highlight sheets alone?"

I let out a frustrated breath. "Easily seven figures."

"Interesting. And how can I help you today?"

"He's in my kitchen, making pasta."

"I'll call in the National Guard." Her bone-dry wit is once again the bane of my existence.

"I'm serious. I blew up his life twice in as many days, but he cooks when he's anxious. Apparently."

"What kind of food are we talking about?"

"Pasta Primavera with egg noodles. From scratch."

"Oh, the suffering you must endure. I have no idea how you manage."

"I called for your advice, not to be harangued. If I wanted to be bullied, I could simply call my father."

"Oof. Low blow."

"Apologies."

"So let's dig into this a little more. You're upset that he's cooking for you?"

I glance back at the kitchen, then linger on how his perfectly broken-in jeans hug his perfect ass. "Not upset. Not exactly. It just feels...wrong-footed."

I linger on his ass for a few more moments until I realize Sherry is still talking.

"Has it not occurred to you that he might want to poison you?"

I can practically see the grin on her impudent face. "Not that I can blame the man."

I roll my eyes and play along. "Honestly, Sherry, if this is how I go, it's how I go."

"I take it your place smells divine."

"It smells like Maialino's in here."

I smile when she grumbles under her breath.

"Are you trying to make me jealous?"

"No. Maybe."

"Hmm." She's tapping something, like a pen on a desk. "So now you're in an uncomfortable position where he's endangered himself and sacrificed his relationship with his family to save you, and all you've done is fire him."

I remind myself that I hired her against my father's wishes for the express purpose of this kind of takedown. I can't believe I ever once thought that was a clever idea.

Sighing, I respond, "I'm guessing there isn't a Hallmark card that apologizes for that kind of thing, is there? One I could stuff full of cash and shove in his direction?"

"I have a feeling if you gave him cash, he'd find it offensive."

I look at my phone as if it's begun translating her words into Gaelic. "Who finds cash offensive?"

"People who like a little more thought with their gifts."

"Then what do I do? I won't have peace until he's been properly compensated."

"Have you updated his title and salary?"

"Yes, and I gave him the raise you told me to."

"I might have a few ideas," she says, followed by more pen tapping. "When is dinner going to be served?"

"I don't know." I hold the phone to my chest. "Mr. Portelli?"

His shoulders shift and tense. Putting down his utensils, he looks at me over his shoulder. "Who you calling Mr. Portelli?"

My throat goes dry. He really looks like a mobster when he's irritated.

Fuck, that's sexy.

When he stitches his eyebrows together, I realize I haven't answered him. "Oh, sorry. Um, Joe—when do you think you might be done with dinner?"

He shrugs. "Twenty to thirty minutes. You hungry?"

"I am, but I'm also asking because Sherry might stop by." Her response is too muffled to understand, but I can guess what she's saying. "Or she may fight her way in. I told her you were creating pasta from scratch, and she's already in the car."

His stern look breaks and he smiles. God, it lights up the whole kitchen.

"I've shared some of my lunch with her before. Tell her to get her ass over here so she can have it fresh."

I turn back to the phone. "Did you hear that?"

For a few seconds, all I hear is a softly muttered, "Yes, yes, yes."

"Sherry?"

"I'm doing a happy dance, don't interrupt me."

I go quiet, listening, and it sounds like she's moving around quite a bit. I'm not sure how many moves a lovely, plump woman of fifty-five has in her, but I'm sure Sherry is as above average in that area as she is with everything else.

"Okay, I'm back. I'll be there in thirty with a solution to your little problem."

"Who said I had a problem? I was just..."

"Overthinking things, as usual. Don't worry. I'll use my company card."

She ends the call, and I tap the edge of my phone to my forehead.

What have I gotten myself into?

TWENTY-EIGHT MINUTES LATER, Sherry walks through the elevator doors, a supremely smug look on her face. She's holding a substantial box, which she went to the trouble of having gift wrapped. Not sure I fully understand the purpose of that or what she could possibly have in a box so big.

"Rand," she says, grinning. "It is nice to see you this evening."

"Rand?"

"It's after hours. We're on my time, not yours."

I nod as I escort her through the hallway into the living room, wondering if I'd like it as much if others started using my first name.

"Oh my God, this house smells like heaven."

Joe comes padding out of the kitchen, still barefoot, still weirdly attractive in his worn-out jeans and tank top. He gives Sherry a little wave from across the space before returning to the kitchen.

She lets out a low whistle under her breath. "I see the problem now."

I turn to her. "What?"

"Not only did he save your life, but he could also practically jumpstart your heart. Who knew he was hiding all of that under his secondhand wardrobe?" she whispers conspiratorially.

"Whatever are you on about?"

"He looks like a Calvin Klein model."

"No. I dated a Calvin Klein model. That man was smooth, refined, and beautiful. None of those words describe Joe. And shh. He can probably hear every word we're saying."

Sherry lowers her voice but seems bound and determined to make her point. "You're right. He's not refined. At. All. He's ruggedly handsome. Dangerously so. I can see why you'd be having a hard time."

"I could fire you," I hiss, fixing her with a glare. "I could so fire you right now."

Sherry snorts, dramatically rolling her eyes. "But you won't. Because you're not an idiot." Grinning, she looks right up at me. "Except for when it comes to how you behave around mobsters, apparently."

"I'm never living this down, am I?" I say as we make our way into the kitchen

Gesturing between Joe and me, she answers, "You pissed off a mobster while begging his brother to give you another chance after behaving so spectacularly awful the day before. Yeah, you've earned whatever you get from me on that."

"This is going to be a learning opportunity for me, isn't it?"

"Yes. One I'll enjoy reminding you of whatever I possibly can."

Joe's eyes dart back and forth between the two of us like a tennis match.

"You talk to him like that?"

Sherry shrugs. "All the time."

Joe laughs, pointing at himself. "I only thought people who weren't long for the job could talk to him like that."

"Generally true, but he knows I'm irreplaceable."

I shake my head at her before addressing Joe. "Unfortunately, she's telling the truth. I read somewhere that it's a good idea to have at least one person in your organization who's willing to speak truth to power."

His eyes dart back to her before fixing me with a wolfish grin. "And is it?"

"Well. Yes." I adjust my stance, a little uncomfortable. "I suppose she's saved me from a disaster or two. She can be some-what more diplomatic than I am. She can also be somewhat less diplomatic when the situation calls for it."

"You don't say."

He's teasing me, and that definitely should not make my cock twitch or heat creep up my neck into my face.

"Why am I being ganged up on in my own house?"

Joe's eyes track the color on my cheeks. I swallow, and his all-seeing eyes track that as well.

"I don't know. Maybe it's because one of them is a literal gang member?" Sherry says, bumping Joe's hip with her own.

"What did you do for them?" I ask, realization dawning. Is this going to be a security nightmare? I wonder why Edgerton felt comfortable enough to leave me alone with him.

"I was a delivery guy. Never knew what was in the brown paper packages, never cared to open them."

"How long did you do that?"

"I guess my first drop-off was when I was twelve, maybe?"

"Really?" Sherry asks, her eyes uncharacteristically shiny. "I'm so sorry, Joe."

He shrugs like it's no big deal he was forced to become an underage drug runner. "My nonna got big mad over that. Made me promise I'd keep myself out of trouble and go to college. Told her real young I wanted to be a legit businessman, wear a suit. My father wasn't having it, but my nonna didn't back down. He promised her that as long as I didn't ask him for money, he'd leave me alone. Wasn't exactly a hard decision."

"Oh."

There's an awkward moment of silence as we all stand between the hallway and the living room, then Sherry clears her throat.

"Little help here, guys," she says, gesturing her chin at the large package she's still holding.

"Oh shit," Joe says, reaching out. "Nonna would smack me upside the head, letting you hold that for so long."

Sherry laughs, and he takes the box, clearly accustomed to carrying heavy things, and sets it delicately on the bar. Turning to me, he asks, "I'm not going to ruin anything by setting this down on your fancy wood countertop, am I?"

I shake my head. "My home is meant to be lived in."

Joe tilts his head at me again, like maybe I've surprised him. I walk on eggshells all day long. I need at least one place where I can just be myself.

Sherry hip-checks Joe, pointing at the box. "Open it."

Joe scrubs the back of his head and then removes... Is that a *knife*? He's had a *knife* in his back pocket this entire time? How did it get past my security? I suppose it doesn't matter because he's only using it to carefully open his present, but I plan on having a conversation with Edgerton first thing tomorrow morning.

Then I look over at the enormous chef's knife he's been wielding for the last hour and decide that Edgerton probably wouldn't let the man stay with me if he thought there was even the smallest chance of violence.

"Holy shit. This is an entire gaming system. With VR helmets." He looks at me. "You are insane."

I shrug and try not to be charmed by how much he looks like every kid at Christmas. "I'm not the one who picked it out. She did."

"Then you are insane," he says to Sherry, giving her a big hug. She looks over his shoulder as he wraps his muscles around her and winks at me.

A shard of jealousy twists its way into my stomach. It's a weak emotion, so I settle myself and decide that I am jealous of absolutely nothing with this man. I have everything. Though his delight in getting the gaming system is probably visible in the outer boroughs.

After thanking me, he declares that dinner is ready, and we all sit around the dining room table, eating Joe's homemade pasta primavera. I've paid hundreds of dollars for a plate of pasta that couldn't hold a candle to this. It's quite literally one of the most delicious things I've ever put in my mouth.

"This is divine," I say, puzzling at another forkful before practically shoving it into my mouth.

"You sound surprised."

I gesture at my kitchen, which, apparently, has magical properties. "I watched you this entire evening. This is literally just flour, water, and egg. And you didn't even make a sauce. You just chopped up the vegetables."

He shrugs. "It's all in the wrist."

Sherry laughs and eyes me significantly. I gesture a slicing motion at my throat, and she laughs even harder.

Still, I've hardly had time for intimate dinners with friends these last few years, and that's what this feels like. Intimate. It's oddly freeing.

I'm reminded of Joe's sharp words during the meeting and how they cut right to the heart of the matter. How I had to go on the attack so others wouldn't see me bleed.

He was right about the cage, of course. It's gilded and beautiful, but a cage, nonetheless. And for as long as my father holds sway over the board, the desire to build the company of my dreams will be crushed, denied oxygen.

I would never tell anyone how hard it is to breathe sometimes.

I make a note to look further into the whole alpha-wolf study. Joe seems to think it's a mantle one can simply put down, but that is not true. Thousands of people are employed at Wolfe Athletics, and I helped Father build an empire based on that persona.

Refocusing on our mini dinner party, I refill Sherry's wine and let Joe heap a second helping of the delicate, fragrant pasta on my plate.

My trainer be damned, I eat every bit of it.

After dinner, Sherry excuses herself, needing to get back

home. Joe picks up the dishes and grouses when Grayson appears and cleans up the mess he left in the kitchen.

"Shit, man," Joe says after the third time Grayson shoos him away. "I'm sorry. I wasn't thinking. Should've invited you and your mom up here for dinner. Next time, okay?"

Grayson smiles, though he knows as well as I how inappropriate that would be.

"Perhaps, instead, I can have you cook this in my place and fill it with these delectable smells."

Joe nods. "Sounds like a plan. Hey, I'm gonna get back into it. I gotta work with this mook here to figure out what to say to the fancy people so their stock pulls out of the dive it's in."

I don't know what a *mook* is, but I'm guessing it's not flattering.

9

JOE

PER EDGERTON'S REQUEST, Rand and I have stayed in his penthouse for the last several days. I have to admit that the guest suite, if that's what we're calling it, is very comfortable. The bed is way more supportive than what I was sleeping on in my fifth-floor walkup.

I thought we'd warmed up to each other with the first dinner, but...no. It's clear we're meant to stick to our respective spaces, using the company's instant messaging platform to communicate ideas to share with the board. He's been open to my suggestions, though it's weird that he'd rather stay on his side of the penthouse than talk face to face.

The only person I've actually talked to during this time is Grayson, and that's only when he delivers my meals. But even those interactions are brief. Based on the regret in Grayson's eyes, I'm guessing Wolfe gave him some sort of directive about what's appropriate.

Honestly, as much as it frustrates me—meals are meant to be shared, for Christ's sake—it makes me feel sorry for a fucking billionaire. I had no idea how close to the truth I was with that cage thing.

Whatever the reason, this is fucking miserable.

After yet another brief, *appropriate* interaction with Grayson, I decide I've had enough with this interminable isolation and pull up the messaging app.

Portelli, Joseph: You know, there's this thing called actual human contact. You should try it sometime.

Portelli, Joseph: Unless you're a robot.

Wolfe Jr., Randolf: Does not compute.

I laugh, then stare at the screen, confused.

Portelli, Joseph: Was that a joke?

Portelli, Joseph: Who is this, and where is the smug billionaire who's been ignoring me?

Wolfe Jr., Randolf: It was a joke. I apologize.

Portelli, Joseph: No apologies necessary. It was a pretty good joke. I lol'd. For real.

Wolfe Jr., Randolf: No, I apologize for not making you feel more welcome. I'm not sure of the protocol in a situation like this.

Who the fuck is this guy?

Portelli, Joseph: I'm pretty sure the protocol would include busting out that VR system and giving it a whirl. Would be rude to ignore Sherry's thoughtfulness.

Wolfe Jr., Randolf: You know, I think you might be right.

Portelli, Joseph: Meet you in the living room?

He doesn't respond immediately, and I wonder if I haven't scared him back into whatever shell he's been hiding in.

Wolfe Jr., Randolf: Yes.

Well, okay then.

I pull on a clean T-shirt from the pile of clothes that Rand lent to me and check my hair in the mirror before walking out into the main area and crossing the kitchen into the living room.

He's standing in the middle of his own space, shifting on his feet as he fidgets with the box of VR equipment. I lock down the urge to give him a hug and meet him in the middle.

"Oh, look. A real, live boy," I say, cracking a smile.

He takes a breath as though he was anticipating something meaner. Squaring his shoulders, he sends me a Very Serious nod. He seems to be at war with himself, like maybe he wants to relax, but there's an inner drill sergeant spit-yelling at him to stand up straight and act like a man.

"Hey," I say, lightly smacking his arm. "Protocol says that when you're greeted with a friendly joke, you throw it back. Or at least crack a smile."

He adjusts a shoulder, then nods to himself. "Hello. Also, no one's called me real—or a boy—in a long time."

I laugh, not sure if he's being intentionally funny or not. "The self-own. That's a bold move."

He finally smiles, and it's vulnerable as hell. Yet another huge crack in his miles-above-everyone billionaire persona. The desire to surround him in bubble wrap is almost overwhelming.

"So...do you know how this works?" he asks, holding out the box for me to take.

I nod and quickly walk him through setting up an account and pairing the two headsets. "I'm so happy Sherry brought this over—I don't even know what made her think of it."

His smile is small and wry. "Did you ever happen to mention VR to Sherry?"

I nod, attaching earbuds to each headset. "I dunno, like once, a few months ago. Do you think she got this because of that conversation?"

"She's very good at her job. Remembers every detail, even the ones you wished she didn't. But I'm glad she was able to get something thoughtful."

"It was very thoughtful."

We go quiet and put on our headsets. Before we get into the

first-person shooter game I've had my eye on, I spy my favorite travel app.

"Hey, before we start trying to murder each other, wanna see something cool?"

"Uh, sure."

I tell him where to go and push back my visor to see his reaction.

"I'm in the mountains," he says, reaching out in front of himself. "Oh, wow, there are mountains behind me," he says, swinging to look behind him.

He spins back around and bumps into his tufted ottoman. I grab his arm to prevent him from tripping and try to ignore the rapid rise of his chest.

"Whoops, let me move this out of the way."

He stands still as I move things around in the living room, making space for us. I touch his elbow, and he jumps.

"Sorry. Just directing you to stand in the middle."

After a few seconds, he relaxes into my touch, his shoulders finally dropping out of his ears. With his headset still in place, I take advantage and really look at him. Despite these flashes of awkwardness, there's something about the way he holds his body that feels like repressed energy. Like his arms. He doesn't let them hang relaxed at his sides. Rather, he keeps them in a slight bend, like a bird with a damaged wing just waiting to heal.

I bet he'd be beautiful in full flight.

I snort to myself—okay, who the hell am I trying to be right now? William Fucking Shakespeare? I shake myself and put back on the headset, hitting the button to start the game.

We're immediately dropped into an intensely violent scene, and I worry it'll be too much for him, but he's into it. Like, surprisingly into it. And whatever part of me thinks I still have a chance at winning is quickly silenced with a bullet between my eyes.

"Wow. Brutal."

I push up my headset, and his proud smirk is more satisfying than a win would have been, that's for damn sure. We go a few more rounds before calling it a night. We've got our first meeting with the board tomorrow, and I'm glad we had a chance to connect beforehand.

You know, for the business.

I REFUSE to take my breakfast in the guest suite again, so I decide to make us a quick frittata.

After knocking out a body-weight workout, I make my way into the kitchen, grateful that the pretty billionaire with the appealing vulnerabilities is nowhere to be seen.

Grabbing the eggs, milk, and some vegetables, I whip up a semi-healthy breakfast. Then just to ensure nobody thinks the penthouse life is turning me into a health nut, I fry up a rasher of bacon to add some flair to the proceedings.

I'm nearly done with breakfast when Rand walks into the kitchen. He's wearing expensive workout gear, sleek and gray, stylish, engineered to wick the merest hint of sweat from his slender body.

My eyes track down his sculpted frame to his shoes, which I recognize from the company's *Amplify* line. Honestly, I don't know why they spend millions of dollars wooing big-name athletes to sell their shoes—they should just put Wolfe on a billboard.

"Whatcha cooking?" he asks, peering over my shoulder as though he's somehow never seen someone make breakfast before.

"Your spinach and mushrooms looked perfect, so I added them to the frittata."

Rand doesn't respond, so I look back and startle, inhaling sharply at his nearness. He's so close I could easily brush my lips along the sharp line of his cheekbone.

After last night, I'm starting to understand that the instant messages and keeping to our neutral corners were about preventing me from having a peek at his soft underbelly. But I see it anyway, clear as day. It's in the sadness around his eyes when his father dresses him down in front of the rest of us, in the restrained excitement over a simple bowl of pasta, and in the private way he smiles when he thinks no one is looking.

But this right here—this soft invasion of my personal space—feels different. Like maybe he enjoys the company of men the same way I do. If I were to kiss his cheek, what would his reaction be? I imagine that kind of affection, if wanted, would be greeted with soft smiles and a sweet nuzzle in response.

Swallowing reflexively, I note that he's got a freckle right above his dark golden eyelashes. Looking back down at the pan, I take a deep breath and gather myself. "I assume you like spinach and mushrooms because they were in your refrigerator. But you don't hafta eat this if you don't like it."

More silence.

I check and, yep, he's still right there. Blinking at me, gifting me with a few more glimpses of that dark freckle.

"What's this mug you've got going on here?" I ask, using the spatula to gesture in a circle toward his face.

His placid look breaks, and he chuckles, crinkling the skin at the corner of his eyes. I don't think that was his intention, based on how he quickly schools himself.

"Sorry," he says, clearing his throat. "You know you don't have to cook for me, right? That the terms of your employment—or your stay here, for that matter—do not cover culinary duties?"

I run my bottom lip through my teeth, straightening my posture. "I know that. I'm just not the kind of douche who's gonna make a delicious frittata with perfectly crispy bacon and not offer you some. Also, I figure we should get our ducks in a row before meeting with the board today."

His Adam's apple bobs, and he nods. "You're right. We should chat through the bullet points so we can present a united front. I do appreciate breakfast—my tyrannical trainer will be thrilled with your choices. Save for the bacon, but I trust you won't rat me out."

I chuckle to myself. "Wolfe, you know I was raised in the Mafia, right? You wanna know the first lesson my Sicilian grandfather taught me?"

The corner of his mouth hooks up into a grin. "Snitches get stitches?"

I shake my head. "Snitches get their firstborn killed. Believe me, your secret is safe with me."

His eyes widen and he takes a step back. It's possible I went in a little hard on the pre-coffee truths.

Laughing, I gesture at the distance between us, trying not to think about how much chillier my skin just got. "You do understand that saving your life means I don't want to cause you harm, right?"

He waves me off. "Of course. I don't fear you in the slightest."

I raise my brow as I start plating breakfast. "That's not to say it wouldn't be smart of you to let me take the first bite though." I hand him his plate. "That was lesson number two from *Nonno*."

He playfully narrows his eyes and uses his fork to give me the go-ahead gesture. Dropping my eyes to my plate, I slice through the frittata with the edge of my fork, then jab the eggy bit of goodness and stuff it in my mouth, chewing slowly.

"*Fanculo.*"

"Something wrong?"

"Everything is so fresh. This is fucking delicious."

"If you do say so yourself."

I wink, and Rand swallows. He looks between my plate and his, calculating. I'm enough of a man to admit that these tiny windows into his persona are endearing as hell. He's trying so hard to look like he's in charge, but now that I've seen it, I can't unsee it. I suppose I should feel superior for having this knowledge, but it mostly makes me like the guy.

There are so many men like him in the mob. Acting like they're not pissing in their pants when half of them just want to go home to *Mama* and forget anything happened.

Grinning like a madman, I finish my bite and reach over to his plate, cutting away a small corner of his frittata. Keeping eye contact, I slowly bring it to my mouth, chewing carefully before I swallow. His eyes track my Adam's apple, his teeth scraping along his lower lip.

He spears a piece of the delicious egg mixture and manages to beat me at my own game. Locking eyes with me, he chews as he smiles, wiping a tiny bit of spinach from his plump lower lip. It's a little fuller than his top lip, and it gives him a pouty, almost bratty look.

He's so close that I'd barely have to lean in to suck that impudent lower lip into my mouth. Picturing it is way too easy: I'd take a few seconds to savor its taste before attacking his entire mouth, grinding against him until he loses his pretense of control and melts against me.

Yeah, I bet he'd like that a whole lot.

I know I would.

Taking another bite from my own plate, I enjoy it thoroughly. When I lick a stray mushroom from the tines of my fork then slide it in my mouth, Wolfe gulps and finally looks away.

Winner winner, chicken dinner. Wolfe definitely wants to see my penis.

And as much as I can imagine crowing over such a juicy detail, I instead feel intensely protective of this privileged truth.

"So, where do you get decent coffee in this joint?" I ask, interrupting him mid-bite. "I might throw myself off the balcony if I have to drink more of that pod crap."

Grinning as he chews, he juts his chin over at some futuristic space machine sitting on the counter.

"What the fuck am I supposed to do with that?"

He raises his brow and sets his half-eaten breakfast on the counter. "Don't touch my frittata—I'm coming back for it. Also, whatever you did with that bacon is really delicious."

I shrug. "Found some chili pepper honey in your pantry, drizzled a little on the bacon right before I pulled it out of the pan."

"Nice." Rand crunches through another bite of bacon before pulling a mug from the cabinet. "Shot, Americano, latte, cappuccino?"

"This thing here makes a cappuccino?" I ask, now the one to look over his shoulder.

He briefly looks back then refocuses on the machine. "It's got everything."

"Fuck, then. Give me a cappuccino."

Taking another bite of bacon, he hits a few buttons. Steam hisses out from the top and grinding sounds vibrate the entire machine. Within moments, a beautiful cappuccino with a foamy head is placed in my hands.

"Go ahead, try it."

His look of anticipation is so cute it's annoying, but my nonna taught me to be a good guest. I take a careful sip and...shit, this is good. Damn good.

"Well?" he asks, his eyes bright like a little kid's. I chuckle at his excitement, and his smile disappears. He steps back, pulling a more neutral look across his face. There's that inner drill sergeant again, yelling at him for showing the tiniest hint of emotion.

Rather than feel sorry for him, I take a few sips, relishing that this billionaire is waiting impatiently to find out if I enjoy his coffee.

Spoiler alert: I do.

"The only person who's ever made better coffee in my entire life is my nonna. So yes, it's very, very good."

"I'm glad to hear it." He allows himself a small, pleased smile and then nods it away, straightening his shoulders. "You don't have to drink the pod coffee. I don't mind making you a cappuccino in the morning."

"And I don't mind making breakfast."

"Deal."

His eyes catch on something, and he reaches his hand out. Part of me wants to flinch, but I still my body as his thumb brushes across my upper lip. It sends sparks across my skin, and I will myself not to bend him over the counter.

"You had some foam there," he says quietly.

"Thanks for the save." I lick over the same spot, hoping for a taste of him.

I don't think he knows what to do when I smile at him. It makes me want to do it even more.

Looking at the time, I take my mug and nod at the table. "Time to prep for our meeting."

He dips his head and grins, then gathers his half-eaten breakfast, following me to the table.

Yeah, definitely playing with fire with this one.

———

AN HOUR LATER, we're well-prepared, dressed to the nines, and riding up in an executive elevator I've never been in. I'm sweating buckets, trying to act confident as we head to the top floor of the Wolfe Athletics building.

When the elevator doors open, I let out a breath, grateful for the familiar warmth of Sherry sitting at her desk.

"I've missed you two," she says, making her way toward us. Where she promptly straightens my collar and smooths down my tie. "You look good in a suit." Her eyes narrow as she eyeballs my shoulders. "Especially one that fits you."

"Thanks, beautiful. It feels a little too fancy for a dock worker, you feel me? You'd think an athletics place would be a bit more casual."

"I don't think the elder Wolfe understands the concept of casual," she says, gesturing to her posh, office-appropriate attire. Switching subjects, she asks, "Have you thought through what you're going to say to the board? Do you have your ideas well in mind?"

I nod and hold up the portfolio I pilfered from the guest room office. "Rand and I chatted through everything this morning. I bulleted my ideas and identified potential avenues to pay for them."

She beams and flicks away another invisible speck of dusk. She seems nervous for me, and I can't tell if that's sweet or slightly terrifying.

"Good, good. Normally I'd have you shoot that over to me so I could create some slides, but we don't have the time."

I adjust my tie. "I appreciate that. If this is part of what I'm going to be doing from here on out, I'd like to come to you for help if you don't mind."

"Of course you can come to me." She smacks my hand and re-straightens my tie. "I just fixed that for you. Don't be nervous. Don't fidget. Don't give them a single foothold to discredit you. That passion you showed in the meeting? *That's* your superpower."

"You sure about that? Pretty sure that's what got my ass kicked to the curb the first time."

"No." She gestures her finger in a circle. "This is exactly the kind of weak language I'm talking about. You didn't get your ass kicked to the curb. You took a stand and told the truth on purpose, regardless of the consequences. You made a decision, didn't you?"

I nod. "I couldn't stay quiet."

"Exactly. These guys don't listen to anyone. Any. One. It's going to feel like you're beating your head against a brick wall the first couple of times, but don't give up. They've spent years locked in groupthink, leaving us with a whole raft of blind spots. Our sales for the last two years have been soft."

"Yet they've increased their profit at the expense of the work-force," I say, lowering my voice. "Working through all those competitor sheets, it was easy to see that we weren't keeping up. Hell, *I'd* started looking at job openings. I'm not surprised we've lost as many people as we have."

"Exactly. And don't you forget it. More importantly, don't let *them* forget it. They'd be damn fools not to listen to you."

She shifts and looks Rand dead in the eye when she says that last bit. I am again impressed with his willingness to let her speak the truth. I wonder—no, scratch that—I *know* that if more people like her were on the board, things would be so much better.

"Are you ready?" Rand asks, straightening his shoulders as he looks toward the boardroom.

He's pulled on his game face, and I gotta say...that's a neat party trick. I mimic his posture, the length of his neck, the barely perceptible snarl of disdain on his lips, and we walk in the door.

SHERRY CALLED IT. This meeting has been a shit show, pretty much from the beginning.

"Your ideas aren't even remotely sustainable. What a farce."

Finding the old, beady-eyed jackoff with the stupid opinion, I fix him with a glare. "That's not true. I spent the last six months looking at our competitors, and we are the only people in this space not offering these options to our employees."

Another guy, two seconds from shuffling off his mortal coil, scoffs. "Which is why our profit margins are so much better than theirs."

My lips snarl as I shake my head. "Those numbers are the most propped up piece of shit I've ever seen before in my life. You can lie to the investors all you want, but don't lie to me. Don't treat me like I'm stupid."

Ford, snazzy dresser and Rand's one friend on the board, lowers his chin. During a break, Rand explained that as the investment genius of the group, Ford knows I'm telling the truth. He's been quiet, but I hope he'll jump in at some point and back me up.

Wolfe Sr., however, plows on. "Oh, yes. Please tell us all about the numbers. I'm intrigued by all the insight you must've gained from your time on the docks."

Oh wow. This absolute piece of shit. I don't let my inner mobster out to play, like, ever, but I'm about to rip him a new one.

"Look here, you motherfucker..." I start, dropping into my Brooklyn.

Rand stands up. "Okay, clearly we've reached an impasse. I think we've all brought up good points—"

I open my mouth to strenuously object to that fucking characterization, but he holds up his hand, darting a nervous look at his father. I shut my mouth, but it hurts to do so.

"But," he continues, "I believe we should all go to our neutral corners and think through our arguments and solutions. We've leaked to the press that Mr. Portelli is working with us, which has slowed some of the hemorrhaging."

Wolfe Sr. snorts. "This is pure theater. Son, don't let yourself be fooled by this man. I paid enough for your college education that you should be smarter than this. We don't let the little people call the shots."

Most of the old people in the room nod in agreement, sneering in my direction. Rand, Mr. Alpha himself, opens his mouth and closes it, looking somehow smaller at the end of that exchange than he was at the beginning.

His dad just condescended to him in front of the executive team, and he hasn't done anything to defend himself.

And that bothers me way more than it should.

10

RAND

THE ROOM GOES SILENT, save for my father's disdainful words about *the little people* ringing in my ears. Frustrated and anxious, I straighten my tie, then loosen it. Then take it off entirely.

I hate wearing ties.

Most of these people genuinely do not care about the human beings who work for us. And to be honest, until I was being shot at by the Mafia, I don't think I'd given it much of a thought one way or the other. We pay people, they work for us, end of story.

But now I hear it—the judgment and disregard. And I can't stand it.

I sneak a look at Jackson. As VP of Human Resources, he's a serious fellow and always careful with his words. He's remained silent this entire time, but every time Joe makes a point, he nods his head ever-so-slightly.

My father noticed, and we'll likely be short one VP by the end of the day, with no lessons learned on my father's part.

And that's the point Joe has been trying to make the entire time. These people who work for us are *human beings*. That seems obvious now, but as far as the company is concerned, they've only ever been assets.

That kind of short-sighted thinking allowed my father, near the end of his tenure as CEO, to approve the manufacturing of our very expensive shoes in places where people were enslaved for their labor. I have no proof that he knew this ahead of time, but I'm not convinced knowing would have swayed his choices.

Joe, on the other hand, is a thing of beauty. If he was powerful in an ill-fitting, wrinkled shirt, he's damn near invincible in well-tailored, luxury wool. He speaks with authority and passion and—sometimes—a flash of mobster. It's sexy as hell.

In comparison, I'm already cowing to my father like I always do. I'd love nothing more than to follow Joe into the fire, but I have no choice. My father holds all the cards.

When the silence continues, I clear my throat. "Okay, we've listened to what Mr. Portelli has to say. I understand these things can get heated, but there's a lot we've learned."

My father purses his lips, and I, as always, school my face when he undermines me.

I glance at Joe, expecting the same derision in his expression. But no. His jaw tenses and he narrows his eyes at my father, shaking his head in what can only be described as disgust.

My father pushes back from the table and stands, imperious as always. "Fine. I have other things I need to attend to."

With that, the meeting is over, and not a damn thing has changed. There's an awkward pause before everyone shuffles off to whatever they have planned for their evening.

Straightening some papers, I chance another look at Joe, and he looks disappointed. Probably in me. When I think about how quickly I was in over my head at the docks, I wonder what his opinion of me must be. Not that I should care what he thinks, but I do. I really do, and that he's seen how weak I really am is almost more than I can bear.

When we get back to the penthouse, I beg off from our dinner and VR games, claiming a headache. Grayson knocks on my door several minutes later.

"Sir. Mr. Portelli says that you have a headache and was quite concerned. He insisted that I bring you migraine tablets and chamomile tea," he says, gesturing to the tray of care items.

"Fucking Joe," I swear under my breath.

"Sir?"

I shake my head. "Nothing, Grayson. My apologies. It was not a good day at the office."

"That so, sir?"

Something about having Grayson standing here—since I am not competent enough to grab an aspirin from my own damn medicine cabinet—makes me feel utterly useless and utterly alone.

I ask myself what Joe would do and snort to myself.

"Sir?"

"Can you... Grayson, when it's just the two of us, can you please call me Rand?" I feel stupid for asking, but it feels important. Really important.

"Of course, sir...Rand. I'm happy to do that."

"Thank you."

We stand there for an awkward moment. "Rand, would you be open to a suggestion?"

Startled, I nod immediately. "Yes. Please."

He takes a breath and sets the tray on a bedside table. Facing me with a smile, he says, "You and Joe have been stuck in this place for days. Actually, you've been stuck indoors for longer than that. Before the security concerns cropped up, you jogged every morning and walked through the park in the evening before coming home."

"Edgerton hates any environment he can't control. He's acting like people are just waiting outside my door, anxious to cause me harm."

"And I respect his position enormously. But I've known you for most of your life, and if we're on a first-name basis, maybe you won't mind me saying that I can see how hard this has been on you." He grasps my shoulder, capturing my gaze. "Rand, trying to follow every rule has left you dying on the vine. You need to take the reins and restore the balance in your life."

I laugh. "You suggesting a jailbreak, Grayson?"

"I would never suggest going against security protocol. Certainly not by yourself." He looks behind us, and when he's satisfied that Edgerton isn't going to pop out of a hidden corner, he leans in, a conspiratorial look on his face. "But I might imply it."

I laugh and surprise the hell out of both of us by draping my arm around him in a half-hug. "You inspire me, Grayson. Thank you."

Grayson bows his head, winking at me as he leaves my room.

Implied, indeed.

I GET UP EARLY and make a cappuccino for Joe and a triple espresso shot for myself, hoping to entice him into a bit of trouble-making. Just as I'm transferring the caffeinated nectar to insulated mugs, he meanders into the kitchen, his rich brown hair sticking out in every direction. My fingers twitch with the desire to run through the unruly strands.

"That smells divine," he says, scratching his belly, revealing a dark happy trail that runs from his belly button to just beyond his hazardously low-slung waistline.

I had Grayson buy him proper pajamas, but they run large. I suppose that wouldn't be so bad if he wore the matching shirt, but Joe prefers his old tank top. The practically see-through one that molds to every cursed muscle.

So. Yeah. Now I've seen the v-cut abs I'd only imagined, and after closer examination of the thin drape of material, I've determined that Joe isn't wearing any underwear. The material is flimsy enough for me to suspect that he's uncircumcised.

I wonder if he likes docking. I've never—

I look up and catch his amused expression. Ignoring the heat igniting in my chest and groin, I plow forward into my plan for the day.

"I'm sneaking out of the building and spending the morning in the park. Wanna join me?"

He leans back against the counter, crossing his impressive arms. "Is that why you put my cappuccino in a to-go cup?"

My eyes glide back down to his pajama bottoms. He shifts his hips, and his cock drifts from one side to the other.

If that's what he looks like relaxed...

"Rand?"

"Huh?"

"I guess we're taking the caffeine to go."

"Yeah, if that's okay with you."

He's definitely uncircumcised.

Joe clears his throat, and I tear my eyes away from his crotch. He arches his brow at me, and I quickly refocus on the beverages. When he doesn't say anything, I chance another look in his direction. Fuck, busted.

Not bothering to hide his bemused expression, he shows a little mercy. "Hell, why not. Give me five minutes, and I'll be ready to go."

"Sounds good."

He heads back to his suite, and I cover my face with my hands. I can't believe I was just staring at his dick. I need to have Grayson book my regular guy, pronto. Meanwhile, I text to let him know we'll be ready soon.

True to his word, Joe is back in the kitchen five minutes later, wearing the hell out of Wolfe Athletics' luxe jogger pants and slimline hoodie. Even our fancy cross-trainers are sexy as hell on him. Our athletic gear is supposed to make people look erudite and wealthy, but he looks like an actual athlete. When he turns to open the refrigerator, I get the full view of his thick, muscular glutes in my joggers.

I'm not a religious man, but God, do I want to worship at the altar of his ass.

"Sir, you rang?"

I nearly jump out of my skin. "Grayson! You scared me," I exclaim, turning bright red.

"Ah, yes, sir. I didn't mean to frighten you while you were...concentrating."

I turn to my loyal employee, whose eyes are also appreciating Joe's assets. I wait till I have his attention, then purse my lips. "Do you have everything set up?"

His mischievous smile shouldn't put me in a better mood, but it does. "Yes, sir. If you and Mr. Portelli are ready, I can take you through my entrance to the commoner's elevator."

"You know, if you're going to openly sass me, you might as well just use my first name all the time."

"Certainly, Rand. And if I may make a suggestion, I believe that Sherry's level of sass also garners her full-time first-name status as well."

Joe lets out a rude guffaw, and I gesture between him and Grayson. "This is your fault, you know. You've infected Grayson with your *Brooklyn* attitude."

Joe drops into his thick accent. "Hey, yo. Grayson, baby, ain't nothing wrong with getting a little Brooklyn in you every once in a while, you feel me?"

Grayson bows his head, barely managing to hold back laughter. "Yes, Joe. I shall keep that in mind."

I throw up my hands. "It's a world gone mad. Grayson, can you please just help me sneak out of my own building?"

"Of course."

We follow Grayson through the service door, and Joe chuckles. "That at least solves the mystery of how Grayson appears out of nowhere."

Grayson grins. "I have my ways," he says, leading us down a flight of steps to a typical apartment hallway.

I hold my finger to my lips then point to the second door on the right. "Edgerton's apartment," I whisper under my breath.

Joe's eyes sparkle with mischief and he gives me a thumbs-up.

We make it to the elevators and head down to the lobby, joined by two other people along the way. The private elevator is nice in theory, but after meeting two lovely neighbors I've never ever met before, I wonder if I've been in too much of a bubble in general.

I'm a little nervous about this next part because Grayson has to distract the building's security personnel. Joe and I stay in the elevator vestibule while Grayson saunters up to the security guard on duty.

Grayson knows how to saunter?

Before I can puzzle on that for too long, I watch as he leans into his accent, cracking a joke. The guard laughs uproariously, and when Grayson places a delicate hand on his arm, the world could end around them, and that man wouldn't notice.

Joe and I silently slip past them and quickly make our way across the street, aiming for the closest entrance to the park. Within moments, we're surrounded by nature, and the sounds of the city fade into the background.

Joe turns to me, laughing. "Who knew Grayson had game?"

"Game? No. Grayson is a gentleman. That security guard, though...he definitely has a thing for Grayson, don't you think?"

"Yeah, he has a *thing* because Grayson is flirting with him."

"He is *not*. You take that back. Grayson does not flirt. He's English, for God's sake."

Joe laughs, his hand landing on his chest. "Whatever, boss."

I linger over the veins on the back of his hand, then remember to respond. "Grayson is loyal, I'll have you know. He would not sully himself with *the help*."

Joe pushes my shoulder. "Grayson *is* the help."

"You take that back! You take it back right now. He is *not* the help. He's *Grayson*. My life would fall apart without him."

"Psst, billionaire," Joe says, crooking his finger at me. I lean in, nervous. "Calling *anyone* 'the help' is dehumanizing and marks you as an out-of-touch one-percenter who deserves to be eaten." He emphasizes this by chomping his sexy teeth together.

Teeth are not sexy, dammit.

More to his point, a now-familiar sense of wrongness lances through me. Before all of this happened, it was so easy—too easy— for me to get away with saying things that are outdated and plain wrong. Even with Sherry, I wonder how often she doesn't say something because she simply has to pick her battles. "Noted," I say sincerely.

Joe smiles and pats my arm, which makes my nipples hard. "Anyway, at least that's one employee you pay well. Considering he's able to stay in the same building."

"I'll have you know that his apartment is part of his compensation package. And, of course, he's well paid. It gives me angina to think about how, in fifteen years, he'll be retired. I can't even begin to imagine it."

"You could retire early. Live a life of luxury."

I pause, looking over at Joe. "Is that really what you think of me? That I would simply luxuriate in my wealth?"

"Well, somebody should. If you're gonna hoard all this coin, at least spend some of it for fuck's sake."

"Believe me, with all of my investments, I've been spending money."

"Whatever, Corporate Ken doll."

He says it like a dig, but his tone is too fond.

Fucking fond. What alternative universe am I living in?

We've already been walking for a while, but Joe stops in his tracks, taking in the surroundings.

"What?" I say, looking around, immediately questioning the wisdom of sneaking past my security.

"Shit, this is Central Park, right?"

"Duh," I say as if it's the most obvious thing in the world... because it is. Despite teasing him, I have to admit that the wonder on his face is kind of lovely, actually.

Pushing his shoulder, I tease, "Wait. You've lived in Brooklyn all your life, and you've never been to Central Park? What kind of New Yorker are you?"

He shrugs as though his truth is equally obvious. "When I was younger, I only ever went to the city to take my nonna to her favorite Broadway shows."

"But you've worked here for a while now. The park is right outside the window."

"It's right outside *your* window, Corner Office. Besides, my boss is what my nonna would call a real *stronzo*. A real asshole," he says, grinning broadly.

I shoot him the finger, which cracks him up. He pokes my chest. "See, you've got a little Brooklyn in you too."

I'd like to have a lot of Brooklyn in me, thank you very much.

Needing to get my mind on something else, I grasp at something he just said. "My mother enjoys Broadway shows too. What does your nonna like? The big productions or the small, artsy shows?"

There it is again. That *fond* smile.

"Big productions all the way. And she liked to see them over and over again. What about your mom?"

"I think she secretly loves the big productions and sneaks off to see them as often as possible. But she tells everyone she likes the highbrow stuff."

"So, like mother like son."

"Excuse me. Evangeline is little more than a sentient mani-pedi. I am nothing like her."

Joe's lip curls up. "You really gonna talk about your mom like that, Mr. I Like Shoot 'em Up Games?"

"Look, not to talk down to you, but you have no idea how these high-society families function. My mother is everything she's supposed to be—pretty and sweet, just like spun sugar, only with more Botox. Her one duty is to photograph beautifully on my father's arm, and she's a pro. Believe me when I tell you that there aren't any hidden depths."

Joe's brow raises thoughtfully. "Look, I get that you've got a family dynamic I don't know nothing about, but I gotta wonder if you've even tried to have a serious conversation with her. Like, how much of what you just said is reality, and how much of it is just you regurgitating something your father said?"

His question stops me cold. The sneering mani-pedi comment was a direct quote from my father.

He shakes his head. "Sorry. I just...I wish I had been given the opportunity to know my mother. My father only ever said that she was a stupid whore who abandoned me and whose only decent contribution to the world was that she had a son instead of a daughter."

Fuck.

"That's awful. I'm sorry, Joe."

He lifts a shoulder, trying to brush it off, but the hurt is visible just under the surface. "I'm just saying—maybe check your assumptions while you have the ability to."

"I will. Thank you."

I make a mental note to check-in on my mother as we walk along in silence.

After a few minutes, Joe turns to me. "Where are we? I mean, within Central Park?"

Grateful for the change in subject, I shrug, looking around. "We're in the Ramble. Is there anything you want to look at in particular?"

"There a place where we can feed the ducks?"

I smile, looking sidelong at this ex-mobster. "Yeah, we can feed the ducks." I point out the path we should follow. "This will take us to the Bow Bridge. You're not supposed to feed them, but you can usually find someone who'll sell you something better than potato chips or whatever."

He grins. "Black market duck food? This I *gotta* see."

When we arrive at the bridge, the morning sun shines in his eyes and sets fire to the edges of his hair. It's enough to make me breathe a little funny.

Just as I'm trying to remember how a respiratory system works, a little girl, maybe three or four, walks up to him with a bag full of feed in her grubby hands. She holds it up like a present, and he smiles down at her, causing her to giggle.

Sweet girl, I know the feeling.

Her mother follows straight away, grinning up at Joe. "She likes to offer the food to big strong men because they'll throw it farther into the lake."

Or maybe her little girl is trying to lure handsome men into her mother's lair.

Joe does the thing that Joe always does and brightens everything around him. Obliging the little girl, he reaches into her bag and scatters the feed far into the lake. A small flotilla of ducks follows the arc of his throw, some of them flying low across the water to get to the pellets before they sink.

The little girl screeches in delight, clapping her hands together, dropping some of the duck feed on the ground at her feet. A few enterprising ducks come up close, and she screams again, backing straight into Joe. He prevents her from falling, and she wraps her chubby arms around his hands, gripping him tight until her mother manages to coax her away with sliced apples and caramel dipping sauce.

As Joe dusts the duck feed and kid dirt off his hands, I sidle up next to him, murmuring, "If that mother runs out of the caramel dipping sauce, we might have a hostage situation on our hands."

Joe laughs, his eyes crinkling at the corners. "Too right."

Does he smell this good naturally, or is that some kind of fragrance? Before I can ask, the mother thanks us for amusing her daughter, then blessedly leaves us be.

That's right, lady. Keep walking.

Joe watches them leave with a soft smile, and I can't leave well enough alone.

"You were good with that little girl. You want kids?" I ask, tossing a few stray pellets of feed into the water.

Laughing as the ducks scramble over each other to get to the food, he answers, "Yeah, I love kids. With the right guy...I could see it."

Even though I already knew he wasn't straight, his easy confirmation sends a bolt of *something*—energy, emotion maybe—through my chest.

"Yeah, me too," I say, the truth tumbling quietly from my lips.

Joe, still looking out over the water, exudes calm acceptance. "The kids or the guy?"

I take a shivery breath and, looking down at my muddy, expensive Wolfe Athletics shoes, decide on the truth. He did bust me looking at his dick this morning, after all.

"Both," I say on a gust of air. "But that's not common knowledge."

He nods carefully. "Your parents know?"

"Sure," I say, turning back toward the path. "Not their favorite subject."

His low chuckle heats my core. "Well, what good is a queer son to a talking manicure and a raging asshole?"

"Exactly." I laugh even though we both know it's not funny. "It's all about the discreet, well-paid hookups."

He side-eyes me. "How do *you* go about setting up a discreet hookup?"

My cheeks heat, but I answer truthfully. "Grayson." Changing the subject, I point to a different path. "I figure we'll wander through the trails for a bit, get some brunch at the boathouse, and get back before Edgerton loses too much hair. Sound good?"

"Sure," he says, allowing the diversion.

I look back, and he's following my lead with a warm smile.

We wind through the Ramble, and I'm quiet as Joe takes in the nature around us. After a while, he continues our initial conversation as though it's what we've been talking about the entire time.

"So that's it, investments? That's what your big money's doing? Have you ever taken, I don't know, an extravagant vacation?"

"I've been all over Europe, Asia, and Australia. I am well-traveled," I say, sounding a little snooty to even my own ears.

"If I were to pull up a map of the Wolfe Athletics offices worldwide, would your travel pattern match?"

"Possibly."

"Well, then, those are just extravagant business trips, and they don't count. Have you ever been to a beach just to go to a beach?"

I scratch the back of my head. "I burn easily."

"But you're not, like, allergic to the sun, right?"

I knock my shoulder into his. "*No.* I used to jog outside."

He raises his brow at me.

"Okay, fine, the sun only ever came up at the end of the run, but I also used to walk through the park after a long day at the office."

"I just hope you haven't endangered yourself with all of this unexpected UV radiation. Here, I'll give you my hoodie," he says, laughing as he takes off the offered hoodie.

I try to ignore how his shirt has rucked up around his dark nipples, revealing more of his finely sculpted abs. I'm not successful. Like, at all.

Joe goes quiet, and I shoot him a quick glance, hoping I haven't been busted twice in the same morning for looking at him in a lustful fashion.

But I don't have Joe's attention at all. I follow his line of sight to a man standing directly in our path. Unlike my utter cluelessness at the docks, my gut tells me that this is about to get violent. And I have no idea what to do.

But Joe does. He cracks his neck, his face hard stone.

The man reaches for his waistband, but Joe's already closed the distance. Knocking the weapon from his hand, he jerks the man's arm behind him so fast that a sickening crack echoes through the trees, followed by the man's screams. I never knew a man could scream like that.

"Look at me, you *fuck*. Stop fucking screaming. Look. At. *Me*." Joe's voice is a cold black sea, and I shiver at the murderous snarl on his lips.

The man, terrified, does as he's told.

"Is this about my father's extradition?"

The man screams when Joe leans into the hold, and he nods. "Yes, *yes*!"

"I don't want to fucking kill you," Joe grits out, and I believe him. "But if you fucks wanna try to drag me back into this shit, I will fucking murder every last one of you. Do you fucking hear me?"

"Yes," the man whimpers.

"Am I fucking clear?" he shouts, spit flying from his lips.

A woman with a stroller rounds the bend, spots the scene, and turns back around.

The man looks like he's going to throw up. "Crystal, man. Fucking crystal."

Joe throws the man to the ground, spitting on his face. "Get the fuck outta here. And tell your crew to leave me the fuck alone."

The guy, probably just a punk kid in his early twenties, scrambles to his feet, his arm grotesquely dangling from his shoulder. He's looking between Joe and his gun when Edgerton and crew come racing to the scene. Joe points out the gun on the ground, which they secure while surrounding the young man with overwhelming force.

Joe turns and starts walking toward me. I step back, not knowing what to expect from this version of him.

"Rand, I'm not gonna hurt you," he says, his voice still doing that intense Brooklyn thing as he lays a gentle hand on my arm. His fierce expression bleeds out and is replaced by worry. "I promise. I just wanna make sure you're—"

"Holy fuck," I breathe out. "You went full mob on him, didn't you?"

Joe shakes his head. "He'd a been dead if I'd a gone full mob on him. And I didn't wanna kill nobody today. Or ever, really."

"Wait, did you just save my life again?" I joke, hoping to diffuse the energy crackling across my skin. Joe doesn't laugh.

"Nah. He wasn't going after you. Which is good for him."

"Why good for him?"

Looking at me intently, letting me see the murder glint behind his eyes, he responds, "If he were going after you, I'd a killed him with my bare hands. And I wouldn't a bothered with the niceties."

His words stun me into silence. Smiling grimly, Joe pats my arm and turns his attention to Edgerton's crew. They seem to be interrogating the man with the broken arm. Meanwhile, I'm horrified and gravely turned on by Joe's promise on my behalf.

Seconds later, we hear sirens, and Edgerton releases the guy, who stumbles in the opposite direction. He and Joe flank me while the rest of the team takes a different route.

The two men march me to the nearest park exit and body me

across the road, dodging cars and cursing under their breaths. They relax marginally when we make it to my building, only letting out a collective breath when we've made it to my private elevator and have begun to ascend.

Staring forward, Edgerton states the obvious. "Mr. Wolfe, I need to ask you to work within the security protocols I've given you. If you don't, I cannot guarantee your safety."

"I apologize, Edgerton. I just needed to get out of this building."

Closing his eyes, I suppose to avoid witnessing my stupidity, he answers, "Sir, you are allowed to leave the building. You are not a prisoner. Just allow me to do my job and put men on you."

"Yes, well, that still feels rather prison-like to me."

"Mr. Wolfe, if you need us to hang back, be less visible, it's not my favorite, but we can arrange it. But Mr. Portelli's situation adds danger in every possible way, and I cannot protect you when you take off like that."

"Mr. Portelli's *situation* is my doing. It's not his fault."

"Yes, sir."

"And if you can't provide adequate security for the man who saved my life, then let me know so I may find the right person for the job."

Edgerton turns toward me, his eyes dark and foreboding. "I assure you my security is more than adequate. Providing that the client isn't actively circumventing it."

"Your security was rather easy to go around, truth be told. And besides, Joe had the situation well in hand."

Edgerton's face takes on a neutral aspect that is entirely frightening. "Sir, if you would like for me to have my team treat you like a detainee, I'm more than happy to do so. As for Mr. Portelli's aid in this situation, I'm grateful. But they were lying in wait for him, and it was a matter of luck that you weren't collateral."

"They?" Joe asks, staring at Edgerton.

He spears Joe with a look, giving him a sharp nod. "You passed their spotters on the way into the park. We found spotters from a different family at two other entrances and convinced them that you were a bad target."

"You convinced them, huh?"

Edgerton's jaw flexes. "If the medical bills cost more than the price on your head, they'll think twice about targeting you. But that's not a guarantee."

The elevator doors open, and Edgerton exits first, then gestures at me to follow. When I stumble over the door track, Joe grabs my arm, steadying me with a hand at my back and walking me into the foyer.

I lean into his touch, hating the downturned angle of his mouth.

Grayson waits in the foyer for us, his eyes a bit wobbly. "I'm so sorry, sir. This is all my fault. I'll have my resignation to you by this afternoon."

I snort, mostly because I don't have it in me not to. "I've asked you to call me Rand, and you're not getting out of my service that easily, old chap. If anyone's to blame, it's me. I knew exactly which protocols I was ignoring, and I went through with it anyway."

Grayson swallows thickly and bows his head. "Thank you, Rand."

Joe, seeing our sorry states, takes charge. "Since we've all been appropriately chastised and are probably hitting an adrenaline wall, why don't we all go to our neutral corners and check-in again around dinner. Sound good?"

Edgerton eyes me before nodding his assent. He and Grayson exit stage right while Joe guides me into the living room.

I turn to him, shaky and uncertain. "Joe, I—"

He holds up his hand. "I'm okay. We're okay. I promise."

I nod, feeling lost and stupid and horribly guilty.

"Come here," he orders, opening his arms to me.

I stumble forward, crashing into the hug, nearly sobbing with relief as his strong arms surround me.

His lips brush my ear as he whispers, "You were never in any danger. He would've never touched you. I wouldn't have allowed it."

Even though I'm aware Joe is a human being like anyone else, capable of faltering, I know in my bones he is telling the truth. That man in the park was not mob enough to go against Joe's brutal instincts.

And a small part of me thinks—hopes—that it's personal. That he's willing to violently, murderously protect *me*.

When he finally steps away from the hug, I rock forward, wanting to chase it, wanting his body against mine for the next several hours. Instead, I stifle the urge and rock back, giving him a stiff nod.

We part ways, each of us going to our own suites. I still feel the heat of his body when I collapse onto my bed and wish I had more than just the memory of his touch to surround me.

11

JOE

THIS MORNING WAS A NIGHTMARE. As soon as I spotted the guy in the walking path, I recognized him from one of the families. Worse, I immediately started mentally preparing myself to kill him if I had to.

I suppose it's one of those skills that's better to have and not need than to need and not have, but I despise that part of me. Most of the time, I can pretend I've never seen the light go out of someone's eyes at my own hand, but there is no denying my ability to murder when someone I care about is in danger.

And when it comes to Rand, I find that I care. A lot.

Seeing his guilt makes it all so much worse. He was a shell of himself in yesterday's board meeting, letting his father walk all over him. When he wanted to be a little rebellious this morning, I was thrilled. I encouraged it.

But Edgerton is right. We were reckless, completely unaware of the number of people right outside our bubble, just waiting for an opportunity to bring me in. Even though I would've protected Rand with my life, I shiver to think how easily we could've been overwhelmed.

We got lucky.

I shiver again when I think about the way I held him. I meant for it to be a grounding hug, but Rand was like a starving man, dying from lack of touch. Every protective instinct came rushing forward, and I let it go on for far too long. Neither of us wanted to stop. If I'd invited him into my bed, even just to hold him, he would have fallen on the chance.

Needing to recalibrate, I stand under the hot shower for several long minutes. Once I start to feel human again, I dry off and fall into bed, letting sleep take me for the rest of the morning.

WANDERING into the kitchen after a restless nap, I catch Rand making a sandwich. He sees me and guilt mars his features. I reach out and rub his shoulder. "Hey, none of whatever this look is. You and me? We're good."

He nods but looks unconvinced, so I try for small talk.

"Whatcha making?"

"A club sandwich. You want one?"

"Fuck yeah."

He grins at the strong language and grabs more bread, toasting it as he fries up a few extra strips of bacon. After he assembles the ingredients, I grab the drinks, and he plates the sandwiches before setting them on the bar.

He's still a little shaky from this morning's violence, but I enjoy that he somehow makes sitting at the bar look elegant. He's even tasteful about the way he places a napkin on his lap.

Chuckling at my mental wanderings, I take the first bite and growl out a moan. "Fuuuck, this is so good. Billionaire's got sandwich skills."

Rand swallows funny and starts to choke. I drop the sandwich and spend the next few seconds pounding on his back until he discreetly coughs into his napkin.

"You okay?"

His face is flush, and at first I think it's from all the coughing, but then I realize he's a little embarrassed. It's silly, of course, because people choke on their food all the time.

Darting a look in my direction, he quickly reaches across the bar for another napkin, which he immediately places in his lap. He unfolds and rearranges it before picking up his sandwich. I guess the guy can't eat unless his napkin situation is squared away.

Huh. Unless the napkin's *covering* a situation.

A quick glance at Rand's face tells me he's still battling some kind of embarrassment, so I let my gaze fall to his lap again. Double *huh*. Maybe that's just an unfortunate fold of the napkin, or perhaps having my hands on him got him a little riled up.

Might hafta explore that a little.

Probably shouldn't.

Anyway, we get back to eating, and I demolish my sandwich in a matter of minutes. I hop up and grab some chips from the pantry, still hungry. Laughing, Rand splits the last half of his sandwich with me, and I inhale that too.

"Damn, that was seriously tasty. Was there a little kick of something in there?"

He nods. "I just stole your idea and drizzled some chili honey on the bacon when you weren't looking."

Endearing as fuck.

"It was really good. Thank you."

He ducks his head, and while that little gesture of deference is a quick shot to my groin, I can tell he still feels terrible about this morning. He's wearing this defeated posture, and I can't help but want to make him feel better.

Time to switch it up.

"Hey, so how'd you get so good at playing video games? You kicked my ass the other day."

Distracted, he responds, "I used to play a lot in college. Best in my frat."

"Yeah, well, I did mostly online classes, so I missed the whole frat experience."

He shrugs, the move refined. "I don't know that you missed all that much."

Walking toward the living room, I gesture at the gaming system and ask, "Wanna shoot something?"

"Uh, sure."

He gets up and spins away from me, going around the other side of the bar to put things away, perhaps needing a chance to calm down.

Once we're in place, he quickly scrolls through the options. Stopping short, he backs up. "Wait, they have *Mario Kart*?"

"Yep," I answer with a soft chuckle.

"Can we play this instead? It's one of my favorite games."

Happy to hear a little joy in his voice, I can't help but tease him a little. "Sure. But only if you play Princess Peach."

He huffs out a pretend annoyed breath and agrees to both. "Fine. I love Princess Peach."

I hip-bump him, which makes him laugh, and it's a sound that warms my chest. Thankfully, once we get started with the game, it's easy to get the hang of the VR version, and soon we're battling it out on a racetrack. Not surprisingly, he's edging me out.

Midway through the last lap, I clip his back tire, causing him to spin out while I jump ahead. He doesn't give up, though, correcting fast, then regaining lost ground, passing Mario and Wario, managing to stay on my tail the rest of the way.

With a couple of yards to go, he maneuvers around me and copies my move, clipping the back of my tire. We both spin out a little, but he recovers faster and flies down the track, getting the first-place trophy. I have to settle for third place, behind Wario.

I take off my headset to spy on him again, holding back laughter as he pumps his fist and grins like a madman.

He pulls off his headgear and immediately shifts back into the guarded version of himself. A nicer part of me would pretend I don't notice the change, but I don't have it in me to let it go.

I stand there, headgear in one hand, the other on my hip, watching until his eyes meet mine. I let him see my amusement, and his eyes immediately drop to the ground.

"Shut up."

"Why? It was cute."

His eyebrows knit together. "No one's called me *cute* since middle school."

"You know—you don't have to hide the soft parts from me. I'm not your dad."

He snorts. "You're not my friend either, Joe. You don't get my soft parts." He says that last part a little wistfully, I think.

"We're at least friendly enough for me to call you cute, aren't we, Rand?"

He rolls his shoulder. "Not if you're going to make fun of me."

Oh man. This guy.

"I was in no way making fun of you. Promise."

Cautious, he raises his eyes to mine, fixing me with a half-hearted glare. I stand there and let him see me. Let him see that I am the same person in every room. His nose scrunches, then his face smooths again.

"Besides, I won. I'm allowed to celebrate."

My smile broadens. "That you are."

We split the rest of our afternoon between VR games and Netflix reruns. He beats me at nearly every game, but I get him to admit that the lead actor in *Lucifer* is pretty damned hot.

I manage to not pull him onto my lap and fuck him until he begs for mercy.

It isn't easy.

We finally pause to watch the sunset over the city, after which Rand asks, "Do you want to play *Mario Kart* again?"

"Actually, I'm starving. Was thinking of putting together something simple for dinner. Maybe a meatloaf and a salad. Sound good to you?"

"Joe—"

I cut him off with an arched brow.

"How many times do I have to explain it? You don't need to keep cooking for me."

"And how many times do I have to explain that I enjoy cooking for myself, and everything I cook is easily doubled. I'm not putting myself out for you. I just enjoy my own cooking. Besides, you made a delicious sandwich for lunch, and I'd like to return the favor."

"Well, you are a very good cook. I just never want you to feel obligated."

Jeez. I get the feeling that people only ever do things for him because he pays them. I wonder if he's ever actually felt cared for.

"What's this look?" he asks, gesturing at my face. "Are you making fun of me?"

I shake my head, letting him see my smile again. "I swear, I'm not making fun of you. Though I have no clue why you think I'd feel obligated to do a damn thing for you. I have exactly zero remorse for the shit show I've caused you. I did have to save your life twice, which, to be fair, has caused me a medium amount of remorse," I say, grinning.

His reaction is to merely roll his eyes at me and put away the gear.

"And I also feel no remorse for how difficult I'm making your job right now. It's possible—but don't get excited about this part—

it's possible I'm aware that yesterday sucked ass for both of us and that what happened this morning was intense and scary. And occasionally—again, I'm not saying that's what's happening here —*occasionally*, I like to soothe that shit with food. Now, I can make exactly half a meatloaf and half a salad if that would make you feel better, but that feels ridiculous."

"What do you put in your meatloaf?"

"Are you allergic to anything?"

"No, but I already had a sandwich this afternoon, and the carbs—"

I cut him off with the gesture. "It's meatloaf. It doesn't matter what's in it. You don't get to pick at it. You don't get to ask for special things. You just sit there and be a good boy and eat what I make for you."

Did I put a little bass in my voice at the end there? Yes. Yes, I did.

Is it possible that I did it to see the pretty flush on his cheeks again? Hm, also yes. I usually go with my better judgment, but not tonight.

It's surreal how the intensity of these last several days has changed our dynamic. In the beginning, all I saw was this towering asshole willing to throw his weight around to get what he wants. By the next day, I saw a man in deep conflict with himself and his persona. And yesterday, I saw a man who's been wanting to do good this whole time. Who's been told that's somehow not manly enough. Who's been shutting himself up just to gain his father's approval.

And maybe I'm the foolish one, maybe he's just doing this all for the good of his company, trying to stop the bleeding. But I don't think so. I think he relishes any opportunity to do the right thing. I think he's been dying to do it.

I don't feel sorry for him as I stand in his multimillion-dollar penthouse. Not really. But I do understand him a little better than I did before.

I've been in the mob since I was born. I never wanted the mob life, but I had to play the game to get high up enough to make my own decisions. I thought I could get away without cost, but this morning reminded me that was a foolish notion.

Maybe I can convince him that the cost of being good to his people is worth the price he'll have to pay with his father. Sometimes it's worth standing up for something, even if there are consequences.

Scratching my neck, I bring myself back to the whole meatloaf discussion. "So, are we okay? Or do we need to call Grayson to prepare you something special?"

"Yes, I'm fine. I suppose the meatloaf is sufficient. No need to call Grayson." Ah, there's the haughtiness creeping back in.

"Sufficient? What kind of bullshit answer is that?" I say, then look at him and realize he's just fucking with me.

"You billionaire son of a bitch." Laughing, I grab him up in a half nelson, messing with his perfect hair.

He stumbles and lets out an adorable squeak, pushing my hands away from him. "Get off me."

I release him and bite my lip when he yanks down his T-shirt. My breathing picks up as I fixate on his discomfort, and it makes me want to soothe and fuck him simultaneously.

Instead of doing either, I spin on my heel and turn toward the kitchen, refocusing on meal prep.

Just as I'm pulling together the ingredients, Grayson walks in. "Oh, I see how it is," he says with an anxious smile. "Trying to edge me out of a job by rendering me useless."

I know he still feels terrible about suggesting we play hooky from the security folks, but he wasn't entirely wrong. Rand needed to get out and see a little bit of the world. Hell, I needed it just as badly. We just should've been smarter about it.

"Even I know that's a lie, Grayson. I know your list of to-dos has got to be a mile long. In fact, I bet you know him better than anyone."

Grayson dips his head. "That I do, Joe."

I tilt my head, waiting for eye contact. "You weren't lying the other day, were you? Rand is a good man."

"Yes. He very much is." Grayson regards me for a few seconds. "And thanks to you, more people will get to see him the way I've seen him."

"You think so?"

He nods, thoughtful. "You put a big crack in that mask of his, and right in time. The strain of wearing it was getting to him. I think your confrontation in that meeting was the last time he could convincingly tell that lie."

I shift, turning toward him. "Yeah?"

"He carries the weight of the world on his shoulders, and I wonder how he's never stumbled. Even in that meeting, he did everything exactly from the playbook he's been given since birth. And some part of him probably believed it. But then he spoke to a man with real power." He gestures at me. "The kind of power that comes from understanding who you are at the core. And very quickly, all of that posturing seems very cheap indeed."

"Do you think he likes being a leader?"

Grayson's smile is a little uncertain, like maybe he doesn't trust himself after everything that went down this morning. Still, he answers in the affirmative. "I think he likes it very much. I think he would like it much more if he could be the kind of leader he was born to be."

"And what kind is that?"

"Nurturing. Gentle. I don't know. Maybe that's what I was thinking when I suggested he find some breathing room. I think he'd enjoy..."

Grayson lets his words die off, but I need to know. "You think he'd enjoy what?"

He shakes his head, then continues. "I think he'd like to *play* sometimes, you know?"

"Play how? Like with the VR games?"

"Sure, that's a start. But from a business perspective, I think he'd enjoy playing with *ideas*. I'd never seen him so alive until this whole incident with you. But in the Wolfe family, notions of play and nurturing, of being gentle, are viewed as female qualities, which, in their mind, is the same as weak."

I thin my lips. "You shoulda heard how he talked about his mother this morning. Told him he sounded like his dad."

"That'll make him think twice," Grayson laughs. "My mother is near the end of her life, and she's still the kindest and strongest person I know."

"Exactly. If Wolfe Sr. tried to tell my nonna—may she rest in peace—that she was weak for being nurturing or gentle, he'd have been dead before he got the words outta his mouth."

Grayson's eyes sparkle. "Not smart to mess with a Mafia wife, I suppose."

"Too right. Nurturing the family was everything to Nonna," I say, then pause, a harsh reality nearly taking the wind out of me.

Tilting his head to the side, Grayson asks, "What just happened, Joe? Your face went sad."

I press the meatloaf mixture into the greased pan and place the homemade tomato sauce on top, just like my nonna made it.

"Eh, just...after she died, the only person left in my life that ever had my back was my uncle. But people are staking out Rand's place, and I can't imagine he doesn't know about it. And I think I need to contact him and find out before I take my next fucking breath. I have to know."

Grayson takes the dish from my hands. "I'll take care of this and put together the salad. You go talk to your uncle. I'm sure he'll reassure you that he's watching out for you."

"Yeah, Grayson. I'd appreciate that. I made enough for you, so make sure to include a portion of salad for yourself as well."

"Joe, one of these days, you and I are going to have a serious conversation about who is supposed to be cooking here."

"Sure, Grayson. But not today." I start to walk away then turn back. "I don't suppose you've got a landline in this place?"

Grayson steps into the pantry and hands me an old-school wireless phone a moment later. Shit, I haven't seen one of those in forever.

"You can use this anywhere in the penthouse, including the balcony. And if you dial star-sixty-seven before dialing, it'll prevent this number from appearing on their phone."

"Thanks, man."

He bows his head and gets to work while I head to my suite.

Sitting on the pretty couch, I pull out my cell to look up my uncle's number and dial it on the old phone, following Grayson's instructions. Not sure what to expect, I'm surprised when he picks up after the first ring.

"Zio?"

"Joe! Are you okay?"

I let out a sigh of relief. At least he doesn't greet me with a string of curses.

"I am, Zio. It's good to hear your voice. I've been worried about you."

"So worried that you nearly destroyed this family?"

My heart sinks in my chest. Okay, maybe it's not all positive.

"Zio, I was trying to save the family. If Sally would've killed that man, you know the heat it would've brought down. You can't just toss a billionaire in the Hudson and wipe your hands of it. Wolfe practically has a small army protecting him—"

"Tell me. How many men are we talking about?"

I hesitate. "I don't know."

"Joey, I know this life has never been for you. But your father is taking this personally. I'm surprised you haven't already been brought back in."

My heart drops into my stomach. "Any places I should be avoiding?"

"Not that I know of, but I worry about you. I can't see where you're calling from—where are you staying? Are you safe? Do you have protection?"

I tap the phone to my forehead, shedding a few tears. If he's surprised I haven't been brought in, he knows there's a plan in place. And now he's trying to verify my location. It might as well be my father asking these questions.

It's my worst fear realized, and I hadn't even considered it until just now.

"Yes, Zio. I'm safe," I say, ignoring the rest of his questions.

"Good, Joey," he says, not pushing for a location. I take heart.

Still, he's chosen a side.

And it's not mine.

12

RAND

JOSEPH PORTELLI IS A PROBLEM. When he was horseplaying earlier, the power of his hold played at something bright and needy in my chest, and that was bad enough. The incident in the park and the way he held me right after, however, awakened something deeper. Darker.

"If he were going after you, I'd a killed him with my bare hands."

I wonder if he has any clue at all how much those words make me ache for the taste of him, long for the feel of his hands bending my body to his will. It took every bit of willpower not to straddle him on the couch and beg him to have his way with me.

Even though I'm driven to distraction, I know something's gotten under his skin. I can't ignore the bothered quiet that's come over him during dinner. His shoulders are bound up, his mouth set in a hard plane, his hair ruffled from running his fingers through it over and over again.

I wonder if it's just this morning's violence or if something else happened while he was cooking. I want to ask, but don't dare.

As soon as we finish eating another eye-rollingly good meal, he makes his excuses. He doesn't even offer to help wash the dishes, which seems so out of character that even Grayson puzzles after him as he leaves for his suite.

I hesitate then decide to approach Grayson at the sink. "Do you have any notion of what might be wrong with Joe? He was in a good mood before dinner, but now something is wrong."

Grayson rubs his mouth, measuring his words in that careful way of his.

"Tell me. I'll be discreet. I think he'll be good for the company, and seeing him unhappy makes me worry."

It's not the entire truth, but close enough.

Or not.

"Good for the company?" Grayson asks, leveling me with a gaze.

"Yes. He's very smart. His ideas have a lot of merit."

"Hmm," he says, going back to washing the dishes.

"Do you know anything?"

He towel-dries a plate, considering me for a few more moments. Once he's put it away, he turns to me fully.

"We were talking about his grandmother—"

"His nonna?" I ask, smiling briefly.

"Yes. His nonna. He said that after she died, the only other person in his family who had his back was an uncle. With everything that's happened, he hadn't considered that his uncle might not still be on his side. He allowed me to finish dinner while he went to his quarters and called him."

"Oh. So if he was upset at dinner...?"

"The news was likely not good," Grayson says, wiping down the counters.

"Thank you, Grayson. If you're done here, I'm in for the rest of the night. Enjoy your evening."

Grayson gives me a sharp nod and leaves for home. Looking out at the empty living room, I pivot back toward the curving hallway that leads to the guest quarters. After hesitating for a moment, I push forward.

His door is visible from the small guest den, and it's partially open. He's undressing, already down to his boxers, revealing beautiful skin and well-defined muscles. He thumbs his waistband, then glances up, a dangerous look in his eyes.

My hand automatically goes to my face, covering my eyes. "I'm sorry."

"It's okay," he says, his voice flat. "I ain't got nothing you ain't seen before."

I peek out from behind my hand, and he's even closer with all of his near-nudity and dark intensity riding just under the surface.

Spreadsheets. Falling stock prices. Mobsters.

"Of course. Um, I was just coming back here to check on you."

"Why?" His eyes are wary, and it's almost enough to distract me from wondering what it'd feel like to run my tongue across his pretty muscles.

"Rand?"

I snap my eyes back to his. *Focus, you idiot.*

"Um...you weren't yourself at dinner."

He flexes his muscles—more like a flinch—and cocks his head to the side. "Not myself? We've had a handful of meals together."

"And several very intense days," I say, pushing back. "Today especially. But something happened tonight between gaming and dinner, something that made you upset. I asked Grayson for details, and he told me you might be having family troubles. I just wanted to ask if you're okay and see if I can offer any help."

"*You* wanna help *me*?" The incredulity in his voice stings. "Mr. Billionaire Daddy's Boy actually cares about helping someone outside of his one-person bubble?"

"*Hey.*" I level him with a glare, and he looks off to the side, jaw flexing. "Regardless of what I said before, I think we *are* friends now, and friends don't do that."

"Friends, okay." He laughs, scratching his bare chest, still looking off to the side. He takes a deep breath and briefly glances at me. "I'm sorry. I'm not good company tonight."

He goes to close his bedroom door, but *nope*. Not gonna happen. I stick my foot in the door and press it open. "What's going on, Joe?"

"Can you just...give me some fucking space or something? I will be better company tomorrow, I swear."

Yeah, he's not getting out of it that easily. "No. We were having fun before dinner, and now something's wrong. Out with it."

He squeezes his eyes shut, pain lancing across his face. After a moment, he opens them and finally speaks. "My uncle knew that there would be people waiting for us in the park, and he didn't do anything to warn me. And he tried to get me to give up the details on your security team."

"Oh."

"Yeah. *Oh*."

"What can I do?" I ask, stepping closer to him, desperate to make it better, to be of some use to him.

A shadow of a grin tilts up the corner of his mouth, but he schools himself.

"Tell me," I demand. "There's nothing too small or too big."

He shakes his head, frustration playing out on his features. "I probably just need to punch something. Or fuck someone," he says, the word *fuck* coming out on a low growl. He finally looks me in the eye, a dark smile playing on his lips. "Maybe I can get Grayson to ring up one of your discreet hookups."

His words feel like a gut punch, and I step back as if he's actually punched me.

"Oh." He raises his brow, amused.

"What do you mean, *oh*?" I ask, jutting my chin out.

"Nothing."

"What?" When he doesn't answer right away, I push his chest. *"What?"*

"You're jealous," he states plainly, as though it's obvious.

Heat floods my cheeks. "I am *not.* I don't have anything...I came back here because you looked sad over dinner, and I felt sorry for you. There's no *jealousy.* I can have anyone I want. I don't get *jealous.*"

He looks at my crotch, raising his brow at the obvious bulge.

A frustrated grunt flies out of my mouth. "Fuck off," I mutter, turning to leave. He's in a shitty mood, and I don't need him accusing me of *jealousy.*

I mean, I'm clearly jealous, but that's none of his fucking business.

I barely take a step before he yanks me back, one arm pinning my chest and another at my throat. "Don't you dare tell me to fuck off," he growls, his hard body a furnace against mine. "Not after everything I've sacrificed for *you.*"

God, he feels so safe.

"Get off me," I grit out, twisting against him, unable to budge or escape the insistent hardness digging into my hip. "Let me *go.*"

He holds me for a second longer, letting me know without words that I am utterly in his control, then releases me. I stumble forward and turn to face him, wishing I still had his arms around me.

He smirks at me, breathing heavily like some kind of beast. "I let you go. Why are you still here?"

I open my mouth, but nothing comes out.

"What do you want, Rand? Why did you really come back here?"

I gulp.

"Answer the question," he says, adding an authoritative edge to his voice that sends ice and fire down my spine. *"Say it."*

Jesus, I have *got* to get out of here. I turn to leave, but my feet stay anchored to the floor.

"Say. It."

"I need you," I whisper, eyes on the floor.

He says nothing, and my face flames red. Goddammit, I can't believe I admitted that aloud. Fuck, fuck, fuck. What am I doing here?

"Rand, look at me."

I swallow and blink up at him.

"Good boy."

The hair on the back of my neck stands on end as my face heats up. Something about that deep, velvety 'good boy'...I wrestle with the fact that I—ah, fuck—I liked it. I inhale with a shaky breath, and he raises a hand to caress my face. I try to pull back, but he keeps me in place with a firm hand on my hip.

"I'm not going to hurt you, Rand."

"What are you going to do then?" I ask, rocking forward, voice unsteady.

"Make you feel good if you'll let me."

I close my eyes, shivering in anticipation. "B'why?"

"Because I need it, Rand. You said you'd do anything. I...I need you to let me make you feel good."

"But it's my fault that you—"

He nods. "It *is* your fault. And I don't know why, but this blush on your face feels like penance. Makes me want to forgive all your sins."

My eyes fly open, and he's so close. So fucking close. I shake my head, denying myself even as I reach out and run my fingers across his powerful abs.

"Rand?"

"Yes?"

"You don't have to do this if you don't want to."

I gulp, and his eyes follow the rise of my Adam's apple. "I know."

"Take your shirt off for me."

Goosebumps travel down my back at his command, and I'm encouraged by the dark smile playing on his lips. With twitching fingers, I reach for the hem and pull it up over my head, then let it drop to the floor. He inhales sharply, his approval washing over me like warm silk.

"You're beautiful," he whispers, smoothing his hand up and down my chest. I stand there, wordless, as he strokes across my sensitive nipples and ticklish belly.

"And one more thing if you don't mind," he says, his eyes heavy-lidded as he leans in, his lips brushing the shell of my ear.

"Anything," I say breathlessly.

"Take off your pants."

My cock jerks at the softly spoken command. I undo my slacks with shaking hands, letting them fall to the floor. He pulls back slightly as if to admire the view.

"Wearing your own underwear, I see. What a good little business-man," he says, tugging at the logoed waistband. I'm already flushed, then blush even harder when he whispers softly, "May I kiss you?"

I nod, needing it more than I realize. I blink, and he's closed the space between us, startling me. Grinning at my response, he brushes his lips against my lips, his eyes never leaving mine.

Inhaling sharply, I revel in his intense focus. With a small growl, he wraps his arms around me, and I go weak at the sensation of his skin on mine. He deepens the kiss, and I open to him, letting him slip his tongue inside.

His hardness digs into my hip.

"Wait." I'm breathless as I push away from our embrace.

He pulls back. Wiping his lips with the side of his hand. "Was that too much?"

I shake my head. "You have to know this is a big risk I'm taking."

"I suppose it makes for good Page Six fodder if the guy destroying your businesses is the one found in your bed."

I gulp and nod.

"Then it's a good thing we're in my room," he says, pushing my briefs down my hips until they fall to the floor. Carefully, I step out of them.

He steps out of his boxers and pulls me in for another kiss. His skin against mine makes me dizzy, and the tight fit of our cocks rubbing together is heaven. I luxuriate in his hold on me until we finally make it to the bed.

Sitting back against his pillows, I watch as he digs into a small kit by his bed, coming away with a pretty bottle of lube. After adding a little to the palm of his hand, he straddles me, lining us up.

He strokes himself, then gathers my cock in his large, rough-hewn palm. His heat and confident grip surge through me as he rubs us together. He leans in for another kiss, and the pleasure from this simple act rips through my body. Within seconds, I'm right there.

"Gonna come," I practically croak, my eyes rolling into the back of my head.

He grins, kissing me before roughly whispering in my ear, "Come for me, Rand."

His simple command destroys the last of my control, and I arch up, thrashing as his hold stays steady, true. Stroking me through my orgasm.

Just as I'm spent, he begins to stiffen, my dick still trapped as his grip gets rougher, snapping his hips as his hand lights up my oversensitive cock. His intense eyes never leave mine, and I witness the exact moment he goes over.

Hot cum splatters across my chest then dribbles down my

cock. Silently, he runs curious fingers through our combined spend. Mixing it, spreading it up and down my torso, pausing here and there to lick his fingertips.

Like a fever breaking, the dark mood from earlier evaporates.

My eyes track his movement as he scoops up a bit of the cooling liquid with his fingers.

"Open your mouth for me," he says softly, the command undeniable. I do as he says, my eyes never leaving his. Gently, he pushes the cum onto my tongue. I moan and suck at his fingers, licking between them, wanting every last drop.

"Greedy."

I nod and open my mouth again. He runs his fingers across my belly, gathering a bigger scoop, this time shoving three fingers in my mouth, all the way to the back of my throat, coating my tongue with it, the taste sharper, muskier on that part of the tongue.

I suck his fingers, swirling my tongue over them. He pushes back farther, teasing my gag reflex. He doesn't go hard, but the soft tickle still causes my muscles to tense, and I let out an embarrassing moan. He grins and pushes farther, biting his lip when I choke and gag.

More cum, and this time he holds the back of my head in place while he pushes his fingers back, gagging me a little harder. Pulling out, his fingers drift over my stretched-out lips. "I just wanted to imagine what you might look like with my cock shoved down your throat."

I moan and nod and undulate beneath him, my dick twitching hard. He looks down. "You like the sound of that, don't you?"

I blink, missing the feel of his fingers in the back of my throat. "Yes," I rasp out.

"These so-called discreet hookups of yours...do they know who you are?"

I shake my head. "I dress differently. Wear a hat."

"Is that because they're fucking you, dominating you? And not the other way around, Mr. Alpha Wolfe?"

My face heats, and I look away from him, rolling toward the edge of the bed.

He puts a firm hand on my shoulder, pushing me flat against the mattress. "I promise, I'm not making fun of you. I'm just trying to get the shape of things."

I swallow and look at the ceiling, his eyes on a burning path up and down my body. His examination stains my cheeks an even deeper red.

"Huh. That's interesting," he says, eyeballing my rock-hard cock.

Shit.

Stroking my face, he leans in and whispers, "Does the big bad CEO like taking it up the ass?"

Yes. Fuck yes. All of the yes. Please God, *yes*.

His amused expression tells me he's reading me like a book, that he knows the answer before I've said the words. Flustered, I bring my hands up to my face. He's gentle as he moves my hands, but his eyes are another matter. They bore into me, reaching down into my very DNA.

"Answer me, Rand," he insists, tipping up my chin so I'm forced to make eye contact with him.

Deeply embarrassed of my answer but compelled by the intensity of his eyes, I nod.

"Use your words, Rand."

"I like it both ways, S-Sir. But, uh, mostly the way you just said."

"Don't 'Sir' me, Rand. I'm just a lowly dock worker." He winks, and my breathing goes funny. "Do these paid lovers of yours know how much it shames you that you need it so bad?"

I turn my head to the side, mortified.

"Turn over," he commands. I bite my lip and slowly comply, afraid and needy as I hit my hands and knees.

"Ah. Such a good boy for me."

I shiver.

He covers me with his body again, his cock pushing between my cheeks as he lays his weight on me. "God, I can have so much fun with you," he says, the timbre of his voice reverberating through my rib cage.

I whine and bury my face into the pillow. He thrusts between my cheeks again, this time harder. "Any hard limits?"

"Nothing in public."

"Mm. Disappointing," he grumbles in my ear.

"It's just...my position. Thousands of jobs..." My words taper off as his dick slides between my cheeks.

"Don't worry, lamb. I'll work around it."

I whine, cursing myself for how much his teasing words turn me on.

His kisses on the back of my neck are fucking killing me, and he whispers once again, "You do know that you can say no at any time, right?"

I nod into the pillow, embarrassed by how much I need to be kept very, very safe.

He hums into my ear. "Stay exactly like this but arch your back. I want a better look at your hole."

I stifle a moan, shaking my head.

"That wasn't a request."

I pound the bed with the side of my fist, then do as he says, arching my back, exposing myself completely to him.

He goes silent for several seconds, and I die a thousand deaths.

"You have a lot of hair here," he observes dryly, lightly circling the sensitive skin with a finger.

When he pulls away, I squeeze my cheeks together and cross

my ankles, bringing the pillow up to the sides of my face. Fuck, my dick is so hard it's almost painful.

"I'll be right back." Tapping the inside of my knee, he commands, "Widen your knees for me."

Groaning, I obey as the air conditioning kisses along my skin. Moments later, he steps back into the room and whistles under his breath.

"This would be such a pretty sight without that dirty, hairy hole. Thankfully, I can fix these things."

A few moments later, he settles in behind me, humming to himself. I shiver when his fingers circle the entrance, accompanied by something slick.

"I have to wash your ass for you, Rand, so I can shave you."

A hot washcloth is run along the same sensitive area. "Just wiping away the soap, dirty boy."

Something cold and wet lands on my hole, and I scream into the pillow.

Smack. I imagine the perfectly red handprint on my ass and nearly come right then and there.

"Now, be still. You don't want me to nick such a sensitive area."

I look back and see him with a razor in hand.

He lowers the razor and looks deep into my eyes, empathy immediately returning to his expression. "We can stop if you'd like."

I shake my head and shove my face back into the pillow.

"Good boy," he says, rubbing my back like he knows I need the praise as much as the other.

Seconds later, he pulls a cheek to the side, and it takes everything in me not to flinch when he swipes the blade across the sensitive skin. It doesn't hurt, and he's very careful not to nick me. Still, it makes my skin pucker and my spine stiffen. Quickly, he moves to the other side, pulling the opposite cheek away as he glides the sharp razor across the minuscule amount of hair.

He rumbles his approval and a warm wet cloth makes me jump again.

"This is so much better. I'm going to need you to make a wax appointment for the future so you can be appropriately prepared for me."

"Thank you, Sir." Shit. "Uh...thank you."

His approving hum feels like every good thing in the world.

Palming my hip, he whispers, "Flip over."

I do as I'm told but pull the pillow with me, covering my face.

"Nuh-uh," he says, tugging the pillow out of my tight grasp. "Look at me."

I lower my chin, shaking my head.

His strong fingers grab my chin, forcing it up. "Open your eyes."

I comply and find nothing but his warm gaze staring back at me. "Thank you, Rand. Good job."

I hate how right it feels to get that kind of compliment from him and to know it's sincere.

"And thank you for making me feel better," he continues. "That was kind of you. I'll let you go back to your room for now."

My eyes grow big, and I look down at my painfully hard cock, then back up at him.

A smug, knowing grin spreads across his face, and his answer shows no remorse. "You've already come once, greedy boy. I'm going to need you to leave that alone."

I protest, but he shakes his head. "I have a big ask for tomorrow, but an even bigger reward if you can do me this favor."

Grumbling, I fix him with a glare. "What?"

"When it's time to get on social media and talk about what we're doing, I want you to apologize. Apologize to me specifically, and then apologize to your employees."

"They're already drafting a statement."

"I understand. And I'm telling you to ignore it. The people need to hear from you directly. Need to see your contrition. We'll have Sherry take a picture of us standing side-by-side, cooperating."

"I said I didn't like it in public," I grit through my teeth.

"I'm not collaring you. I'm not stalking you in the lobby. This is just an apology. And I'm confident you can handle this for me."

"Are you seriously not going to do anything about this?" I ask, pointing at my angry cock.

He shakes his head. "When there's nobody around, I'm going to fuck you in that big fancy boardroom of yours. So all you need is a little patience." He helps me out of his bed and gently pushes me toward the door.

"I really fucking hate you for this."

Suddenly his hand is around my throat, fingers pressing into my pulse points just enough to remind me who's in charge. Whispering into my ear, he growls, "No. You don't."

Letting me go, he hands me my things as he pushes me out the door, then chuckles when I look back, jaw to the floor.

"Go to bed, little lamb."

I race to my room, collapsing naked onto my luxurious bed. I'm tempted to ignore him and take myself in hand, but I know he'll know, and I don't want to figure out how long he'll make me wait for my next orgasm.

My phone buzzes on my nightstand, and I pick it up, hating whoever's trying to make me use my brain at a moment like this.

Joe: *Are you okay with what we did?*

I smile and roll my eyes, appreciating what he's doing, even though it's unnecessary.

Rand: *Yes. Sexually frustrated, but I'm good.*

Joe: *Do you need anything?*

Rand: Permission to jack off? Your rough hand on my cock? Your cock up my ass? All of these work for me.

Joe: Denied. Anything else? Water? Herbal tea?

Rand: Jerk.

Joe: You really wanna be disrespectful to me right now?

Rand: No. And thanks for asking. I'm going to try to sleep now.

Joe: Good luck. <devil emoji>

What the hell did I just get myself into?

13

JOE

IT'S THE WEEKEND, and even though there's another meeting
with the board, Rand declares that we don't need to wear suits to
the office. He's wearing slacks and a cashmere sweater that fit his
lithe body perfectly. I chose an expensive pair of jeans and a nice
Henley from the collection of clothes he lent me. Edgerton
accompanies us as we take the secret passage between the two
buildings.

We haven't talked about what happened the night before.

As we exit the elevator, Sherry takes one look at us and grins
knowingly. Standing, she hands Rand a stack of opened mail and
messages.

"Nice outfit, *Rand*."

"Thank you, Sherry. And not to steal your first-name-outside-
of-regular-work-hours thunder, but if you could just call me Rand
from now on, I'd appreciate it."

Her smile is deeply satisfying. "You got it, boss."

"And how has your weekend been?" Rand asks, trying to avoid
looking awkward, therefore making it doubly awkward.

"Restful. Yours?" she asks, eyeballing me.

His cheeks color and he loses eye contact. "Um. Not restful, but mostly good."

She raises her brow at me, and I give her a little shrug. Not much use in trying to pretend around this one.

"Joe, I see that your new clothes fit you nicely."

"Oh, thanks. Rand lent me like a half a closet's worth."

She taps her lips, and I know right away I've got it wrong. I turn to Rand, and he smiles his arrogant, king-of-the-world smile.

"You bought these for me?"

"Well, I had Grayson purchase them, but yes."

"How much did you spend?"

"It's irrelevant."

I look at Sherry for backup, but all she does is laugh. "You're hooking up with the boss, but you're going to draw the line at clothing? Okay. Just know that you are really bad at this sugar baby thing."

My mouth flies open. "I. Am. Not. A. Sugar. Baby."

"He is *not* a sugar baby," Rand says. *Far from it,* he mutters under his breath.

Sherry shrugs. "Okay, fine. But neither of you denied the hooking up thing."

Rand's cheeks go blotchy. "Why haven't I fired you?"

"Because you would literally fall apart if you did."

I snort-laugh, and Rand smacks my shoulder, then immediately steps back, looking concerned. Rolling my eyes, I grab his belt and drag him into his office, Sherry's laughter following us inside.

"I can't believe you did that in front of Sherry," he says, smacking my shoulder again, then following that up with another apologetic grimace.

"Why are you flinching? You're acting like I'm going to put you over my knee and wallop you in front of the staff."

He shrugs. "I don't...know what we're doing. What I'm allowed to do to you. What you're allowed to do to me. And I'm a jittery, horny mess," he says, pointing at the bulge in his expensive slacks. "I hardly slept last night."

Ah. Communication would have been helpful. That one's on me.

"You're allowed to do whatever you like to me, within reason. And our dynamic from last night was seasoning, a way to help you remove the mantle of responsibility for a few moments. It's not an entire lifestyle. We're in this crazy whirlwind together, and we're just having fun."

The tension in his shoulders visibly loosens. "Oh. Okay. I just...this morning. You didn't make breakfast. You said you would, and when you didn't, I thought maybe you wanted to put some distance between us."

"I'm sorry for that," I say, gently pushing him up against the wall, grinding our hips together. "It's only because I'm making you wait until after today's meeting. If I'd made you breakfast, I would have had you ass up over a barstool before you could say *cappuccino*. I fucked up by making you wait, and it's torture not being able to have my way with you right now. Fucking. Torture." I time that last bit with a couple of hip thrusts to emphasize the largeness of my mistake.

He grins, grinding back at me. "Now you know how it feels."

Someone knocks on the door, and I pull away from him. "True. Also, I tend to go with the flow. Find out whatever little kinks make you hum and sparkle in the moment, and then lean into them. If you need something a bit more structured, we can do that too."

He shakes his head and sneaks a kiss. "I liked it. Like you said, I can put off the responsibilities of being CEO and just let you take over for a second."

I palm his neck, then pull open the door for Sherry, who holds up her phone. Time for the next phase of taking on Wolfe Athletics.

WE'VE BEEN in this boardroom for hours, and Rand is sitting at the head of the table, squirming.

It's a very minor squirm, barely noticeable, but I see it and my mouth waters a little at the thought of rimming his freshly shaved ass. Every time he adjusts, he shoots a glare my way, and I merely smile. He's definitely cursing me out in that brilliant mind of his.

Unfortunately, the only thing going well in this room is my delicate torture of Rand. This conversation I'm supposed to be having with this team of executives isn't really a conversation at all, and nothing has changed since the last time we met. Whenever I bring up something reasonable, something that demonstrates value in the employee, I get shouted down.

Actually, no. Not shouted down. They are wealthy, entirely convinced of their rightness by virtue of the size of their bank accounts. I need a fucking master's degree in subtext to understand these people and their genteel snobbery. God, it's exhausting.

So, yeah, I've been told without a single declarative sentence that I'm a communist, a socialist, and one person seems to think I'm an anarchist.

That's fun.

I stubbornly push forward. "I know this has been a challenging morning, but I'd like to jump into healthcare since that is something everybody, including everyone in this room, needs."

"We offer excellent benefits," Wolfe Sr. intones, entirely dismissive of the subject.

I shuffle some papers around. "You offer high deductible insurance that, in many cases, ends up being just as expensive as paying out-of-pocket."

"Yes, but with catastrophic illness, there is significant coverage."

"Coverage, yes. But only after a deductible that most families can't even begin to afford."

The man who looks like he's held together by a team of medical experts sniffs. "If people cannot handle their finances, that is not our concern."

I tap the papers in front of me. "Which brings me back to the point of salary. The average apartment in Manhattan goes for two-thirds the average monthly salary of a Wolfe Athletics employee."

"More than half of our staff live in the boroughs and New Jersey."

"Excellent point," I say, shifting another piece of paper to the front. "The average commute time for a Wolfe employee, roundtrip, is two hours, which means it takes a minimum of fifty hours a week to be a Wolfe employee."

"How people get to their jobs is none of my concern."

"It should be your concern. There's a lot of lost opportunity there. And based on Mr. Wolfe's speech," I say, flicking a look over at Rand. He flushes, shooting me a warning glare, "this company has the audacity to further require more than even that. You want more time, and you don't want to pay for it."

"We are paying for it," says Wolfe Sr., clearly bored. "That's what the salary is for. Salary includes overtime."

I shake my head. "That's the line companies use to run their staff on less than a skeleton crew. Salary covers a standard work-week: forty hours. That's it. Overtime should be comped one way or another."

"For as long as I've been doing business, that's what salary means."

I lean forward on the table, nailing Wolfe Sr. with an ugly grin. "Imagine my surprise that you are not up on current trends." Rand chokes on his water and carefully flicks the beads of moisture off his expensive sweater. I stifle a smile and continue. "Which explains why Wolfe Athletics is no longer competitive."

Wolfe Sr. draws himself up, entirely self-important. "The hell you say. Our sales rival those of the big-name sports brands. In what way are we not competitive in the market?"

I scratch my eyebrow and shake my head. "The job market, Mr. Wolfe. We are woefully behind in the *job* market. You can't sell the product if there aren't people here to support its manufacture and distribution."

He gestures dismissively at the notion, daring me to make my point.

Fine.

"This market correction that Wolfe Athletics is going through right now? It's painful. But the bigger loss will be the people and their institutional memory. The people who've already left took with them terabytes worth of knowledge that resides only in their memories. It wasn't saved anywhere, and now it's *gone*. And some of that knowledge is more valuable than what you lost in stocks. So you are welcome to ignore every fucking idea I have, but there is no solution to your hemorrhaging value that doesn't include better treatment of your employees."

"In what world do you understand profitability better than I do?"

"This is emerging data based on interviewing the people who left. I found out where they were going and identified trends."

"Mr. Portelli, conversations with your friends does not a data set make."

"I agree, Mr. Wolfe. Which is why I avoided my closest associates. These are early numbers, but they match the trending I've been seeing for months now."

Rand speaks up. "It's true, Father. Joe's been watching our competitors, and he knows how they operate."

Wolfe Sr. pins me with an incredulous look. "Oh, please. Tell me how my rivals operate."

"Gladly," I say, sneering at this self-righteous prick, half-tempted to tell him to meet me out back. "They're circling this company, waiting to take every scrap of value from it as you crumble in on yourself. So somebody in this room needs to help the rest of you pull your fucking heads out of your fucking asses or suffer the consequences. I don't give a shit either way."

Rand clears his throat and raises a brow in my direction. I take a step back and a deep breath. I know these people don't care about anything except that goddamn profit margin. Wrangling my frustration and shoving it into a lockbox, I refocus on dispassionate facts.

Approaching the table, I aim for a better headspace. "Three years ago, Elite Athletics started offering high-dollar customizations for their shoes."

The dumbest guy in the room cuts me off. "Those customizations are entirely ridiculous. They render the shoes practically useless in an actual athletic environment."

I ignore him. "They made twenty million from those ridiculous additions last year, the same year they started paying for their employees' deductibles. The deductibles cost them fifteen million, leaving them with a five-million-dollar profit on the solution they used to pay for everything."

I shuffle the papers till I find the stat I'm looking for. "If you turn to page twenty-five, you can see we lost seventeen employees to Elite Athletics specifically. They weren't even offered that much more in salary, often taking jobs directly correlated to the ones they had here."

"Who are these people?" Wolfe Sr. asks, looking down his nose at the handout he's ignored this entire time. "We had everyone sign a non-compete clause as part of their employment here."

I hold my tongue. There's a loophole in the clause that Wolfe's competitors have been taking advantage of for years. They can hire someone for the mailroom and then, on day one, *promote* them to essentially the same job they had at Wolfe Athletics. I'll let them spend their own money trying to figure that out.

The idiot can't open his trap soon enough. "That's cheap economics, Mr. Portelli. We would never stoop to such depths. Perhaps your online classes didn't prepare you sufficiently for the realities of elite business environments."

I shrug. "You might be right. But according to CNN, you lost almost a billion dollars in the first twenty-four hours after that video went viral. Proportionately, it's one of the worst stock melt-downs anyone's ever seen. What's funny is that if you were to hire sufficient people to do the job and pay everyone here a wage that's workable for living in or near the island of Manhattan, it would've cost you maybe ten percent of that."

They shift in their seats and look to their beleaguered Chief Financial Officer. He nods.

"Thanks for that confirmation, Dan. I know I seem like a guy who just managed to stumble his way from the docks into a board-room, but I do know a thing or two. For instance, this is the beginning of a sea change. People leaving their jobs for greener pastures is becoming the norm. The people in this room support and vote for politicians who oppose universal healthcare and paid family leave. You're thinking only about the bottom line, forgetting entirely about the lost opportunities."

"What lost opportunities?" asks Wolfe Sr., though I doubt he cares for the answer. I'm going to give it to him anyway. Maybe it'll help someone else on this board figure shit out.

"The opportunity to work with people who are fully engaged. To work with people who aren't having to choose between medication and keeping the lights on."

If Wolfe Sr.'s expression is anything to go on, he could give a cold shit about whether or not people like their jobs. I get the distinct feeling that he's upset about working with actual people who have actual needs.

It's frustrating, but when I look around the table, the others are reviewing the provided data and paying attention. Fine. I decide to talk to them.

"Every Wolfe Athletics employee is overworked because you won't hire enough people, and underpaid because, well, that's just the Wolfe Athletics way. The fact that you lost a billion dollars means nothing to me. That's an amount of money so high over my head I can't even begin to imagine it. But I do know what it means for someone to worry about feeding their family. And if you continue to treat your employees unfairly, you'll deserve everything you get."

14

RAND

GOD, I want Joe to ream me on this fucking table.

He started the meeting out sounding like he usually does—professional, with a little Brooklyn on the side. But there's a bit of mobster creeping into his voice, and he has a room full of millionaires and billionaires shifting uncomfortably as a result.

It's the sexiest goddamn thing that's ever happened in this room. So far.

Speaking of shifting uncomfortably, as much as I want Joe to shove his hard cock up my ass and keep going till he finds Oz, he's also why I'm hating life right now. My asshole itches like a motherfucker, and my cock is an achy, leaking mess.

"Mr. Portelli, we've listened to quite enough of your, frankly, immature ideas for how to steer our company to success. I've been doing this for forty years, and giving into employees' whims isn't what got me here. If they don't like the way we do business, they can start their own company."

He gets up to leave, and I hold up my hand, stopping his progress toward the door. "Father, the reason for bringing in Joe is to have a visible representation of our willingness to listen to our employees. May I remind you that we lost another half a billion dollars in value since then, and that has only slowed because we leaked that he's working with us. Regardless of your opinion of his ideas, we must stop the bleeding, even if the cure is distasteful."

Joe, picking up on my cue, nods and stands, equal height with my father. "If you want social media to stop attacking you, you're gonna need a photo op. And you're not getting one from me without at least one of the things that I talked about today. Raises are your cheapest option, but extended healthcare pays dividends in the end. Your choice."

My father's lips curl, his body language stiff and unbending.

Ford, my one friend on the board, clears his throat. "Mr. Portelli's solutions are less costly than another night of stalling out at this lower stock value. It's cheaper by an order of magnitude that I'd rather not admit out loud."

Jackson, who managed to survive another day as VP of HR, shifts in his seat, looking at Joe. "None of this makes a difference without a strong statement in favor of work-life balance and employees' rights, along with a commitment to making sure that our products are ethically sourced."

"Won't that just remind them of that slave-labor debacle?" my father asks. He's definitely going to have Jackson fired before the end of the day.

Jackson, apparently, has started reading from Joe's handbook. "Sir, they're already making the comparisons on social media. So it's helpful to remind them that we stopped those practices, though there is a large contingent wondering what we did to clean up the mess we left. I asked Ford to check with his people and run some numbers. Buying people out of their *indentured servitude* costs less than a hundred thousand dollars. Now, I know that the State Department doesn't want us to do business with enslavers, but we created this mess, and it might be one of the faster options. Maybe even bring over someone, a manager perhaps, to demonstrate our commitment to making a difference."

My father blinks at Ford. Before he can say anything, I cut him off. "Jackson, make it happen, take it out of my profit share. Do it now. See if we can pay mercenaries to free the people caught up in this instead of the people holding the chains. But do whatever needs to be done to make sure they are safe. We can work it out with the State Department after."

Jackson excuses himself and leaves the room, stopping to nod at Joe.

"I'd like to ask everyone to leave the room, save for my son," my father says, his voice so cold I can't remember it ever being warm.

The boardroom clears out, with Joe at the tail end. He grips my shoulder as he passes me, a symbol of support I don't think I've ever had in my father's world.

As soon as the door is closed, my father stands in front of me, cool, as cruel words leave his mouth.

"We are men in charge of our destiny, and you can't even handle one single employee. Did you hear him? He's making demands of us as though he has the right."

"The question is, did you hear what he said? He doesn't care that we're wealthy. Our wealth is so far beyond his existence that it doesn't matter. I think it's safe to say he represents a lot of people. People want decent benefits, a living wage, and some semblance of work-life balance."

"People have always asked for handouts, Rand. You can't let yourself be swayed by misplaced sympathy."

"Father, these are basic human needs. Calling them handouts doesn't negate that. You may be satisfied with doing the legal minimum, but the people are starting to notice. We've been greedy, and this is the reckoning."

"You sound like Jackson," he says, muttering *beta* under his breath.

"Not that it matters, but I looked up the study that Joe talked about. Did you know that this alpha-wolf theory is based on debunked science?"

"It's not about the science, Rand. It's about creating a structure that people can fall in line with. It makes it easy for people to listen to us and give us their money."

I've always thought of my father as smart, cold, and cunning. I'm starting to realize that he is nasty and vicious down to his core. Fine, I'll put it in a way he'll understand.

"Father, do you know what happens when an alpha wolf shirks his responsibilities?"

My father's thinly disguised disdain is awful, and I shudder to think about what I'd have become had I continued to follow his business model.

"When an alpha couldn't or wouldn't care for the pack, a beta would rise up and kill that wolf, thus becoming the alpha. Looking at our ledgers, social media, and sales...who do you think is winning?"

My father pales because, while he doesn't care about the science, the numbers cannot be ignored.

"You can sit here and try to be right, or you can listen to the man who has the ability to destroy our business. It's your choice, but this is not going away. And while there is only a very tiny window of opportunity to make this better, everything you've said only makes this worse. Joe could not have been clearer. Why is this so hard? The numbers aren't lying to you."

"It sets a precedent."

The hard, disapproving set of his mouth used to send a chill down my spine, and maybe this is just a temporary reprieve, but it doesn't affect me the way it used to.

I gesture to the Manhattan skyline. "The precedent has already been set. We are so far behind precedent that we look inept. Every social media platform has taken and run with this."

"What do I care about Facebook and Twitter?"

"Have you not been paying attention?" I close the gap between us. "Are you really that daft? Are you really so out of touch that you don't understand that the video between Joe and me went flying around on social media at the speed of sound? The billion and a half dollars we've lost is social media's doing. You don't have to like it, you don't have to be involved in it, but you do have to respect it. And if you don't, so help me God, you will single-handedly tank this organization."

"No, son. I believe that distinction goes to you."

I shake my head. "False. Everything I said to him was everything you ever taught me. Go listen to it. I dare you. There's not a single word I said that wasn't something that first came out of your mouth. I wanted to handle myself differently, but I had your marching orders in my head. Following your example has only served to make me a terrible CEO and a horrible human. I've spent the last several days with Joseph Portelli, this guy from the docks that you've been looking down on, and I know more about being a better human from him than I learned from you in my entire life."

"How dare you speak to me this way," he says, looking down his nose. "I groomed you for this position, and I can take it away. With the snap of my fingers, I can gather the board and have you dragged out of the building."

I remember what people said about my little performance at the company meeting, and I decide they're right. *No more.*

"Do it. I dare you. Do you know what I have not and will not sign? A fucking NDA."

My father's eyes go wide at the language. A Wolfe never uses coarse language. It's unrefined.

Well. Fuck that, obviously.

Putting on my coldest façade, I tell a complete truth. "I could go to any one of the news outlets within walking distance of this building and end it all for you."

His fingers strangle the top of one of the fancy leather chairs, making it creak. "You would never."

My lip snarls in disgust at the thought that I could've very well gone my whole life regurgitating my father's bullshit.

"I very much would. And since you've decided to hold that over me, may I suggest you implement every last one of his suggestions right now. Call the board and get them to approve every single one. If you don't, this house of cards will tumble down right on your head. Here's the thing: I can take that man and start *any other* fucking business in the world. I could sell bespoke shoelaces, and if I put him on my board, it would be wildly successful. Billionaires, overnight. Go ahead, test me. *I dare you.*"

I fist my hands, willing them to stop trembling. I can't believe I've just laid an ultimatum at my father's feet. And it's not a bluff. I'll fucking do it.

Because I'm right.

No. Joe is right. He's been right this whole time.

And it's exhilarating.

My father straightens his shoulders, looking at me with dead eyes. "Fine. We're reconvening tomorrow. I'll step aside. Take your shot with the board. And if you try to bring this company down, I'll blackball you from here to Tokyo."

He walks out, leaving me in the large boardroom alone. I brace my hands on my knees, trying to catch my breath.

I can't fucking believe I did that.

Joe slips in, shutting the door behind him. "Are you okay?"

I straighten up quickly, a little too quickly, and he's immediately there to steady me.

"You made several very good points today," I say, ignoring his question. "They were hard for the board to hear, but you had the numbers to back you up. My father is angry because he can't manipulate these numbers to look good for him. And I've requested that he follow all your suggestions, not just one of them."

"How'd that go?"

"He threatened to have the board kick me to the curb."

"Shit. Rand. I don't want you to lose your job," he says, moving to comfort me.

I hold up my hand. "I reminded him that I have not signed an NDA and can start my own company. The smartest thing I could do is have you help me lead it because we'd both become dangerously wealthy overnight."

His mouth hooks up into that heart-stopping grin. "What makes you think I'd want to work with you?"

"Well, you did make me come really hard last night, so I figure we could probably work out a business relationship."

He laughs, and something about that settles my racing heart. I swallow hard, and his brows stitch together. He reaches out, grasping both of my hands. "Are you really okay?"

"I will be."

"What's going to happen now?"

"No doubt my father has already gathered the board members in his office and is delivering the bad news. He's also going to try to have Jackson fired, but he doesn't have the votes for that either."

"What's next?"

"We get another chance to talk to the board tomorrow, and they'll vote on the initiatives."

"That sounds amazing. Why do you look so sad?" he says, cupping my jaw.

I put my hand over his. "I knew my father was a hard, unfeeling man, but some part of me always looked up to him. And today, I lost the ability to do that."

Joe checks that the coast is clear and then surrounds me with his arms. "I'm sorry, Rand. Truly."

Resting my head on his shoulder, I shake my head. "He never even asked me about what happened yesterday. I had Edgerton share the report with him, and...nothing."

I look at the vaulted ceiling and the ridiculously expensive bespoke lighting fixtures, blinking back tears.

"Wait. He didn't call to check on you?"

I thin my lips, hoping the stupid tears stay in place. "Nope."

Joe tightens his hug. "I'm sorry," he says, kissing my forehead.

An idea takes hold, and I step out of his embrace. "I know that you didn't want to post anything until we got the final approval from the board, but I think we need a head of steam going into tomorrow's meeting."

"Yeah?" he asks, troublemaker smile at the ready. "You wanna post now?"

I nod. "I really, really do."

He rubs his hands together. "Let's do it."

I pull up the pictures that Sherry took of us and, without over-thinking it, I type up the sincere apology that Joe and my employees deserve. Joe reviews it, makes a couple of quick suggestions, and I post it on all of my social media.

Shaking his head, he pulls me in for a strong kiss. "Damn, that's sexy."

I inhale sharply, my cock instantly aware. "I'm a man of my word."

Joe palms the hard, aching length as he growls in my ear, "So am I."

15

JOE

I STEP out and do a quick sweep of the area. The executive suite is all but abandoned, and I take the liberty of telling Sherry to go home for the evening.

She looks between me and the door to the boardroom, a smile playing on her lips. "Security's on a precise rotation. They come through here at eight and thirty-eight past the hour, like clockwork. Do with that information what you will."

My eyebrows hit my hairline, and she pushes my shoulder. "I knew from the second you stood up at that stupid meeting that things were going to change. But I didn't know if it was a good or a bad thing."

"And?"

"It's good, Joe. You're good for him."

I'm pleased by her assessment but don't want her to get it twisted. "Hey, we're just—"

She shakes her head as she holds up a hand. "I don't want the details, Joe. I'm just telling you what I'm seeing." She gathers her things, then heads toward the exit, tossing over her shoulder, "And for what it's worth, he's good for you too."

Sweeping into the elevator, she turns and sends me a wink, tapping her wrist as the doors close.

I take a deep breath, letting it out slowly. A part of me wants to deny the gravity of her words, but there's a lightness in my chest, and I want more of that.

Slipping back into his office, I close the door most of the way, stopping just shy of letting the latch click. I walk up to Rand and dip my fingers into his back pocket as I pull him toward me.

"Hey."

"Hi." His response is adorably shy. "She knows what we're doing in here, doesn't she?"

"Well, I told her to go home, and she gave me the security guard schedule, so..."

Ducking his chin, he rubs his forehead. "Fuck, that is so embarrassing."

I know he's telling the truth because he's beginning to tent his pants. I do love this little kink of his.

"Hey," I say, palming his cheek, directing him to look at me. "How careful do I need to be around security staff and Grayson?"

He takes a big breath like someone about to leap off a cliff into unknown waters. "Grayson busted me looking at your ass yesterday, so the cat's already out of the bag there. I would never hide anything so important from Edgerton or his team, but I don't trust building security—here or in my residence—to keep my confidences."

"Good to know."

I bring him in for soft kisses, knowing they're not nearly what he wants. When he starts to whine, I lean in and whisper in his ear, "I'd first like to bend you to my will for a little bit since it seems almost everyone here already knows what I'm doing to you anyway." He glares at me, and I wink back. "Second, since time is tight, I'll wait till we get back to the penthouse to make up for all the dirty things you're going to do for me. Both of those things okay?"

Rand's breath is shaky as he nods his head.

"You know I'm going to need more than that."

"Yes. And if you're talking about aftercare, or whatever, I don't need it. You know my limits, though, right?"

"Nothing in front of other people."

"Yeah," he says on a relieved—aroused—breath. "And I'm good with tapping out or saying stop."

"Stop or tap out, got it," I confirm. Brushing a knuckle under his chin, I direct him to look at me. "And even if you don't need much in the way of aftercare, I do. If you could just let me know, for my own peace of mind, that I didn't go too far and I'm not actually a terrible person, I would appreciate it."

He nods, and I raise my brow.

"Yes, Joe. I'll make sure you know how much I loved this."

I check the clock on the wall, and Sherry's words spur me forward. Cupping his face, I kiss him sweetly. "You did a good job today. You helped me remember what was important."

He shivers, touching his forehead to mine. "I just wanted to make you proud. Make myself proud."

"You did." I take his lips in another heated kiss, my hand drifting up toward his neck in a firm grip.

He moans softly against my mouth, shifting against me. I pull back and suck on his fat bottom lip, alternating between teeth and tongue as he hardens against me. When we're both good and worked up, I end the kiss. His eyes track mine, a little lost, needing direction.

"Strip for me," I command, putting a little bass in my voice.

He hesitates, and I raise my brow. Letting out a shaky breath, he pulls the cashmere sweater over his head, folding it neatly before setting it on the conference table. Toeing out of his shoes, he undoes his belt and pants then yanks out the tail of his button-down. His nervous fingers falter on a few of the buttons before he's able to slide it off his broad shoulders. He's a little less neat with folding the shirt.

Grabbing the open edges of his slacks, he starts to lower them before stopping to check out the door. "Wait, it's not closed all the way."

I grab his face, a little rough as I turn him to face me. "The door is my concern. Do you trust me?"

He nods, his eyes flitting back to the barely-there crack.

"Your words, Rand."

Just as quickly, his eyes meet mine. "I trust you. I'm sorry."

Grinning, I pat the top of his head. "Now be a good pet and take off your pants for me."

He glances at the door again, but his expensive pants hit the floor with a clink of the belt buckle, followed by the soft woosh of his underwear.

"Socks too."

He steps out of his pant legs, then bends over, awkwardly pulling off each sock, sending me a baleful glare when he nearly loses his balance. Finally, he stands up straight, entirely nude. His dick bobs out in front of him, a drop of precum hanging from his tip for dear life.

"Take out my cock, and let's see how fast you can make me come."

Rand's eyes flick again to the door behind me, and I grab his chin. "If you don't trust me, we don't have to do this."

He refocuses on me, his eyes glazed with lust.

"The sooner you take care of me, the sooner I can take care of you. On your knees, billionaire."

He carefully kneels and unbuttons my jeans. The sight of an outrageously wealthy man on his knees for me...I admit it does great and terrible things for my ego. More than that, however, is his submission. So fucking beautiful.

"Unzip me but leave my clothes in place."

He inhales sharply and works down the zipper, awkwardly shoving his fingers inside to move the underwear below my balls, fishing out my cock.

"Mm, that's my good boy."

Biting his bottom lip, he looks up at me, seeking permission. I nod. He takes my limp cock into his mouth, sucking on it, swirling it with his tongue.

"Don't forget my foreskin, baby. Get your tongue in there."

He immediately follows my instructions, dipping his tongue under the sensitive skin, swirling it until my eyes roll back.

"Take it all in."

He obeys, and I stifle a groan as his hot mouth engulfs me. Grabbing his head, I begin fucking his face. He gives off another low moan.

"Baby, you have to be quiet." He blinks up at me and nods, his mouth still stuffed full of my half-hard cock. I continue thrusting, holding his head steady so he can't move it.

"Fuck, you're so hungry for it. What a little slut you've turned out to be."

His cheeks heat in my hands, and he starts to struggle as my erection fills his mouth.

"Shh, shh. Don't fight it. Open your throat for me."

He grabs my thighs, and I feel the back of his throat relax a little.

"Good boy, keep going. I know you're thirsty."

I deepen my thrusts, and he gags hard. His eyes water and drool drips down his chin. I pull him off my cock for a few seconds to allow him a couple of gasping breaths, then thrust back into his waiting mouth. Fuck, the sound of him choking on my cock is going to end this before it begins. I pull away, and my stomach tightens with need when he chases after my erection. I hold his head back.

"Poor baby. Look who's not used to a big dick."

He bats away my hands, swallowing me, doubling down on the mind-blowing suction. Grabbing his head, I fuck the back of his throat, and he chokes, coughing as more drool runs down his chin.

"Looks like I'm going to need to train you how to properly take a long, hard cock."

He responds with a hot little grumble. *"I can do it."*

He tries to deepthroat me again, only to gag even harder. Holding his head in place, I shallow my thrusts. He fights me to go deeper, so I pull away.

"Hm. Maybe we should start from the beginning."

"I don't need—"

"Suck on the head like a pacifier."

His face flames red. "I'm a grown man."

I condescendingly pat his cheek. "Grown men know how to take a dick."

"My lovers have always been satisfied."

My billionaire is strenuously objecting while he's on his knees, bare, his face red and messy with drool, hair a complete mess. Fucking hell, he's perfect. I flick his nipple, hard, and a thin string of precum connects to the floor.

"You've paid men to tell you that you're good in bed when I'll tell you you're lousy at it for free. Now suck the head and try not to choke to death."

He goes silent, but his glare is loud. I paint his lips with my own leaking tip. His tongue slips out, tasting me on his lips, his eyes darkening. Finally, he acquiesces, taking in just the head of my cock, sucking on it like a baby. He even makes the suckling sound, pulling hard as his ears turn bright red.

"See," I say, nearly breathless as I brush the hair from his forehead. "You've got it."

I let him suck me until I'm about to detonate, then I pull away. "Do you want me to help you go deeper?"

Clenching his jaw, he nods. I'd worry he wasn't into it, but his dick twitches with every word I say.

With an evil grin across my lips, I direct, "Lie face up on the conference table with your head at the edge."

He's frustrated and adorably fumbly as he climbs on top of the table, looking like a freshly born farm animal as he sways on his knees. Finally stable, he gets into position, lying flat with his head right at the edge. I grab his shoulders and pull him toward me, far enough so his head is just off the end. His long body is exposed and helpless, and his hands are fisting and unfisting against the smooth wooden surface.

"Open your mouth."

He does as asked, and I slip my cock between his willing lips. Pushing in slowly, I'm able to get my entire length in his mouth without gagging or choking him. Pity. I miss the sound of him struggling to take me.

"That better?"

He nods, swallowing against the head of my cock.

"See. Sometimes guys just need training wheels for cock-sucking."

He snarls at me, then opens wide when I push in and hang out at the back of his throat, pulsing. He starts sucking, intensifying the sensations.

"There's hope for you yet," I say, stroking his jaw.

I pull out and stroke back in, watching his throat fill as I fuck it. Wrapping my hand around his neck, I squeeze every time I bottom out.

Out in, out in, his throat taking to his training like a champ.

I edge myself a few times and finally pull out. He gives me another little whine, and I shush him. Cracking the door to the executive suite again, I'm pleased to note the area is still empty. After a quick time check, I leave the door open just a sliver more than before. I turn to find him in exactly the same spot, head still hanging off the edge. His eyes track the slightly open door, but he says nothing.

"Since I went to the trouble of preparing it last night, I've decided I want your ass."

His eyes widen as he licks his lips.

"Get up and bend over the table for me."

He rolls over on his belly, awkward as he gets up on his hands and knees before shifting over the edge. Standing, his cock bobs in front of him, painfully hard.

"Were you a good boy last night? Did you keep your hands off your dick?"

"Yes. And fuck you for that, by the way."

Slapping his ass, I enjoy the sharp report that echoes through his grandiose office. I toss the packet of lube on the table. "You're welcome. Prep yourself."

Grumbling, he leans forward, bracing himself with one hand while sneaking a couple of lube-slick fingers between his cheeks.

"Here, let me help you," I say, spreading his cheeks for him.

His jaw tightens, and he bites his lip, his face flushing a gorgeous red. He's practically flying now.

"Fuck, what a pretty asshole. Someone took great pains to make sure of that."

"Thank you," he grits out, impaling himself on two fingers.

"Make sure to get them deep enough, but don't hang out on your prostate. That's cheating."

He shoots me another glare over his shoulder but does as I ask. He begins to thrust his fingers in and out, and I still his arm.

"Tsk, tsk. Don't be impatient. Add a third finger."

"I'm not a virgin," he hisses. "My ass doesn't need this much prep."

"Well, it doesn't belong to you, now does it?" I ask, smacking what's mine.

Grunting, he adds a third finger, glaring at me the entire time.

"One of these days, you're going to be the one ass up, and I'm going to get you back for all this."

"Don't threaten me with a good time," I toss back, grinning confidently.

He looks back again, confused and panting as he fucks himself.

"I'm vers." I shrug, loving the surprised O on his lips.

"Payback's gonna be a bitch."

"I'm counting on it." I shift my hips forward, increasing the pressure on the fingers in his ass, covering him with my body so I can whisper in his ear. "But that day? Is not this day."

I pull back and move his arm out of the way, enjoying the slick sound of his fingers leaving his body. Leaving my jeans in place, I roll on the condom and stroke lube up and down my length.

"Okay, now bend over." He immediately complies and, fuck, I love it. "All the way, Rand. Put your ear to the table."

He does as I ask, placing his hands at the sides of his face.

"Spread your cheeks."

Knocking the table with the side of his head, he complains, "Why do you like that so much?"

"I dunno. Why does it embarrass you so much?"

He shuts his mouth as he shifts his weight to the side of his face, glaring at me. I stifle a groan when he pulls the globes of his ass apart with elegantly tapered fingers. Biting my knuckle, I admire his perfect hole on display just for me.

Slipping my phone out of my pocket, I snap a quick picture.

"What did you do? Did you take a picture of me like this?"

Ignoring his question, I grab his hips, kicking his feet out wide. I take another beat to enjoy him—fuck, he's glorious—before thrusting into him. The side of his face makes a little squeaking noise on the slick wood surface, and he grunts but pushes back against me.

"You're perfect, you know that?"

His pleased smile makes me want to fuck with him even more.

"And now, I can pull up a picture of my billionaire all bent over and waiting for me any time I want. Maybe with my next guy, I'll put it up on the TV so we can both enjoy your hole while we fuck each other."

His face flushes an even deeper shade of red, and he grits out, "Fuck. You."

I slam into him again, causing the table to screech along the floor. He grunts as I bottom out, his fingers losing some of their grip.

"Spread 'em wide, Rand. I need access to my hole."

He glares when I take another picture, and I thrust into him again. Thrust, pulse. Thrust, pulse.

Rising on his tiptoes, he pushes against me in rhythm, rubbing his ass against me.

"Ooh, that's my needy bitch. You need every inch of me you can get, don't you?"

He whimpers and spreads himself wider for me.

"Tut, tut, Rand. Give me your words."

"Y-yes. I need every inch. Please. Harder."

"Then get up on your hands and brace yourself," I growl. He loses his balance because I'm still hammering into him, but he finally manages to push up onto both hands, rocking back with each deep thrust. Leaning my weight onto him, I wrap one hand around his throat and the other around his desperate cock.

"Please. *Please*," he begs in a high, suffocated pitch, pushing back, fucking himself on my cock.

I wish I had hours to do with him as I like, but a promise is a promise, and building security will be here in exactly seven minutes.

I apply light but firm pressure to the arteries in his neck as I squeeze and pull at his cock, thrusting into him. He pushes back against me, then forward into my hand, fast and hard. His breathing hitches and I loosen my grip on his neck for a few strokes to give him a nice headrush before increasing the pressure once more.

When his hips start to go off rhythm, I release his neck, pulling us upright and shoving us forward until his thighs press against the edge of the table.

"I gonna come," he chokes out.

I clap my hand over his mouth, still thrusting. "Give me a few more seconds, baby. I know you can do it."

He shakes his head, but the straining of his muscles tells me he's trying so hard to hold back for me. Jesus, he's going to be the death of me.

"Come, Rand."

His strangled cry nearly sends me into the stratosphere, and every muscle in his body arches against me. He clenches hard, and I stroke him through the orgasm, savoring the sound of his cum splattering on the fancy conference table.

The muffled sound of his ecstasy, the heat of his skin against my clothes, the nearly painful grip of his ass pull the orgasm from my body. I pound into him until I spill my entire load, wishing I could see my cum leaking from his used hole.

Time is ticking, but I'm not finished with him yet. "Look at this mess you left on the table. People work here, for God's sake. Lick it up."

He seems willing but looks back when I don't pull away. Still inside him, I tighten my grip on his hips and arch my brow. Breathing hard, he leans over, tightening around me.

"Time's a-wasting, billionaire. It's better when it's warm."

He shivers around my cock as he braces himself and leans forward, taking a tentative lick.

"You can do better than that," I say, pushing his face in it. "Lick it up like you mean it."

I wait till he nods before letting him up. Breathing heavily, he begins licking up his cum in long, satisfying stripes.

"Oh, yeah," I growl, draping myself over him, thrusting. "Now that's a good boy."

He moans and practically makes love to the table with his tongue, chasing every drop. I caress his neck, feeling his pulse race under my fingertips. It seems that even post-orgasm, our little back and forth is enough to keep him going.

When the table is properly spit-shined, I slip from his body, the tip of the condom hanging from my half-hard dick, full of cum. Standing, I face him toward me and lick the cum from his cheek and nose, then help him into his underwear and slacks, tuck him in, belt him up, and straighten his hair, lewd as my spent cock brushes him with every move.

I lean in for a kiss, exploring him gently as his breathing returns to normal. "Take off my condom and lick me clean."

He kneels and does as asked, then disposes of the evidence. I pour him a tumbler of water. "Drink."

He complies, downing it in one go, still quiet and a little dazed-looking. I pull him into my arms and nuzzle into his hair. "You okay, baby?"

He nods, snuggling against me. "You were perfect. Fuck, I don't know how, but you just get me."

I let out a deep breath, happy he enjoyed it. He whines when I pull away too quickly, and I place a finger on his pretty red lips.

"A security guard will be by in about thirty seconds."

His eyes go wide, and I wink at him. "I told you. I've got you."

We walk out of the boardroom and across the suite to the bank of elevators. With a shaky hand, Rand swipes his badge, one of the doors opens for us, and we step inside.

Just as the doors close, a security guy rounds the corner, heading straight for the executive suite.

Rand turns to me, his mouth in an adorable O. I hold up my finger, glancing at the discreet video camera in the corner. I know he needs reassurances, but I've first got to get him to the penthouse.

We take the elevator down to the security level, where Edgerton is waiting. His eyes dart between us before he ushers us into the tunnel entrance. Rand is perfectly quiet, looking at his hands as we make our way to his private elevator.

Once inside, I turn to Edgerton. "What kind of security do you have in this elevator?"

"Sound and video, along with some enhanced safety features."

"And who owns the media? Who has access to it?"

"Just me."

Rand glances over at me, nervous. I open an arm to him, and he quickly slips into the side embrace, gripping me tightly.

"You still okay?" I whisper into the side of his head as I run my fingers over his cashmere-covered rib cage.

With his lips pressed together, he gives me a quick nod.

"Just a few more minutes until Edgerton does his walk through the penthouse, okay?"

"Okay."

Edgerton, to his credit, schools his face as the elevator doors open. He steps into the space with a nod in our direction and immediately begins his sweep. He's mostly checking the logs for potential visitors while looking for recording and tracking devices.

As we wait in the foyer, Grayson greets us and, like a practiced professional, doesn't outwardly react to the fact that his boss is attached to my side in an intimate embrace.

"Grayson, I think you can take the afternoon," I say, looking to Rand for confirmation.

Distracted, he nods. "Yes, Grayson. Thank you."

Grayson heads out, taking the service door by the elevator.

A few minutes later, Edgerton joins us again. "Everything's secure. Do you plan on going out any time this evening?"

Rand shakes his head.

Edgerton looks between us again, then wordlessly makes his way out the service door.

Rand, still a little cum drunk, rests his head on my shoulder. "That had to be the hottest fucking sex I've ever had. My legs feel like Jell-O, and I need you to snuggle me, hardcore." Side-eyeing me, he asks, "What the fuck did you do to me?"

I shrug. "Gave you what you needed, that's all."

"I pay guys to top me, and they still treat me like the CEO. You've never treated me like the CEO, even when you call me a billionaire."

He finally looks at me. I smile.

"People forget that CEO is just a hat like any other. Same with sub and Dom and top and bottom...I mean, when did people stop asking which hat they wanted to wear *today*? This hour? This minute?"

He stitches his brows together. "Never heard it put that way."

I hold out my hand, and he takes it. "Now you have."

We make our way into the living room, and the couches look like the perfect spot for some aftercare. I turn to Rand. "I don't know about you, but I want to be in some jammies. Want to get changed and meet back here in three minutes?"

Rand bites his lip then pulls me in for a fierce kiss. "Deal."

We laugh as we run to opposite sides of the enormous penthouse. I race through my little suite and grab my new flannel pajama bottoms and my old college tank top. Stripping in record time, I yank on the tank top, then shove my legs into the bottoms, pulling them up as I run to the kitchen. I fill up a fancy sports bottle with water and grab one of Rand's wooden mixing bowls, tossing in snacks and comfort food from the pantry.

I make my way back into the living room, sliding on my socks, coming to a stop in front of Rand. He's stretched out on the couch, hands behind his head, looking smug.

"Fuck, you're sexy," I say, knowing it'll make him blush.

He lowers his head, smiling. "I don't know why I get this way around you. It's annoying as hell."

"Annoying? Might want to have a conversation with your penis about that. He seems to really enjoy it."

He laughs and grabs the bowl of goodies from me. "Shut up."

"First, drink," I say, shoving the sports bottle in his face.

He rolls his eyes but takes a few deep swigs, then selects fruit snacks from the bowl before offering it to me.

I scrunch my nose. "I'll get some in a bit, but I need to get some touch time with you if you don't mind."

He nods, and I lean back in my corner of the couch, beckoning him. He crawls over and lies on top of me, his head on my chest. I run my hands up and down his back, grateful for his weight.

"This feels so good," he mumbles into my pec. "I just feel so fucking safe with you. Even when you're pushing my face into my own cum."

I tighten my arms around him and tangle my legs with his. "It helps me to hear that," I say, kissing the top of his head.

He looks up at me, smiling. "Wait, did you not enjoy making me lick my cum off the table?"

"Oh no, I loved it. I just need to make sure that you loved it as well. And that you know that I'm not trying to be some controlling asshole."

"Do you know how I know you're not an asshole?"

I shake my head. He kisses my chest. "I don't feel bad about myself around you."

I groan as he trails his kisses up my neck, past my chin. Hovering over me, he looks me in the eyes, smiling sweetly before kissing me. It's perfect and exactly what I need to come back to baseline.

"Did you like that I took you so close to being discovered by the security guard? I thought it might give you a little extra thrill right at the very end. Like the perfect espresso after a delicious meal."

He snorts. "It did get my heart pumping again." Burying his face in my neck, he presses his hard-on against my thigh. "That answer your question?"

"Mm, it does," I confirm, shifting my thigh up and down his length. "Anything you didn't like?"

He goes quiet, and I run my fingers through his hair. "Tell me."

He scrunches his face in a very non-billionaire way. "Can you erase the pictures you took of me?"

"Of course," I say, reaching for my phone. "I was kind of improvising with the pictures. Should I just leave that off going forward?"

"I hated it *and* it scratched that itch. It's on the keep list for now."

"Sounds good," I say, pulling up the pictures for him to see.

He narrows his eyes at me. "Those are just selfies."

I wink. "I didn't have your permission to take the real thing. But sometimes the illusion is just as effective."

"God, I hate you."

"No, you don't," I say, kissing his chin.

He lets out a little grumble. "No. I *don't*. But you know what this means, right?"

"I have to take real pictures next time?"

Big sigh. "*Yes*."

I set down my phone and wrap him up in my arms. "Oh, he's so put out when I spoil him."

He shimmies up and starts kissing me, sliding his still-hard cock against mine. "Shut up."

I chuckle and thrust up. "Can I take care of that for you?"

He bites his lip and nods.

We flip so I'm on top, pulling off his pajama bottoms to

maneuver between his legs. Resting my head on his thigh, I grab the base of his cock, taking the top of it into my mouth, gently sucking on it as I jack him off.

"Mm," he says, squirming under me, his body warm. "Cozy little blowjob."

He runs his hands through my hair, and I love this sense of easy togetherness. I fondle his balls, pulling on them with one hand while I continue milking him with the other.

"Coming," he whispers.

He thrusts up, and his warm cum fills my mouth. I swallow quickly, then reach up for a kiss, plunging my tongue into his mouth.

"Can I?" he asks, palming my cock. I nod, and we kiss for several minutes while he strokes me nice and smooth until the orgasm is right on top of me. I deepen our kiss as I groan and spill into his hand. Pulling my tank top over my head, I wipe up our mess.

I grin at him until he pulls back with a confused look. "Hey."

I kiss him. "Yes?"

"You jacked me while you were blowing me."

"Yeah." I bite back my grin.

"That means you can't deepthroat either."

I wink, and his mouth falls open.

"You made me suck you like a pacifier."

His disgruntled face is one of my favorite expressions. Biting back a laugh, I crook my finger at him, and he comes face to face with me, glowering. Wordlessly, I point down to his cock, already starting to fill again.

"You motherfucker."

"Don't do anything with that until I say so."

His peevish mutterings make me smile, and I hold him until we are comfy and warm. Our soft drift into slumber is interrupted by the buzzing of his phone.

Sleepy and disgruntled, he glances at the screen then turns off the ringer before setting it facedown on the fancy ottoman. "I forgot that I blew up my father's marketing strategy."

"Oops."

He shrugs. "These last few days have been insane. I'll deal with it in the morning."

We laugh, then fall asleep, wrapped up in each other.

16

RAND

I'M NOT SURE WHY, but giving up my sexual power to Joe for a few brief moments has given me power—real power—everywhere else. For instance, it's the day after he railed and defiled me in the boardroom, and I'm once again standing up to my father.

We've taken a break, but Father has cornered me, his cool disapproval evident.

"We had a specific marketing strategy in place, which you've destroyed with this amateur-hour social media post." Scanning my attire, he shakes his head. "And you look like you're about to take a run in the park, not manage a crisis of your own making."

I wonder if the man has ever been wrong about anything in his whole damned life.

It was a good post. The first picture was simple. Me looking straight into the camera, no cheesy corporate smile, no fancy suit, no alpha mask to make me feel superior. Joe took the picture, and I...I just looked happy. Determined.

The second picture really tells the tale though. It's Joe and me sitting across from each other. Sherry took that one, capturing a moment before the second meeting with the board.

Joe had been passionately explaining the critical needs of our employees, and in the picture, he's pointing at something on the paper in front of us. I'm leaning forward, listening intently. There's something interesting about this picture. It isn't staged—Joe actually looks a little frustrated—but it shows our mutual respect.

I love this picture of us.

I refocus on my father and smile. "Your strategy was bullshit. And this outfit is from our clothing line. We're an athletics company. We should look athletic."

"Are you saying our marketing department can't do their job?" he asks, ignoring my very good point about the clothes to ask an actual question.

"No. The opposite, in fact. I'm saying that you and the board have hamstrung the marketing team, and they are doing their level best with the bullshit you've given them. Our post freed them to make better decisions."

"*Our* post? Are you actually buying into what this Portelli guy is saying?"

I nod. "I am. He's a good man, and he's right. You should listen to him."

"He's a mobster, Rand. He'll always be a mobster."

And thank God for that, I mutter under my breath, remembering our night together in vivid detail. A warm hand lands on my shoulder, and I glance up to see Joe. He looks proud of me, and I feel it in my toes. I nuzzle my cheek against his hand, and he winks at me.

My father looks between us, and he shakes his head like he's never been so disappointed in his whole life.

Joe turns to my father. "You're right, of course. I was born into a mob family, and some of that shit is innate. I just redirect what I learned and focus on the good."

My father gives Joe an up-down that would intimidate a lesser man. "I understand my son thinks you saved his life. You and I both know that all I had to do was arrange for a sizable transfer of cash into your father's bank account, and all of this drama could have been avoided."

Joe's smile is sad. "My father would've taken your money and sent Rand back in a body bag. He wouldn't go after you, or your mistresses that you think nobody knows about, or your wife. No. With the future of Wolfe Athletics in his hands, he'd have simply killed your son and taken your one true love—your business—to its knees."

For the first time ever, my father seems nervous. He adjusts his collar. "If he had done that, I would have paid another family to wipe out every last one of you."

Joe grabs my hand, kissing the back of it. "And that, Mr. Wolfe, is why I saved your son's life."

There's a moment of quiet as my father absorbs Joe's simple truth.

"I never wanted any part of the mob life. I wanted a fancy job in Manhattan. Wish I'd realized sooner that you corporate guys are more gangster than we ever could be."

The meeting is about to reconvene, and my father pulls himself back together. "However true that may be, I still hold the purse strings. If we cannot come to some sort of accord, a simple meeting of the board will swing the entire decision my way."

"I think it's funny that you keep bringing up the board," Joe says, crossing his arms. "If you could use them against me, you would have already. You would've called a vote, had me fired, had Rand stripped of his title, and taken over as CEO. But you haven't done any of that."

My father's face goes to stone.

I hold up my hand, shaking my head. "That's not true though, is it? You did hold a vote. Yesterday. You held a vote, and you lost."

His eyes flash rage, then go cold as if it never happened. But I saw what I saw.

"We are not finished talking about this," he grits out.

"We are, actually," I say, trying to keep the shiver out of my voice. "We're voting this afternoon on all five measures. Vote however you want, but this is happening. And once we get the go-ahead, if I find that you are working against me in the background, if I can't make the deals I need because you've called in your old cronies, if you make somebody wait even an extra day for health benefits, you'll pay for it. This is not the day, and I am not the one."

Joe catches my eye, his look pure intent. Pointing at me, he grins as he mouths *Alpha*.

I shake my head and point to myself. *Rand*, I mouth back.

He bites his knuckle, and I cannot wait for him to destroy my ass again tonight.

My father catches our little exchange and disgust plays out across his features. "You are my greatest disappointment."

"Why, Father? Because I want to take care of our people while making a shitton of money?"

Sneering, he grits out, "When you let them win, they lose respect for you. You have completely lost the upper hand, and this company will descend into chaos, you mark my words." With a shaking hand, he wipes the spit from his lips. "And when they find out you're fucking the guy from the docks? Good luck."

A sliver of fear rolls through my belly, but Joe squares up and my father takes a step back. Leaning in, his eyes black pools, Joe's words sound like murder. "If you're thinking of outing your son, don't. *Don't do it*. I promise you will not like my reaction."

My father takes another step back, though it hurts him to do so. "Are you threatening me?"

Joe closes the distance. "I am absolutely threatening you. Just like Rand, I learned at the feet of my father. The most important thing he taught me, Mr. Wolfe, is that there are a great many things worse than death. And when I'm protecting Rand, I am capable of all of them."

Just as my father opens his mouth to retaliate, Ford bursts into the room, looking ecstatic as he carries a donut in one hand and a coffee in the other. "Joe, Rand, did you see what the market did after your post? Holy shit, we're going to make so much money."

He's wearing a pair of perfectly tailored bright-blue chinos and a white linen button-down with a hot-pink kerchief tied at his neck and is so perfectly unaware of the power struggle he just walked into. I send a helpless look to Joe, whose face cracks into a wide, genuine smile.

He pats my father's arm before answering Ford. "I saw it, buddy. I might even buy some bit dollars, or whatever you call them."

Ford turns to me, utterly pained. "Rand! What are we going to do about him? He's practically prehistoric!"

My father looks like he's about to swallow his tongue, but he refuses to say anything in front of the one board member who sides with me one hundred percent of the time.

I shrug, dizzy from the switch. "You know, he's teachable, our Joe. Maybe you sit down with him after this vote and show him the basics."

His eyes light up. "Yes! I am so excited about this afternoon. *God, I love money.*"

Joe laughs, and Ford shoulder-bumps him. "It's not just the money, Joe. I promise."

"Mm-hmm," Joe says, turning his grin to my father. "You billionaires are only ever worried about the one thing."

Ford pouts. "I'm telling the truth! I can't wait to see what happens when employees begin to thrive. I bet it'll be something special." Turning to my father, his green eyes sparkling, Ford continues, "I know this has been a tough negotiation, but you have got to be so proud of Rand's leadership. He's gonna take the Wolfe family name into the next millennium."

We turn to my father, who pastes on an approximation of a smile. "It'll be something."

The rest of the team joins us and are equally jazzed by the numbers we're seeing. We have a bit more back and forth between the old guard and the new, but by the end of the hour, we've flipped enough board members to win the day. All five measures pass, with my father abstaining from the vote.

I wish I could be in a more celebratory mood, but one look at my father tells me that he's not done with me. Not by a long shot.

17

JOE

RAND'S BEEN quiet since the vote, and I know his father's disapproval is the reason. He seems happy to have found his stride as a leader, but it's early days, and every son wants the respect of their father.

Thankfully, I know how to help him get out of his head about it.

"Did you touch yourself last night?" I ask as we walk past the foyer into the living room.

Rand shivers, shaking his head. "Fuck you again for that."

"You could, you know. Fuck me."

"Ahem. Rand." Grayson rounds the corner, his cheeks pink. "I had not anticipated your early arrival, but dinner is almost ready."

I grimace and mouth a quick *sorry* to Rand. His mortified expression is too fucking adorable.

"Take the rest of the evening, Grayson. And thanks for getting dinner started. I'll take it from here." It's not my place, and that's why I do it.

Grayson's eyes dart to Rand, who gives him a small nod. With a small click of his heels and a stately bow, Grayson leaves us to our evening.

"So now you're bossing around Grayson?" Rand asks, unzipping my hoodie with a grin.

I shrug. "I wanted him out of here before I did something very, very indecent to you."

"I'm all ears."

Grinning, I go to my knees and tug down his waistband, gently scooping his dick and balls out of his underwear. Taking his soft cock into my mouth, I give it a tentative suck, and he immediately begins to plump, his moans filling the cavernous room. I move down, kissing and sucking at his nuts, enjoying the grunt of protest when I use my free hand to hold his cock, lightly thumbing under his head.

"More, please. More," he begs, trying to thrust his hips for more traction. I lighten my hold even more while lapping at his balls.

When he whines again, I firm my grip, cranking him several times before taking him into my mouth, sucking hard. He lets out a shout and hardens further, coaxing me to take more of him, thrusting his hips, fucking my face.

I pull off him with a wet slurping sound. "Watching you take your father down a notch—it was glorious. It made me so fucking hard, seeing you stand up for yourself like that. He was flabbergasted."

He laughs. "I know! It was the best thing ever."

I nuzzle his belly then look up the long line of his body, catching his eyes. "The best...ever?"

"Oh no! I mean..."

I suck a little hickey in the valley between his groin and his thigh, laughing. "I know what you mean. It was impressive. It turned me on."

His eyes widen. "It did?"

I nod. "Yeah. I got to see the real you without all the posturing. You were every bit the leader you needed to be, just being your authentic, passionate self."

He scratches the back of his head, smiling shyly.

"You liked it, didn't you? Standing up for yourself like that."

"I did."

Cocking my head at him, I ask, "That the only place you wanna get bossy?"

He reddens. "No. Maybe. But not right now. If that's okay."

"Oh, it's always okay. I'm perfectly happy with our current arrangement. I'm just saying that if you want to turn the tables on me, I'm sure I'd deserve and enjoy it in equal measure."

"Good to know. I do have one request."

"Name it."

"Can we go to my room?"

We haven't yet done anything in his bed, so this seems significant. He holds out his hand, and I take it. "Of course. Since we shared our statuses, you still good to go without condoms?"

His jaw tightens. "I can't wait to have your cum dripping out of my ass."

"Me too, baby. Same limits?"

"*Yes*," he says, leading me to his bedroom.

I'm pleasantly surprised by his inner sanctum. There are no cool edges here, only an inviting combination of slate-gray walls and furniture, transposed with a thick white duvet and fluffy white pillows. He directs me past the bedroom into the ensuite bathroom, which has more of the pretty gray with white accents and the fanciest fucking shower I've ever seen.

There's gotta be at least a dozen showerheads pointing toward the middle. I imagine standing there, pummeled by all that water, every inch of my body getting sprayed and massaged.

"Strip," I order, my voice laced with mob and steel.

He does as requested, slipping off the shirt before pulling his undershirt over his head. He quickly pulls down his pants, his hands shaking. Stripping down to nothing, he crosses his hands in front of himself.

"Don't cover yourself. Let me see you."

He lets his hands fall away, and his natural blush moves from his chest up to his neck as I look him over. I twirl my finger in the air, and he dutifully turns in place, letting me enjoy every artistic curve of muscle up and down his lanky frame.

"Bend over. I want to examine your hole."

He whimpers, then bends at the waist, automatically reaching back to spread his cheeks. I reach between his legs, pulling back his cock and balls so I can see them nestled under his ass.

"Mm. So fucking pretty," I say, lightly circling the puckered skin with my middle finger, watching him struggle between embarrassment and horniness.

His cock thickens and his balls draw up nice and tight. I spit on his hole, then watch it drip down, clinging for a second to his cockhead before dripping on the floor. I keep him in this position, teasing his length with my fingers and the brush of my hard cock covered in expensive athleisure joggers.

"You've got some kind of space-age shower in here, sweetheart. Stand and set it up for me."

I support him as he straightens up, amused by his little wobble after the head rush. I remove my clothes as he taps a black panel outside the shower, lighting up a hidden interface. He hits a few buttons, and the shower turns on with a powerful woosh, and I look forward to the promise of excellent water pressure.

I kiss him as the water comes up to temperature and steam fills the space. When we enter, a groan leaves my lips. So perfect.

He leans in, whispering, "The showerheads are programmable. I want to show you something."

"That sounds very promising."

"It is," he says, tapping at the screen with all the controls.

Looking over his shoulder, he grins. "At the risk of sounding bossy, put your hands on the wall in front of you and spread 'em."

Laughing, I do as asked and am immediately rewarded with pure fucking bliss.

Two of the jets are perfectly aimed at my taint and balls. He hits a few more buttons, and another set of showerheads bite at my nipples. There's a pair at my shoulders, helping reduce the tension there, and the final two beat down on my scalp.

"You are a very dirty boy," I say, spreading my legs farther apart.

Rand hums a little self-satisfied tune to himself and goes back to the panel, making a few more adjustments. The jets tickling my balls shift up until they're nearly pounding at the puckered entrance of my asshole.

"How's that feel?" he asks, ducking under my arms to stand in front of me. I mourn the loss of my nipple jets but mind it a little less when his happy eyes meet mine.

I bite the inside of my lip as the pulsing stream of water lights up every nerve ending. My voice is shaky as I respond. "Like I'm a whole new person. Spread my cheeks for me."

He presses his face into my neck, and I can feel his smile on my skin. Wrapping his arms around me, his fingertips drift down to my ass as he obeys my command, grabbing a cheek in each hand and pulling them apart.

Fuck, that water pressure is going to be the death of me.

I shift back and forth, trying to take advantage. "Jesus, Rand. It's like this shower is fucking me."

"Is that okay?" he asks, blinking up at me. His little innocent act doesn't fool me one bit, but it does make me harder.

Pinning him against the wall, I take him in a rough kiss. At the same time, I angle my ass to get a bit more of that solid pressure in the back. I edge myself for several minutes, nipping his lips and neck when his hands threaten to lose their grip.

Finally, I step back from the kiss. "Wash us."

He lets go of my ass and produces a bar of soap, finely milled, smelling of man and leather. He runs a luxurious washcloth over my body then his, carefully cleaning every inch.

When he tosses aside the washcloth, I take him in a heated kiss. "Good boy. Now, eat my ass."

He presses another kiss to my lips, then dips under my arms. The nipple jets are in full force again, riding me hard, and I grit my teeth, groaning in pleasure. His satisfied chuckle makes my cock twitch.

He circles around behind me, and I glance over my shoulder as he kneels, spreading my cheeks. I wait for it and am not disappointed.

"You...you're...*hairy!*"

"Baby, I'm Italian."

His glare could start a forest fire, and I wink back. "Don't be shy. Get all the way in there. My hairy hole isn't going to rim itself."

Grumbling, he begins to assault my ass with his tongue. I loved the water, but his hot tongue aggressively lapping at my hole is another experience entirely. He pauses for a moment and stands, hitting another button on the panel as he curses me under his breath. His ears are a blotchy red, and his elegant cock is as hard as I've ever seen it.

As he kneels again behind me, a new set of jets seem to cradle my balls.

"Fu—" I cut off the attempted curse as his tongue breaches me. "Fucking good boy. *Yes.*"

The pulsing rhythm of the water changes, bringing with it all new sensations. I shift my hips so my cock can get in on the action.

He pulls back. "Am I doing this right?"

I look over my shoulder, nodding as I bite my lower lip. "Get the fuck back in there."

He gives me a private smile that sends another wave of lust and pleasure through me, with a dark edge of emotion that seems to creep up whenever we're in the same room.

Before I can think too much about what any of that means, he goes back to eating me out like his life depends on it, licking and nipping at the sensitive nerve endings. After several minutes of this, pushing myself to the edge and pulling back, adjusting my stance so the various parts of me shift in and out of the intense, pulsing streams of water, I'm almost out of my mind.

Finally, I step away from his talented mouth. I'm breathing heavily and everywhere the water touches my body is too much.

"Turn it off."

Looking rather pleased with himself, he rises carefully and hits a button on the panel.

"Dry us off."

After running luxurious towels over our bodies, he leans in for a kiss that gets heated in a second.

"Grab your ankles," I command, flicking one of his sensitive nipples.

Flushing, he leans over, and I grab his towel, carefully drying any stray droplets that I find. "Good. Now let's get into bed."

He takes my hand and leads me into his room. I flop onto the luxuriously plush bed, grinning up at him, my hard cock bouncing with me. He grins and leans in to take a few quick sucks with his perfect mouth.

"Prepare my hole." He shivers at the bass in my voice and immediately grabs the bottle from his nightstand.

Turning away from me, he spreads the lube on his fingers, then reaches behind himself, pulling back a cheek so I can watch him.

"Rand, baby. You aren't paying attention."

He turns around, the worried scrunch of his brows entirely too endearing.

I tilt my hips, and his eyes go wide. "But...*your* cum in *my* hole," he whines.

"I didn't say that'd be tonight."

"But..."

I point to my cock, which is both girthier and longer than his. "If you're worried that yours is so small, don't. I haven't made a man fuck me in a while."

He glares at me, a bit of that haughtiness flashing through as if to remind me that he's still the billionaire in this situation. "I am *not* small."

"*Oh, Mr. Billionaire, you're so big.*" I snort, shaking my head at him. "I told you to stop listening to the men you paid to fuck you. But don't worry. Your cock is *sufficient*. Like a training cock until I need something with a little more heft to it."

He fumbles the lube, spilling some on his fancy duvet as his chest rises and falls rapidly, his neck an adorable scarlet.

I bite back a laugh when I hear him mutter *not small* under his breath. I rearrange myself so I'm laid out like a king, propped up against a large stack of pillows.

"Just because you're smaller than my usual boys doesn't mean you can slack off with preparation. Tongue my hole, then really get that lube in there. You'll want to lie on your belly to get the right angle."

Rand somehow still manages to look like a billionaire while lying flat on his stomach. I lift my balls, and he pushes his face into my undercarriage, extending his tongue as far as it will go. I tilt my hips up a bit more and shove his face closer to my hole.

"Still good?" I ask, loving him in this position.

A mumbled *yes* filters out from between my thighs as he continues to lick at me, each swipe of his tongue a little more urgent than the last. Smiling, I drop my heavy balls on his cheek. He grumps at me, so I do it again.

Once I've got him breathing heavily, I cradle the back of his head and draw him away. "Good boy. Now lube up your pinky finger. That's all I'll need for that small cock of yours."

I check on his cock, and it's still rigid, a fat drop of precum sitting on top.

Chuckling, I adjust so he can reach behind my nuts and massage my taint and hole. After a few seconds, he pushes in his pinky.

I grimace from the minor stretch, but I'm beyond ready. He leans forward, giving my head a little suck as he hooks his pinky against those sensitive nerves in my ass. Jesus, fuck, I forgot how good that shit feels.

"Time for your gherkin, baby."

He removes his fingers and fits the head of his cock against the barely stretched opening, slipping against it a few times before pushing it through the tight ring of muscle.

Fuck, he's so much thicker than his pinky.

I school my face as he slowly pushes forward, pausing at the thickest part of his flared head. Brat.

I grab his hips and complete his thrust for him, throwing him off balance. Grinning, I strengthen my grip, angling his hips just so as I slam him into me.

"Fuck," I mutter, continuing to fuck him with my ass.

Still glaring at me, he falls forward into a kiss, sucking my lower lip into his mouth, teething at the plump skin as he begins to thrust in time with my hands, back and forth, back and forth, letting my lip go when the tight ring of muscle finally gives way.

"Oh my godddd," he says, his voice like charcoal sex.

I may be in charge, but all I've got in me at this point is a head bobble and Lamaze breaths as he continues to bottom out, moans and pleasured sighs tumbling from his mouth.

Without thinking, I wrap my legs tightly around him, hooking my ankles together behind his back.

He loses his balance again, flattening out against my chest.

Soon enough, though, he finds a rhythm and grabs the sturdy head-board to drive his hips forward. I bite my lip, tasting blood as more sounds pour from the back of my throat, the pit of my stomach, the bottom of my soul.

I squeeze tight around him, then roll us until he's on his back. Now that I'm on top, I'm fully impaled on his not-small-in-the-slightest cock. We lock eyes and fuck...this angle is so different, the sensations more intense. When he hits that patch of nerves from this direction, it's all I can do to not immediately explode.

"I'm gonna come on your chest," I growl, rolling my hips until his eyes flutter and roll to the back of his head. "Jack me."

He fumbles again with the lube, spilling a little too much into his palm before taking me in hand. Finally, he begins to coordinate the thrust of his hips with the jerk of his hand, and my orgasm begins to spin up.

"Joe," he whines. "Please. I'm so close. Please..."

I drive my hips down hard. "Fuck, keep begging me."

"Please fuck my cock. I'm so close. I'm going to die if you don't make me come. Please let me come. *Please.*"

I cry out with each upward thrust paired with a firm, slick grip. Rand arches under me, flooding my body with his heat, and I go off like a firework, my cum landing on his cheeks, lips, neck, nipples. I rock back and forth on him until we both shudder.

I collapse on top of him and kiss him stupid. After a few moments, I step into the bathroom for a quick clean-up and run a washcloth under hot water.

"Hey there," I say, pushing the hair off his forehead as I rejoin him in bed. "You okay?"

I clean my cum from his chest, and a lazy smile makes its way across his lips. "Yeah. More than."

I finish cleaning him off and make him drink some water before we snuggle down in bed.

"I'm going to sleep so well tonight," he says with a dreamy quality to his voice. "I hope I was...top enough for you."

I palm his ribcage, finding his eyes so he can see the truth in mine. "You were perfect. And your cock is perfect. I hope you know that I was just..."

He waves me off, a supremely satisfied grin on his face. "You tricked me, inspecting my hole like that, then making me rim you with all that hair."

I growl in his ear. "You liked it."

He shivers. "I did. It got me so nervous and horny and embarrassed, and I've never been so fucking hard in my whole life." He comes in for a hard kiss, loving on me. "I can't believe you let me come inside you."

"You liked that?"

He stretches out, getting comfortable as he fits his head under my chin. "Yesss. I've never been fucked from the bottom like that, and then seeing my cum drip down your leg when you went to the bathroom made me feel all claimed and possessive at the same time."

Pulling the duvet up around us, we quickly begin to drift off. The last thing I see before I fall asleep is his pleased smile.

18

RAND

I'M in that delicious state of half-sleep, where I'm aware of things going on around me, but I don't really want to wake up, don't really want to open my eyes or move from this bed that smells like Joe.

The aroma of fresh coffee fills my nose and rough fingers card my hair. I blink up and see Joe wearing a roguish smile, dressed to perfection, holding a mug of coffee.

"Thought I'd let you rest a little extra after last night." He sets the coffee on the bedside table. I rub my eyes and stretch my back, sitting up against a stack of pillows that perfectly cradle me.

I pick up the mug and sip it, making eye contact with Joe as I do. My cheeks heat as I remember what we did, and I want to taste his cum so badly.

Pulling back the covers, I reveal my naked hard-on. Joe smiles and leans forward, taking me in his mouth, gently sucking the sensitive head of my cock. He pauses to suck on a finger, which he edges up behind my balls, circling my hole.

He slips inside, just to the first knuckle or so, teasing me as he increases the suction on my cock. I moan, and he pushes farther inside, hooking his finger, pressing on the spot that makes me see stars.

"Not going to last," I say. "Unless you want me to."

My dick still in his mouth, he shakes his head, then pulls back with a pop. "No, we've got a lot of work to do today."

I bury my fingers in the hair on the back of his head, and I feel his throat relax as I delicately scratch his scalp. He looks up at me with his gorgeous brown eyes, and I fuck his throat, losing control a little.

Okay, maybe he can *deepthroat.*

He grabs my thighs in a bruising grip, and I shout as I come in wave after wave. I shout again when he reminds me of my prostate, rubbing against it, sending more cum down his throat. I finally let go of his head, and he sits back on his haunches, looking so proud of himself.

"I like the way you look in my bed, Joe."

He skims up my body, delivering a cum-soaked kiss. "I like the way you look when you're coming inside my mouth, billionaire."

"You're welcome to stay in here anytime you want," I say, pulling down his waistband and underwear to get at his thick cock.

"C'mon, Rand. We gotta get moving," he says, thrusting into my hand.

Grabbing the lube from the nightstand, I stroke him to full hardness. "Can't have you talking to the company unsatisfied. It's bad for business."

His breathing goes heavy as I find a good rhythm, slicking him up and down, up and down. "Fuck, Rand. You're so good at that."

He gives in, lying back on the bed, coming on a shout as I finish him off with my mouth, swallowing everything he has to give me. He wraps his powerful arms around me, plundering my mouth until I have to tap out for air.

The softness in his eyes layered with the passion and strength he's shown since our first day together send my feelings headlong off a cliff.

Finally, having lazed in bed far too long, he nudges me.

"Come on, drink your coffee. We've got a company culture to change."

I CATCH Sherry's eye when the elevator doors open, and she looks at the two of us with affection I don't think I've ever seen in her before.

"Hey," I say, realizing what she's got on. "You're wearing something from our luxe line too."

She stands and holds out her hand for Joe to spin her around. Where he and I have mixed in well-tailored dark wash jeans and sharp button-downs with our Wolfe Athletics gear, she's in head-to-toe athleisure, and it makes me so damn happy.

"Figured I'd do my part to support you."

Joe leans in and kisses her forehead. "Thanks, Sherry. You're one of the good ones."

Her cheeks pink up and she gets a little flustered before directing us to our inboxes for the final versions of today's presentation to the company. I know the feeling.

Boy, do I.

Joe looks around and reaches for my hand, threading his fingers with mine, quickly kissing the back of my palm. "Let's do this."

19

JOE

THE AUDITORIUM ISN'T AS PACKED as the last time we were here. When I think of everything that's transpired in the short time since then, my mind boggles. I peek at the crowd from backstage, and there's a nervous energy in the audience.

The company's theme song begins to play, and people settle into place, quieting down. I look at Rand, and he smiles as he scruffs my beard.

"This is not my strong suit," I admit, grateful for his hands on me.

"Are you actually nervous, Portelli?"

I raise my brow at him. "You trying to start something, Wolfe?"

He swallows thickly, cupping my junk. "Maybe."

"We'll see how troublesome you are when I'm back on top tonight."

His cheeks flush, and he briefly looks away.

"I do like it when you get shy around me," I say, gripping his hand.

I'm not sure what this thing is between us, and I don't know that now is the right time to consider it, but I know it isn't just fucking. These small touches we give each other are intimate. They come naturally. And nothing about this feels casual.

I peek out into the audience and spot Edgerton and his guys at the exits, a reminder that there will, at some point, be a confrontation with my father. And I wonder if there'll ever be a time when I'm not straddling these two worlds.

The music drops off, and my attention goes back to the stage and its single spotlight in the middle. My buddy, Garza, moonlights as backstage crew for St. Ann's in Brooklyn, and I asked him to work in a little drama for the occasion.

It seemed like a good idea at the time, but right now, it feels like I'm walking through the blackness of space toward the only bit of light on the planet. I can barely see the people in the audience, only the shadow of them from a castoff of the spotlight.

Shooting Rand one last look, I step out onto the stage.

My expensive cross-trainers sound sharp against the wood as I finally hit my mark under the spotlight. The gasp in the audience takes me by surprise. I look over at Rand, standing there all elegant and cool, and he gives me a single nod. Supremely confident in me, it seems.

Smiling in spite of myself, I face my coworkers. The greeting I practiced seems stiff and impersonal, so I start the conversation with my friends the way I always have. "How *you* doing? Miss me?"

The resulting laugh is deeply satisfying, and I shift in place, sneaking one more look at Rand, whose proud smile nearly undoes me.

"Me and Garza—we wanted to do this whole thing with the lighting, but now that I'm here, it feels like I'm in an interrogation room. Do you mind if I switch things up? I can't see any of you, and it's freaking me out."

More laughter and clapping. Without me having to say

anything further on the subject, Garza brings up low lights around the house, softening the dark stage.

"There you are," I say to the audience, grinning even bigger. "Never mind, now I can see every one of your ugly mugs. Maybe this was a mistake."

Garza switches back to the spotlight, and the laughter is even louder this time. I can't help it. I laugh along.

"Ha, ha, Garza. Put the lights the way you had 'em."

A light chuckle filters out over the audience as he brings back the low lights.

Before I can get into my speech, someone, I think Tony from the production team, pipes up, "So what the fuck, dude? Was this some sort of setup?"

I shake my head. "Garza was sitting next to me that day. He can attest to the fact that I hadn't planned a damn thing."

"I kept telling Portelli to shut the hell up," he yells from the back, netting another laugh.

When the laughter dies down, I continue, "True story: the day after our confrontation, I was up, back on the docks at five-thirty a.m. Then this one," I say, tilting my head to the man offstage, "had someone take him *on a helicopter* to come talk to me. Apparently, calling out their corporate bullshit caused a tiny kerfuffle in the stock market."

I follow this with a *what can you do* gesture, and the crowd laughs again.

"So, no, this wasn't some crazy stunt. This was me hearing someone spout some really tired bullshit and being unable to deal with it anymore."

The audience goes quiet, but it's a different kind of silence. Thoughtful.

"And it turns out when a video of you taking down a CEO goes viral, they suddenly want to hear what you have to say."

More laughter.

"So I did the Brooklyn thing and told him straight up what needed to happen to change the culture here at Wolfe Athletics."

Carla from the AV team illuminates the big screen behind me with the simple list.

That nets a gasp from the audience. I'm guessing the first bullet, the one about giving everyone a market-based salary adjustment, is the biggest shocker.

"Now, let me tell you something. When I said these five things in Wolfe's big fancy office, they nearly laughed my ass out of the room. Trust. But then they lost another half a billion dollars in value and stopped laughing."

Heads nod throughout the auditorium.

I realize that the plan to have Rand just come in at the end is flawed. We need to present this to the team together so they can see the difference in him.

I turn to Rand, raising my brow. "You know what this means," I say, not caring that the audience can hear me.

He shakes his head at me, biting back a smile.

I lean into the mic. "Look, I'm about to go off-script. I'm supposed to show you this presentation all by myself, but I think that makes it look like this was all my idea. And that's just not the truth. I worked with a lot of people, including a lot of you. I think our CEO should join me on stage and help me out. Rand?"

The team shifts in their seats. It's not a bad thing. I think they want to see what he has to say.

He glares at me, but there's a playfulness that I've come to recognize in him. I beckon him with the slightest raise of my brow, and he walks out on stage, sheepishly waving to everyone in attendance.

"Real talk, I don't think he was his best self during our confrontation. But, having worked closely with Rand for a while now, I can tell you that under all that posturing is a very good man. And I wouldn't be here if that were not the case."

I step to the side and let him take center stage. He looks out at this company he helped build and bows his head. Then lifts his chin and scans the audience, almost as if he wants to look everyone directly in the eye.

"Mr. Portelli here is correct. That last meeting was not a good day for me. But neither were the days and weeks and even years leading up to it. I didn't realize I was stuck in an old way of doing things. And if there's one thing I learned from Mr. Portelli, it's that if Wolfe Athletics is to be competitive for years to come, I've got to be willing to challenge my perceptions."

"I swear to Jesus, if you keep calling me Mr. Portelli, I'm gonna get whiplash looking for my dad."

The company laughs, and so does Rand, shaking his head. "And that's one thing I also want to change. The formality of our dress code puts a layer of distance between you and me. My name is Rand, and you'll notice I'm not wearing a ridiculously expensive suit. We're an athletics company, for Christ's sake. Let's act like it. And if we pass each other in the hallway, I would prefer it if you told me *good morning, Rand* or *fuck off, Rand,* instead of some insincere greeting to the lifeless Mr. Wolfe."

Everyone laughs, slightly shocked.

"Yeah, Joe's rubbed off on me, can you tell? Pretty sure my father is somewhere in the back having a heart attack because I just cursed in front of the entire team. But, even if this doesn't mean anything for the bottom line, this just fucking feels better, you know?"

Everyone gets to their feet, clapping. Rand holds his hand to his heart and bows his head, his face beaming. I don't think he's ever felt like this before. I know I haven't.

And in that moment, I'm struck with another truth.

He's someone I could really fall for.

Hell, it's already happening.

20

RAND

I WANTED to throttle Joe when he called me out on the stage, but it was honestly brilliant. After breaking through the wall I'd built between my employees and me, Joe and I were a perfect complement to each other as we covered the pillars of our corporate reset.

Now it's the end of the day and the sun is still out. I want nothing more than to make the quick walk home outside, but Edgerton insists on taking the tunnel. Joe gets quiet when I argue about some goddamn oxygen, and I wonder if our security weighs heavier on him than I thought.

Edgerton accompanies us to the penthouse, checking it out as is customary before leaving us alone with a brief smile. He was in the audience during today's meeting, and I think he liked what we had to say.

As soon as the door closes, Joe pulls me into a kiss that goes on forever. Walking me backward to the living room, his kisses push me down onto the couch, and his body feels like home.

We roll up side-by-side on the deep cushions, kissing and

putting our hands on each other, holding on for dear life. It's comfort, and Joe seems starved for it.

Carefully, I pull back from his kisses. "What's going on, Joe?"

He shakes his head, pulling me closer to him as he rests his forehead on my chest.

"Were you upset that we couldn't take a walk outside?"

He tugs me closer and lets out a sigh. "No, it's not that."

"Are you sure? Because we've been relegated to heavily secured indoor spaces for the foreseeable future, and it sucks to be told that it's dangerous to be outdoors."

Avoiding the topic, he kisses my chin, the corner of my jaw, my cheek before capturing my mouth in a deeper kiss. Several moments pass before I remember we need to break the surface.

Patting his chest, I pull away from his lips, pressing soft kisses to his eyelids.

"Joe, darling, if you asked me a question, and I avoided answering it, what would you do?"

"I dunno. Would there be making out? Because if there's making out, I'd totally let you get away with not answering the question." His smile is sarcastic, but it doesn't reach his eyes.

"Bullshit."

He pulls back, narrowing his eyes at me. "That's my line."

"It's a good line. And I call bullshit. What's going on?"

He pushes his face into my neck, kissing the sensitive skin.

I wrap my foot around his ankle, keeping him in place. *"Joe."*

Gritting his teeth, he finally answers me. "Maybe it doesn't seem like much to you because you have security around you all the time. But I know my father isn't going to give up, which means this heightened security is now more or less a permanent fixture in your life. Who wants to live like that?"

I cradle his face and kiss his cheeks because his lips are too dangerous. "Joe, I want you to imagine for a moment that you're a billionaire with a security issue. What kind of security would you have? Would it be bargain-basement? Unqualified friends and family? Or would it be the most badass team of motherfuckers you've ever seen?"

"Probably the last one," he says, chancing a look into my eyes.

"Exactly. We had an amazing day today, and the fact we needed a little extra security to get through it means absolutely nothing to me."

"Maybe it doesn't mean anything to you, but it does to me. Rand...I'm really starting to care about you, and I know it's ridiculous because we just started getting naked with one another, but..."

"But this is something, isn't it?" I mentally cross my fingers.

He nods. "It is."

I interrupt whatever he's going to say next by sticking my tongue down his throat because I'm so fucking happy. When I finally collect myself several minutes later, I respond, "Good. Because Sherry's already calling you my boyfriend."

"Is she now?"

I nod, giving him my Very Serious look as I ignore the pounding in my chest. "I'm pretty sure that makes it official."

Joe grins. "Wait. So are we actually dating?"

"Unless you want to disappoint Sherry," I joke, trying to hide the huge grin that threatens to split my face in two.

"Well, no. Of course not." His smirk only lasts for a second before his face turns somber. "It's just...you deserve everything. I love spending time with you, but I hate that you have to live a smaller life because I've got this big dangerous thing in my world."

I flick his forehead, stealing another one of his moves. "It's a dangerous thing in *our* world. And what if I've been living a smaller life this whole time? Going from my uber-exclusive penthouse to my private elevator to my secret passageway to the executive suite, bypassing the entire world. What if an ex-mobster is exactly what I needed?"

He tugs at the hem of my shirt. "I was never officially a mobster to begin with."

"Eh, agree to disagree. You scared the shit out of my father, and that is hard to do. And I swear, that guy in the park was bound and determined to drag you back to Brooklyn, and you broke his arm with your bare hands."

He shrugs. "I didn't break his arm. I just violently ripped his shoulder out of its socket."

I laugh, probably a little harder than I should. "Oh, just a torn rotator cuff then. I'm sure he'll just be in a brace for the next six months."

"Sounds like you've got a hard-on for the guy who tried to kidnap me."

"Nuh-uh. Fuck him for trying to take you away from me." I pull him close to me. "*Mine.*"

He snorts. "Yep, that's me. Some billionaire's boy-toy."

"Ouch. Take that back," I say, smacking his chest. "My boy-toys were always paid. You fuck me for free, remember?"

He laughs. "Okay, I'm sorry. Boy*friend*, not boy-*toy*. Even if you did go and spend way too much money on my wardrobe."

"We're not getting into that again. Besides, this was an amazing day for Wolfe Athletics and a really good day for the people who work there, and you're the one who made that happen, and we should celebrate."

"Can we celebrate by holding each other on the couch for a while longer?"

"Can I get a hand job out of it?"

He leans in and kisses me deeply. "Mm. I can arrange that."

21

JOE

"YOU'RE PACING," Rand says, grinning at me.

"I'm not pacing. I'm just working out my speech."

"While pacing."

I've been out on his enormous wrap-around balcony—not pacing—trying to fucking memorize yet another speech. Amusement lights up his eyes.

"What's so funny?"

"You weren't nearly this nervous to speak in front of everyone at Wolfe. That was easily twice the number of tonight's attendees."

"I knew the people in the crowd at work. But this is a *gala. You* were the one scheduled to give the speech."

"Call it payback for going improv on the first speech. Maybe that'll teach you."

I narrow my eyes at him and resume the not-pacing.

We've spent the last few weeks focused on putting policies in place and finalizing a schedule we can share with the team. It's been exhausting and frustrating, and the most fulfilling work I've ever done.

More importantly, things have settled down on the security front. No other families have come sniffing around, and even though the extradition order is still active, I think my father is willing to let me be. At least for the time being.

Meanwhile, I don't sleep in the guest suite anymore, and when I wake up, Rand is always wrapped around me.

I can't tell if it's just the crazy circumstances or if we would've hit it off in a bar. I'm not sure. But the soft touches and shared breakfasts and homemade dinners sure do make me smile. Hell, it's put my heart in a whole different stratosphere.

But this speech is gonna be the death of me.

Rand shakes his head, his posture relaxed. "Joe, listen to me." He puts his hands on my shoulders, his eyes focusing on mine, warmth crinkling in at the edges. "You are exactly who they need to hear from. There will be CEOs from fifty of the biggest corporations in the United States, each easily ten times the size of Wolfe Athletics."

My stomach drops as I look out over Manhattan. We're so high up that even the sounds of the city are muted. "You're supposed to make me feel better, not like I want to throw up."

He shakes his head again. "I'm not saying that to make *you* nervous. I'm saying it because you make *them* nervous. That little viral video of ours? It made all of them want to throw up. Because this little uprising has legs. It has *meaning*. You can help them make sense of it. You can help them navigate it."

"Who needs help navigating this? Just pay your people enough and treat them like human beings? It's literally just two things."

"It's not just two things, Joe. It's a million things that distill down to those two things. And when I say they don't know where to start, it might help you to know that a not-small percentage of American CEOs exhibit psychopathic traits."

"Excuse me?"

"It's true. I'm not talking about a murderer hiding around the corner with a knife behind their back. I'm talking about people who genuinely have a hard time understanding human emotion. It's why America loves them in that position. When your focus is only on the money, you don't have to care about the human element. But now, the money is making them care about the human element, and it's the one thing for which they are woefully under-skilled. They literally need instructions."

I shove my hands in my pockets. "It's like the mob. The most successful people can kill, break the law, ruin lives without remorse. My father has never once been remorseful."

"So you already know how to work with someone who has these traits. You already know that you can't appeal to their hearts. You must appeal, once again, to cold hard cash. So when you tell them what to do, don't forget the numbers."

"I know. I know. Sherry helped me with the speech. I've got it squared."

"I promise, they need you more than you need them." Rand reaches out and pushes my hair off my forehead. "Hell, I need you more than you need me."

I lean in and give him a gentle kiss. "I definitely need you, Mr. CEO. I wouldn't know the first thing about talking to people at this level. Thanks for calming me down. And for the suit. I can't believe you spent that much money on me."

Rand lifts his eyebrow. "I'll have made more money by the end of this sentence than that suit cost me."

My eyes nearly bulge out of my head. Shit. I can't even...I have no frame of reference for any of that. "I just want you to know that I'm not trying to take advantage of you. I appreciate the new wardrobe and that you've let me live here, rent-free."

"During the length of this conversation, my money will have made enough money to pay for the cost of living in this penthouse. For an entire year."

I open my mouth to protest, but he puts up a hand. "You are

the one thing I cannot buy, Joe. And because I know you will never take advantage of my wealth, it makes me want to be generous with it. So please, shush, and let me do nice things for you."

It's my turn to blush, but I try for a stern expression anyway. "Okay, but...don't overdo it. And for some reason, you talking about how much money your money makes over the course of a sentence makes me want to put you on your knees."

He checks his wrist, telling time on a watch worth more than most make in a year. "I think we've got time for a quick blowjob," he says, his crooked smile making my chest warm.

"No, you don't," Grayson says, walking out onto the balcony. "I don't have any spare suits if things get messy. So keep it in your pants until later tonight."

I chuck Grayson's shoulder. "Man, I thought we were friends, and here you are, cockblocking me."

"I am doing no such thing, Joe. I'm keeping things running on time and on schedule. You two can whip your cocks out later."

Rand's surprised gasp makes Grayson and I laugh hard. He's right, of course. The elevator doors open just as we make our way inside, and in walks the night's security team.

Edgerton takes us through the security protocol for the evening. At Rand's insistence, the organizers have increased their security protocols and beefed-up general security.

"Beyond all that, I'll be on the periphery with a backup team, should there be a need."

I assume that means he'll be set up in a van with a bank of computers and listening devices, waiting to take out any bad guys. The thought amuses me, but I hide my smile and nod along in all the right places. I finger the folded-up speech in my pocket, trying not to sweat in yet another ridiculously expensive suit.

Finally, we make our way downstairs and into the car. Before I know it, Rand's usual security guy, James, is holding open the car door for me, and I'm stepping out onto an actual red carpet. The American Museum of Natural History has been transformed into a gorgeous, star-studded event space.

Rand is already out of the car and trips a little on the edge of the carpet. I steady him with a neutral hand on his shoulder, but it's all I can do not to grip his hip and make damn sure he's solid.

"You okay?" I ask out of the corner of my mouth.

"Yep. Apparently not finished making an ass of myself."

"Psh, nothing compares to the alpha-wolf speech you gave. You could go sprawling out on this red carpet right now, and that speech would still have you beat."

The tips of his ears redden beautifully, but I know to back off.

"Sorry, wasn't trying to make you blush on the red carpet. Promise."

"Suuuure," he whispers back, his private smile telling me he didn't mind it one bit.

Flashing lights refocus us, and we stand next to each other, trying to look like allies, business partners, never mind the fact that every nerve inside of me hums and sings with his nearness.

Paparazzi are everywhere, flashing lights, calling our names. It's a bit of a shock when one of the business journalists yells out, "Mr. Wolfe! You and Mr. Portelli seem to be getting along. Have you developed a friendship?"

I stiffen, not sure how he'll take that kind of a question. But his posture, still relaxed, never changes. He smiles at the reporter then looks at me before nodding thoughtfully, looking like the consummate professional.

"I once heard that if you don't bring a diversity of thought into your executive spaces, you will die from the shot you don't see coming. And it's not easy when somebody points that out to you. It usually involves a pretty large ego check. Mr. Portelli could have been the kind of person to gloat about being right. But he's not. Wolfe Athletics was dying a slow death, and we didn't know it. He saved us from that. So, are we friendly? Absolutely."

I try to remember my poker face, and when he sticks out his hand, I don't pull him toward me and fuck him on this very nice carpet. I simply shake it and give him a bland smile. And hope that the recording equipment doesn't pick up the cha-cha in my chest.

We finally make our way past the gaggle of reporters and into the entry rotunda, where the gala is being held among soaring dinosaur fossils. If I thought the red carpet was the hard part, I was wrong. While Rand was right—there are fewer people here than at the company meeting—this is a different atmosphere entirely. Fancy, big-name people are everywhere: oligarchs, actors, sports heroes. My eyes nearly bug out of my head.

"Is that Eanes?"

Rand follows my line of sight, putting his hand on my shoulder. "Weston? Yeah. Wanna meet him?"

I turned to look at him, wide-eyed. "Do I want to meet Weston Eanes? Uh, *yeah*."

"Looks like he's talking with his manager now, but we can circle back around when he's not as busy."

I nod, my head still on swivel.

His hand still on my shoulder, he asks, "Are you okay? Still nervous?"

I snort. "Yeah, I'm nervous." Looking at his hand on my shoulder, I continue, "Maybe don't touch me. I've been fighting a boner since I saw you on the red carpet, and I don't want to terrorize all of the fancy people."

He gives me a nod and an understanding smile. "Message received. It's hard to keep my hands to myself."

I let out a big breath. "You have no idea."

Smiling, he dips his head, cheeks coloring. "Sorry, not sorry." He looks across the room, up-nodding someone. "If I leave you to your own devices, would that be easier or harder?"

I shrug. "I'm a big boy. Go schmooze. I'll flit about the room like a social butterfly."

"Of all the things in the world I can picture you being, social or butterfly-like in any capacity aren't anywhere near the first hundred responses."

"You wound me, sir."

"Get the fuck outta here," Rand says, laughing as he pushes me into the crowd.

22

RAND

IT'S smart to put some distance between Joe and me, if only because there's a real possibility for accidental dry-humping in the coat-check closet if we're not careful.

I scan the room, and everyone oozes elegance and sophistication except for Joe. He's gorgeous in his well-tailored suit, but he still looks like a mobster. In fact, I've decided that the nicer the suit, the more dangerous he looks.

And tonight, he's lethal.

God, I want him to fuck me while wearing that suit.

Unfortunately, with thoughts wandering down so many lovely paths, I nearly run over my texting buddy.

"Mads! My apologies, I didn't see you."

Mads grins up at me. He's of average height, on the skinny side, and has a head full of shiny, thick, wavy black hair. His skin is a deep velvet brown, and his smile lights up a room, even one this large and grand. He's part firefly, part absent-minded professor, and very much the opposite of me.

"No shit, Rand. You're way off in la-la land. What gives?"

"Got a lot on my mind these days. It's nice to see you in person though. Feels like I haven't seen you in forever."

"Same," he says, giving me a fast, hard hug. "It's been crazy."

"What's been going on with you?"

He shrugs. "We're working through a government contract that I can't talk about, but it's eating my lunch. I should've stayed in the private sector."

"And leave all of those defense dollars on the table? I think not."

He shakes his head, looking around the room. "Let's change the subject, eh? Tell me about this Joe person. We haven't caught up since everything went down. Is he really staying at your place?"

"How do you know that?"

"I have my sources. Anyway, he's kind of yummy, isn't he? Looks dangerous in that suit tonight."

My eyebrows stitch together. "You saw him already?"

"Are you kidding? Everybody here is talking about the guy who tore down Wolfe Athletics and is now rebuilding it with his bare hands."

"Hey now, there's a whole bunch of us working together on the rebuild. It's actually kind of incredible."

Mads' large brown eyes scrutinize my face as his lip ticks up at the corner. "Looking kind of wistful there, Mr. Wolfe."

"You'll be happy to know that you were right about the alpha thing. I had no idea how much it was holding me back. He's shown me an entirely new way of looking at the workforce. It'll revolutionize business in Manhattan...if people are willing to listen to him."

Mads tilts his head. "You like him."

I nod. "I do. He's a good man. Genuinely decent. Even though he does look like he might kill us all in that suit."

Crinkling his nose at me, Mads shakes his head. "Don't try to pull a fast one on me. You *like him* like him."

"Oh, shut up."

"Not when your eyes go all anime when you talk about him."

I grumble under my breath, wondering how a guy I spend more time texting than speaking to in person can read me so well.

"Ha! I'm taking your little mutter as confirmation. So...you're sleeping with him?"

"*Shh.*" I grab his jacket and drag him over behind one of the large columns. "Say it a little louder, why don't you? One or two of the Fortune 500 crowd didn't hear you."

"Shit, man. I was fucking with you. You really are sleeping with him?"

I rub my face and spy Joe across the room, charming the hell out of some high-society lady. She needs to remove her hand from his arm, or I'll remove it for her.

Jesus, calm down, Rand.

"It's a little more than that," I say, shielding my eyes from him.

"*Oh,*" he intones on a hushed whisper. "Is this...*serious?*"

My eyes meet his, and knowing infuses his face with warmth.

"We both agreed it isn't casual."

"Oh my *God.* This is so dishy. I never get the good gossip," Mads says, his hands held together in prayer. "They keep everything from CEOs."

"Well, everything except for all of the money."

"Oh my God, he's turned you into a social justice warrior."

"Are you saying that like it's a bad thing?"

Mads' grin is sneaky. "Not at all. Welcome to the team."

He fist-bumps me, and I'm awkward with it.

Shaking his head, Mads can't help but give me shit. "You are such a nerd. You should probably restrict your fist-bumps to emoji and save yourself the humiliation. Seriously, how did you get such a hottie?"

"I'm a billionaire, Mads."

"Yeah, but he's a *badass.*"

I smile to myself. He really is.

"Oh my God, *what is that look?*" Mads inhales sharply. "You have to tell me—does he give you everything you *need?*"

Mads and I don't spend a whole lot of time on our personal lives, but when we realized we'd be friends, we got really clear on the fact that we both like men who are a little more in charge.

I bite my bottom lip.

"You *dog!* Do you know how hard it is to find somebody who will top a *billionaire?*"

"Turns out all you have to do is insult them," I say, laughing.

"Oh my God. The sun is shining out of your face when you talk about him. You're disgusting!" he says, smacking my arm. "I'm so fucking jealous!"

"Look, don't jinx it. I'm not going to assume anything, but this might be a thing. It might be...real. Even if we don't know how we'll navigate it."

He tilts his head from side to side. "You'll figure it out. But you can't leave me hanging. What's he like in bed?"

"There is no way in hell I'm going to talk about my sex life."

"Please. I'm in such a dry desert right now. Please give me something. A single detail. *Anything,*" he says, palms up in supplication.

I roll my eyes. "Fine." After a quick scan of the room, I lean in. "He's fantastic when he's in charge. But he's not this macho asshole. Sometimes..."

"What? Sometimes...?"

"Sometimes, he actually needs me."

Mads' eyes go wide. "That deliciously toppy-looking mother-fucker is *vers?*"

I nod. "He has no embarrassment or shame about asking for what he needs."

"Imagine that," Mads says, knocking his shoulder into my arm.

"And he cooks. Like pasta, from scratch."

"I swear to God, if you don't marry him, I will." He pauses, then punches me in the arm. "Are you telling me you've been eating homemade pasta and haven't invited me over? Not even once?"

"We've been kind of isolated at the penthouse. But I'll invite you over. As long as you never speak of marrying him ever again." Leaning in, I point at myself. "*Mine.*"

Mads' jaw drops. "I have *never* heard you talk about a man like this."

Pushing his shoulder, I scoff. "You've known me for a year. You don't know."

"Oh, I *do* know. I'm jealous, but I'm super excited for you."

I blush a little. "Enough about me and my fabulous sex life. Of which you should *totally* be jealous. How are you doing? What about that thing with the...?"

He runs a hand through his pretty hair. "Stalker? Yeah, that's still going on."

"What the fuck? Who do you have running your security?"

"Somebody incompetent, apparently."

I dig out my money clip and slide out a business card. "You need to hire the security company I use. The guy who owns the company, Edgerton, is no-nonsense."

"And you're happy with him?"

"Tell you what. This whole experience with the video brought out some frankly scary elements, and I trust him with my life."

"Shit, that sounds nice. The company I'm working with is acting like I'm crazy. Which, to be fair, I might be."

"No, you're not. You're very smart."

"Well, smart and crazy aren't mutually exclusive, and I'm pretty sure this whole thing has pushed me over the edge. I was convinced I saw the guy out on the red carpet, and I nearly did a drop and roll to get away from him. Then I looked again, and it was some old guy. He's in my fucking head."

"Doesn't mean he's not a threat. Call Edgerton. He'll know what to do. He won't treat you like you're crazy, I promise."

Mads takes the business card from me and surprises me with another hug. "Thanks for not trying to make me think it's all in my head."

"Anytime, friend. I've gotta get back to it, but let's not let so much time go by between visits."

"Deal."

This time when he holds out his fist, I get the bump right on the first try.

23

JOE

RAND and I circle each other throughout the cocktail hour. He spends a lot of time with a gorgeous man who hugs him. Twice. But then Rand looks at me as he's talking to the guy, and I have a feeling my ears should be burning.

Whatever he's saying is making him incredibly happy.

I'm looking at him again when I run, quite literally, into a trim, elegantly dressed man.

"Sorry, wasn't paying—" I cut myself off when I see who I've nearly knocked down.

This isn't some random man in a nice suit. This is Luciano Stefano, the newly crowned head of the Stefano family. Mortal enemies and begrudging allies of the Portelli family.

The answering smile is a shock, and I swallow thickly, wondering if I'm about to die. I can't look away. I've seen pictures of him in the news, but he's a different vibe altogether in person.

Where I look like a goon in a suit, he fits in with this crowd. He's the love child of Sicily and old-school Hollywood, with a beguiling openness to his expression and pretty morning-after eyes fringed by eyelashes so dark and black they're almost feminine.

I step back and thin my lips. "No offense or injury meant, boss," I say, uncomfortable with that word in my mouth.

"None taken. And I appreciate the recognition, but maybe not in a room full of billionaires, eh? They know who I am, but they don't necessarily like to be reminded." Even his voice is elegant.

I remind myself that as fancy as he looks and sounds, it's no accident that he's here tonight. "Of course..." I trail off, not sure how to address him.

"Luca," he says, holding out his hand. Going against everything I've ever been taught, against every fiber of my being, I accept his hand and shake it.

Somebody take a picture. The Portelli and Stefano families just made physical contact without bloodshed.

"Of course. Luca." I close my mouth. I dare not make any small talk because I'm flying blind here. He's approached me with an agenda, and I'll let him make it known.

"I hear you're persona non grata with your family these days."

My jaw tightens. "Sometimes you make choices based on what's good for everybody, not what's popular."

He nods. "The Portellis forget that they don't just bring heat on themselves when they go off-script. But you always understood that. Which is why I haven't questioned your presence on my island. Though I did notice that you didn't come visit me first."

I shift, catching his men at every exit. Jesus. Does Edgerton know about these guys?

"You're right. I didn't. To be honest, I wasn't sure that it was my place, and you were dealing with your father's funeral. Again, no disrespect intended. And my condolences."

"None taken. And your condolences, while appreciated, aren't necessary. I'm not exactly unhappy that he's dead."

Luciano Stefano is known for his razor-sharp honesty, so his words aren't all that shocking. The fact that the late don and his oldest son didn't get along isn't exactly a state secret. I am surprised, however, that one of the younger uncles didn't take over.

Though looking at the man in front of me, murder in his refined fingertips, I take that back. I'm not surprised at all. I'd bet my shiny new salary he's got family at the bottom of the Hudson.

"I'm curious. Why wouldn't you feel it's your place? You're a Portelli."

"Yes, but I'm just the bastard. I was never more than a dock worker to my father."

He taps his lip with a manicured finger. "I think it's strange your father doesn't embrace his bastards. They would only strengthen his hold on his territory."

His use of the plural is purposeful. I'm the only bastard my father ever acknowledged. He's telling me there are others. A brutal truth designed to test my reaction.

I school my face, not allowing anything to make it to the surface. "Eh, he's old-fashioned that way. Probably only let me work the docks because I look too much like him to deny me."

Luca nods. "Maybe. Though I didn't come to you tonight to discuss old news."

"Oh?"

"I'm here in part to warn you that your father's not done with this. He's not going to take the win and be grateful."

"I wouldn't expect him to. He doesn't know he won."

"He's going to try to force your hand, get you to Brooklyn and keep you there."

My eyes track the movement of his men around the room. "That was my assessment of the situation as well."

"Our families have an agreement. We return your people to Brooklyn. You return our people to Manhattan. Easy."

I shift, noting that his men have taken an interest in our conversation.

He holds up his hand, as much to me as to them. "You're listed as a relative, not a member of your father's organization. Relatives have always been exempt. I mean, who was I to prevent your nonna—may God rest her soul—from seeing *Wicked* seven times, am I right? Besides, you've never killed anyone in my family, and your quick thinking saved all of us a lot of heartache."

I lower my head, listening intently.

"Still, this is a rather large inconvenience. Like most of the families, I ignored the general request. But now your father is contacting me directly. He's specifically calling in the treaty between our two families, and I'm telling him it doesn't apply. You can imagine how he's taking that."

"Not well."

I grind my jaw, re-evaluating which of Luca's guys I can take down quickly. Not a single one of them would go down without a fight.

He steps in close. "Let me be clear. I don't care about the intricacies of the Portelli family dynamics. It's none of my business. But you're under my jurisdiction now, and he can't just walk in and take you."

"Your jurisdiction?" I ask, uneasy in the extreme.

"Yes," he confirms without further explanation. "And I must apologize for the incident in Central Park. You handled yourself well, which is not a surprise, but the families involved overstepped. I recently made it devastatingly clear that you are to be left alone."

I blink like a cow, finally sputtering out, "Thank you. Security's been pretty intense. You've given me peace of mind."

Luca's smile is disarmingly genuine. "I'm happy to hear that. I do, however, have a warning for you. If your father blows everything up to get to you, if he brings the fight to my island, I will notice. And I'm not going to care who's on the board if I have to clear it. Capisce?"

Mobster movies like to show guys who look like me, pinching their fingers together, saying *capisce* all dramatic-like. It's kinda cringe if you ask me, and it's why I never use the word—I'd be a whole-ass stereotype at that point.

But Luca says it delicately. Like you have to lean in to hear him say it.

I flex my fingers, willing myself not to look at Rand. "Any advice?"

"Yeah, you and your billionaire need to be more subtle. He's looking at you like he'd bend over for you wherever. I don't think the fine people in this establishment have it squared, but it's clear as day to someone like me that he's important to you."

I run my hand over my mouth. We've been so stupid. I look Luca in the eye as I give him a sharp nod, knowing that a denial would be seen as disrespect. "Thank you for the warnings."

"Of course." His expression shifts and the hair on my arms stands up. "I do have a favor to ask in return. Two, in fact."

Dread locks my muscles and squeezes the air out of my lungs. This is the real purpose of this conversation. I'm about to be in his pocket and there's no way out of it. Maybe there never was.

I smooth my expression. "It's only fair. What can I do?"

"I like where you're going—making these tycoons sit up and notice the little guy. My sister's like you. She doesn't participate in the family business, but she's a feminist. And she protects her own."

Mobsters don't talk about family members unless they're equally mobbed-up, so I'm surprised he's brought her up at all.

"She's got a kid, twenty years old, sharp. He's a genius, truly. He's also on the autism spectrum. He'd be a real boon to anyone who hired him, but people don't take him seriously because he can't look them in the eyes. Has particular environmental consid-erations. My sister won't let me address the administrators who keep dismissing my nephew's skills. I don't mind telling you that the inability to fix this for him makes me...itchy."

I cover my shock as oxygen returns to my lungs. It's one thing to mention a sibling, but it's unheard of to discuss the particulars of the more vulnerable members of one's family. This means he's trusting me not to share this information with my family, who would absolutely use that knowledge to their advantage.

I'm probably staring at this point, mostly because I don't know what his play is. I decide on parity.

"Yeah, I wouldn't like that either. Got a young cousin who's on the spectrum. Had a few conversations with her school administration so they'd make the accommodations she needs."

Luca grins. "Thought I liked you. So, you see, my nephew needs a mentor. He's a real numbers guy, probably someone Wolfe Athletics could use in their corner."

I nod because I have no other choice. He gestures over to Ford. "That's your finance guru, no?"

I check out the youngest member of the Wolfe Athletics Board of Directors. He's been a crucial tie-breaker vote for several of our ideas. A warm, quirky presence in an otherwise stuffy space. His eggplant-colored suit is perfectly tailored and set off with a simple white button-down and sparkly turquoise tie.

"Yes. He's our newest board member, but he's already working with our CFO to identify ways to pay for the changes we want to implement."

"Excellent. I'm sure he'd love to meet my nephew. And because I'm efficient, he's my second favor."

The muscles that were just beginning to unlock freeze up again. "I don't do the wet work. I can only present your nephew in the best light possible."

He shakes his head, laughing softly. "I don't want to threaten him, Joe. He'll see that my nephew's got the goods. Of that, I have no doubt. I just want to get to know him better. What's his story?"

I draw my brows together, confused. I've never heard word one about Luca Stefano's sexuality. And I wonder how much of our shared sexuality is why he's chatting with me at a charity gala and not, say, in a dank warehouse with electrodes taped to my junk.

He sees my expression and winks. "What can I say? I like everything, but mostly beautiful men. And tonight, I really like him."

Shaking my head, I blurt out, "I *really* can't make him fuck you." Grimacing, I hold up my hands. "No disrespect, of course."

Luca's pretty eyes narrow, and my blood pressure spikes. I can fucking hear my own pulse. When he touches my arm, it's all I can do to not jump out of my own skin.

"I need you to hear me on this, Joe. I never *make* anyone do anything except keep their promises. Not even the people on my payroll. Nobody gets forced to do anything."

I don't think I could wipe the shock off my face if I tried.

He raises a gesturing hand. "Happy employees make more money. I spoil them rotten and charge a premium. Besides, do you know how many times someone on my books has alerted me to something going on in my territory? You know why I showed up tonight?"

"Because I'm causing you all sorts of drama?"

His laugh is unexpectedly warm, and I hate not knowing what that means. "True, but you haven't done anything wrong. On the other hand, one of my girls said that Randolf Wolfe Sr. was in a mood over some Portelli guy and got rough with her."

"Shit. Is she okay?"

He nods. "Nothing too bad, but he's been suspended, and his security team has been given a warning."

"I bet he's unhappy."

"Quite. But it worried her handler enough to tell me. I put a few things together and decided I needed to see what you were about. Didn't hurt that a certain money guy was also going to be here."

I laugh, shaking my head. "Glad you like the work I'm doing then."

"Me too."

The Portellis could learn a thing or two from this guy. My father runs girls in Brooklyn, but they look hard, unhappy, ripe for any of his enemies or, hell, an agent looking to make RICO charges stick.

The Department of Justice quietly gutted the Mafia of old, turning the screws on people in high places to turn state's evidence. It's been a successful tactic, leaving the mob a shadow of what it once was. The Stefanos are the only family who hasn't had someone turn state's evidence. I'd assumed there was a trail of dead informants leading to this man's door, but now I'm not so sure.

Refocusing on the request in front of me, I glance over at Ford. He's sporting a fresh haircut, and his fingers keep running up the new fade, a nervous habit. Still, he's rather dapper tonight, despite his appealing awkwardness.

Fuck it. I know Luca is a man of his word. If Ford doesn't bite, he'll walk away. "Follow me," I say, aiming toward the intended victim.

Luca's brow raises at the order, but he falls in step with me. We reach Ford as he lands a punchline, and the guy he's talking to —who looks like royalty and just as inbred—laughs.

His laughter comes to an abrupt halt when he sees and recognizes Luca. Closing his mouth, he gives Ford a quick wave and dips his chin in his direction before speed-walking somewhere else.

Shrugging off the weirdness, I clasp Ford's hand. "Hey—how's it going this evening?"

His grin is wry and his green eyes twinkle behind his geek chic glasses as they follow the man across the room. "Eh, I'd rather be at my Saturday night D&D game. Colbert was going to drop by, and he's always good for side quests."

His eyes flick to Luca, appreciating his features for a few seconds. He swallows hard, running his hand through his hair. "Honestly, I'd take working on a spreadsheet formula before drudging through another conversation about cryptocurrency. Fuck's sake, just buy in now, people."

I laugh to myself, wondering if unfiltered honesty might be the one compatibility between these two.

"Well, I might be here to rescue you then. Luciano Stefano, meet Ford Bradley."

Recognition crosses Ford's face, and his Adam's apple bobs nervously. Like he might know exactly who he is.

Luca shifts, instantly more elegant and charming. "Ford. How lovely to meet you. My friends call me Luca."

"Oh, uh. Hello. Um...my friends call me Ford."

I hold back a laugh and Luca looks utterly bewitched.

"Anyway, I wanted to introduce the two of you because Luca's nephew is also more of a spreadsheet fellow, good with numbers, probably not big on small talk. Been looking for a foot in the door."

"Oh." Ford blinks up at Luca, a mixture of terror and—maybe? —arousal on his face. "Um...where did your nephew go to school?"

Luca beams like a black light. "London School of Economics. Just graduated top in his class. Looking for something ground level. He's quiet and a little quirky, but he's a sweet kid."

Ford takes a deep breath and nods to himself. Putting his palms together, he plasters on a smile. "What I wouldn't give for a quiet, well-educated intern." Pointing to himself, he jokes, "And there's something to be said for quirky and sweet."

Luca winks at me then puts his arm around Ford's waist. "Here, let me grab you a drink from the bar, and we can talk about him."

Ford's eyes become two large moons and, once again, I'm not

sure if he's feeling excited or slightly assaulted. I raise my brow in his direction. He gives me a nervous smile before letting his eyes drift down Luca's elegant figure.

With a shuddering inhale and perhaps the tiniest whiff of regret, he steps out of Luca's embrace and pulls a card from his wallet. "I'm afraid that duty...uh, calls. But feel free to have him email his résumé to me, and I'll be happy to chat with him."

Luca bows his head, gracious in defeat, just like he said he'd be. "Of course. I'll have him contact you directly, so you don't have his very biased uncle trying to twist your arm."

Ford's eyeballs about pop out of his head, and Luca steps back, his hands up. "Metaphorically speaking only. If he works out for you, great. If not, that's okay too."

Ford gulps and blinks, nodding a little too rapidly. "That sounds good, Mr. Stefano."

"Luca," he reminds him gently.

"Luca," Ford says before practically melting away from us.

There's more disappointment in Luca's eyes than I would've guessed, but his wry grin remains in place. "You win some, you lose some. I just wish I hadn't terrified him. I swear, I'm a nice guy once you get to know me."

I snort. "Yeah, once you get past the bodies piling up in the Hudson, you're a real charmer."

Shit, I can't believe I just said that.

Luca raises his brow at me, then chuckles. I think he actually likes me, which is weird. I catch sight of Ford looking back at us, biting his lip before slipping back into the crowd.

I grin at the surprisingly *human* mobster in front of me. "Looks like he's interested and terrified in equal measure. Do with that what you will."

Luca's eyes track something across the room, and he leans in. "You think so?"

Rubbing the back of my head, I respond, "Maybe. Some guys

are timid and need a gentle approach. Not, you know, putting your hands on them from the word *go*."

I immediately suck in my lips, pretty sure I'm about to have a bounty put on my fucking head for telling the head of the Stefano crime family to keep his hands to himself.

Instead, his expression becomes thoughtful. "Yeah, you're right. I'll keep that in mind. I've seen him at a couple of these things. He's nervous but sure of himself. Like a bird, so colorful. And...I like the glasses."

A man appears at Luca's side, one of his security guys, if I had to guess. "I like glasses too, boss."

He's good-looking, around the same age as me, with tattoos, dark hair, and a sexy scar across his brow. But there's something off about his eyes. They're a pretty blue, but they have this intense energy about them.

"Fuck, Hopper. What'd I tell you about sidling up to me like that?" Luca says, smacking the guy's arm. "Your RICO guy here?"

My ears perk up. "You got an agent on the take?"

This Hopper fellow laughs like I just said the funniest thing in the world. Hell, even Luca laughs.

"Nah, nothing like that. He's on the up and up. Gets frustrated when I spot him—it's like a little game we play. But he ain't here tonight."

"You got something for me then?"

"Yeah, boss. Just want to let you know that my Spidey sense don't like it in here no more."

"You see something?" Luca asks, leaning in.

"No, boss. Just...the energy in here just shifted or somethin'."

Luca nods. "Good enough for me. I did what I came to do. Most of it, anyway." Looking at me, he up-nods. "You good here?"

"Uh, yeah. Luca. Nice chatting with you."

"Thank you," he says, handing me a business card. "And same.

Keep my number on you and call if you need back up. Hopper here is never wrong."

I look at the card in my hand, solid black with only a phone number in gold lettering. Yeah, I'm in it now.

"Will do." Turning to the man who looks like he might eat children's souls for breakfast, I dip my chin. "Thanks for the heads-up."

He pats my shoulder the way a toddler pets a dog—with far too much force and enthusiasm. "Anytime, Joe."

That's fucking fantastic. The serial killer on Luca Stefano's payroll knows my name. Just...great.

Right as they walk off, the emcee of the event, a gregarious woman of stout figure with more jewelry and finery than I've ever seen on another person, finds me.

"Are you ready for your speech?" Her smile is genuine, even if her hair is piled so high on top of her head she looks like a Victorian lady.

"I am," I say, wildly recalibrating my conversational parameters as I reach into my pocket. I pull out the folded piece of paper that contains my speech and hold it up for her to see.

"Excellent," she says, clapping her hands together. Sticking out her elbow, she says, "Well then, will you accompany me backstage?"

"I'd be happy to."

I wind my arm around hers, and we arrive at the large, makeshift backstage area, made of tall stands of rich, velvet curtains. There's a lounge area for speakers and a staging area for the catering crews.

"Good luck out there," my gracious host says, patting my shoulder. "And a little advice: I'm sure your prepared words are great but don't forget to be yourself."

I kiss the back of her hand. "That is excellent advice. Thank you."

She blushes and makes her way to the audience.

Rand peeks out from behind a curtain, scanning the area before walking up to me. I breathe out, a little surprised by how much I need him here. He leans in and whispers, "You've got this. Show 'em how it's done."

We're alone, so I chance a kiss, and he pulls me in for a hard but brief hug. The layers of desire and emotion in his eyes fuel me, infusing me with confidence. He sneaks back into the audience, and the warmth in my chest expands, knowing he'll be watching.

Taking a deep breath, I push through the heavy velvet fabric and walk onto the sparsely lit stage. Unfolding my speech, I smooth it out on the podium and clear my throat.

I can do this.

24

RAND

JOE WALKS backstage followed by thunderous applause, looking relieved and still a little shaken, with no clue about how much of a difference he just made.

I beeline to him, and he stiffens, looking around.

"Fuck that," I growl under my breath, reaching him in full stride and pulling him into a hug before landing a deep, searching kiss.

After a few seconds, he pulls back from the kiss, breathless. "Hi."

"Hi. You were fantastic up there. You had them eating out of your hands. Did you hear Weston cheering you on?"

"I think I got some cousins in Long Island who heard him," he says, looking pleased.

I kiss him again, just because I can.

He pulls away, his eyes sweeping the space.

"I'm sorry," I say, taken aback by his response. I thought he'd be proud of me for kissing him in semi-public.

His eyes snap back to mine and he holds up his hand. "Normally, I'd be all over you right now, but—"

Several members of the event staff make their way through the space, completely unconcerned with us. His eyes follow them all the way out of the space.

"Joe? What's going on?"

He looks around the room then kisses me tenderly. "I'm sorry. I was approached by another don this evening. He asked for my help and then told me it was clear that you and I are an item, which might get noticed by the wrong people."

My heart starts to race. "Was he threatening you?"

Joe shakes his head and seems confused. "He was, like, warning me. And he wanted me to introduce him to Ford."

"For what purpose?" My mind immediately goes to several unsavory scenarios.

"Maybe get a job for his nephew. Maybe get him a date with Ford."

"How'd that go?"

"Not in Luca's favor, at least on the date front."

"Ford rejected him?" I ask, incredulous as the terrible scenarios multiply.

"Yep. He took it surprisingly well. Said he never forces anyone to do something they don't wanna do."

My brows lift. "So...gay mobsters?"

He laughs, kissing me again. "Gay mobsters." His eyes dart around the backstage area again, and he puts his forehead to mine.

"Is his warning the only reason you're not kissing me right now?"

"Mostly. But I do worry about people finding out. They'll think I'm a gold-digger or that this whole thing was a stunt." His searching eyes land on me. "As soon as we figure out what this is, I want to get ahead of the story and say who we are."

"You're mine. Boom, figured it out."

Joe laughs. "Did you just say, 'Boom, figured it out?'"

I shrug. "Yeah. I know exactly how I feel about you."

"Oh really? And how does the billionaire feel about the lowly dock worker tonight?"

"You know, we should role-play that one of these days."

"I like it. Answer the question."

Smiling, I wrap my arms around his neck. "How do I feel about you?"

He nods.

"Ooh. All sorts of boyfriend-y things."

"What kind of boyfriend-y things?" he asks, kissing my nose.

"I dunno. I think that living together makes it feel like we've already been together six months, so I'm already sorta, kinda... smitten-ish."

Joe sucks his lips in, trying not to laugh, and I poke his ribs. "Stop being mean."

"No, no. I'm not being mean. It's cute. You're a cute billionaire. Who's apparently smitten-ish over me."

"Ah, jeez. I'm going to regret telling you that, aren't I? You're totally going to use it against me."

"Maybe."

"Whatever. You're smitten-ish too. Don't try to deny it."

He gathers me in his arms, his dark eyes pretty and intense in the low light of backstage. "No, baby. There's nothing *ish* about how I feel about you."

"Ooh, are you full-on smitten?"

Joe shakes his head, his expression serious. "I'm way, way past smitten."

I gulp. "Yeah?"

He palms my jaw, bringing me in for another secretive kiss. "Yeah. *Mi sono innamorato di te.*"

My heart pounds in my chest. *Innamorato* is a love word. "Did you say that you're falling in love with me?"

"Fallen. Past tense. I know it's too soon, but—"

I touch my fingers to his lips, smiling so wide it almost hurts. "I'm past tense with you too."

Laughing, he pulls me into another kiss, and we lose ourselves in it. I feel surrounded by him, like I'm drowning and flying, and I can't believe no one told me love could feel this good.

Another parade of catering staff interrupts our curtain time, and we pull away from one another.

I look down at my watch, and a slightly mischievous notion spins up. Joe up-nods me. "What's this look?"

"You've done your speech. I've shaken the hands I needed to shake. What do you say we get out of here?"

"Doesn't the marketing team want me to stay around to glad-hand for a while longer?"

"Fuck it," I say, grinning when he raises his brow at the language. "Be mysterious. Disappear. Leave them talking about you. I want you to make love to me."

Joe's answering kiss is deep and powerful enough to knock me off balance all over again. "You're the boss, *mio amato*. Let's get out of here."

I laugh, dizzy and high from our furtive declarations. Grinning as he grabs my hand, Joe pulls up his phone, sending a quick message to our driver and security team. Everyone checks in, and we start making our way out.

There's a secure pickup zone in the back, so we hold hands as James escorts us through the grand museum. We get a little lost in small touches and pointing out pieces to each other, and James sends us a small grin.

Finally, we make our way out to a loading dock, and while the smelly dumpster leaves something to be desired, at least there aren't any photographers. The driver pulls up, and James strides forward to open the door for us.

The driver rolls down the window, and Joe stops me at the bottom of the stairs. "Hey, James. Who's this new driver?"

The soft *thoot* and muzzle flash don't register right away, even as James falls. The single drop of blood oozing from the small black hole in his forehead is equally surreal, and my heart starts knocking against my ribs—*danger, danger, danger.*

Joe shoves me back toward the stairs.

"*Get the fuck inside.* Get help. Don't worry about me."

My feet start moving before I understand what's going on. I reach the top of the stairs as the driver and two other guys drag Joe off to the side. I pause, my legs like rubber as I watch him fight back with everything he's got, bare-knuckle brawling despite the overwhelming odds against him.

"Get the fuck outta here, Rand!"

His words are a cattle prod to my spine, and I nearly make it to the door when I'm tackled by two men, one enormous and the other thin and wiry.

"Fight back!" Joe spits out as he's being pulled back in a chokehold.

As they drag me down the steps, I twist and yell, throwing my elbows until I wrangle myself free. Hitting the ground with a thud, I ignore the sharp pain in my knees as I scramble to my feet.

Half running, half tripping, I make it to the first step before my legs are taken out from under me. I swing my elbows with a little more force this time, hitting the wiry guy's nose with a wet crunch. He drops my foot, and I kick out, landing a blow to something softer, the big guy's stomach.

Holding his bloody nose, the skinny one opens the door to my car. I flail as the big guy drags me over, violently shoving me inside. I register a blow to my head, but I brush it off, gripping the door-frame like grim death. With blood dripping down into my eyes, I blindly kick out again and again, making contact with soft and hard body parts.

Finally, they grab my legs and yank me away from the doorframe. The big guy pins my arms behind me with one hand while shoving a chemical-soaked rag against my nose and mouth. Already breathing heavily from trying to escape, I can't help it as I inhale lungfuls of whatever is on that rag. It's terrifying how quickly the fight goes out of me.

Cursing, they finally manage to get me into the back of the car. Just as the skinny one opens the driver's door, a series of low, menacing pops come from the side. My two would-be kidnappers scramble away, leaving me in the back seat. The skinny one is blown back by an invisible force, landing with a crunch of gravel. He stays down.

I realize, belatedly, that he's been shot. And is probably dead.

As my head begins to make sense of things, Joe comes racing into view, his knife in one hand, an enormous gun in the other. He's immediately beset by the big guy, and my heart falls to my stomach. The sounds of violence are more terrifying than I would have imagined, made somehow worse by the fog in my head.

Joe raises his gun, but the guy knocks it away with his meaty fist. I'm shivering, my stomach in revolt, horrified that I'm about to see the man I've fallen in love with lose his life.

Joe glances my way for a split-second, and in that brief moment, I see someone I've never met before. The incident in Central Park was nothing like this. His eyes are darker, his features harder, and his demeanor is cold as ice. I don't know this version of him at all.

His face contorts into a murderous sneer, and he plunges his knife into the man's gullet, ripping up and to the side. Yanking the blade from the man's body, he drops to a crouch to slice at the man's ankles. The large man falls like Goliath, and I don't know what's more startling, the sound of his body hitting the ground or how the ground shakes when he lands.

Scrambling to sit up, I search for a weapon to defend myself.

Spotting a Billy club in the front seat, I lean over to grab it just as Joe slams the door shut. My world goes silent as I sit back, gripping the club tight in my fist.

I suppose the dampening effect is a coveted feature in luxury vehicles for city driving, but the violence is somehow more frightening without the soundtrack.

With nothing but the Billy club to defend me, I sit back and feel useless—helpless—as I watch Joe rear back and kick the man on the ground, again and again until he's satisfied. The car shakes as something lands on the hood with a dull *thump*. I chance a look out the front window to find a guy I don't recognize fighting off two more men.

With a panoramic view, I watch as Joe calmly picks up his gun and dispatches the two remaining attackers with that same flat look on his face. He checks in with the guy I assume is event security. They nod together, looking like they've reached an agreement. The security guy starts heading to the passenger side when Joe lifts his gun a final time and puts a bullet in the back of his skull.

Jumping at the muted sound, I'm reminded of the time I saw those twenty-six seconds of the Zapruder film of the JFK assassination. Only this is much, much worse.

Horrified, I watch as Joe checks the gun, reloads it, and stands sentinel for several long moments. Finally, he pulls his phone up and makes a call, his words unintelligible through the tempered glass. Shaking his head, it's clear that he disagrees with the person on the line.

He cuts off the phone call with a snarl and leans down. When he stands, he's got the keys in his hand and finally approaches the car.

Wordlessly opening the driver's side door, Joe slides into place, locks the doors, turns on the car, and reverses out of the narrow drive. I open my mouth to say something, then think better of it.

As we clear the main building and turn onto the street, Edgerton and his squad rush the scene. He looks over at us as we pull away, his lips thin. Joe starts driving through the city in the opposite direction of my building.

I still don't recognize the man driving the car.

25

JOE

I RECOGNIZED my father's men, and this was exactly the scenario I'd feared the most. They weren't coming for me. They were trying to take Rand. I think he surprised them by fighting back as hard as he did. I shiver to think what they would've done to him to get me to come to Brooklyn.

I didn't want to kill those men.

I didn't fucking want to kill those men.

But they put their hands on Rand, and everything went red after that.

As we drive toward Tribeca—the opposite direction from Rand's building—my decision is made. If my father wants me to go to Brooklyn so bad, I'll go to Brooklyn. But I've got to get Rand home first.

If Rand says anything to me on the way over, I don't hear him. We dump the hired car on a side street in Tribeca, then walk to Soho. Rand points out the blood spatter on our white shirts, which we remove and toss into trash cans.

From there, I spy an unlicensed taxi and hail it. If the colorful and pierced taxi driver thinks it strange that two suited but shirt-less men are her fares, she doesn't say anything.

Edgerton will probably take my tongue out with a rusty knife later for taking such a risk, but I've got three bloodied guns in the various pockets of this expensive suit jacket and not much else in the way of options.

We finally make it to Rand's neighborhood and have the driver drop us off a block away, then wait for her to turn the corner before we start walking. We reach his building's portico in minutes, and I let out a gust of air, too fucking relieved as we walk through the doors.

Rand's eyes seek out mine, concern knitting his brows together. "Where's my Joe?" he asks, kissing me gently. "Did I lose you back there?"

I blink, swallowing thickly. "Not permanently. But Joe's not in right now."

He tilts his head and takes my hand, leading me through the fancy, high-ceilinged lobby. Passing the plush seating areas and dense greenery, I scan the space, looking into the dark recesses for boogeymen that never appear.

Halfway to the elevators, we're met by Edgerton and two other guys I recognize from the security team...plus Hopper, Luca Stefano's probably-certifiable right-hand guy.

"What the hell is he doing here?"

Edgerton holds up his hands. "Don't ask. Tell me you didn't drive the car here."

I shake my head. "Left it in Tribeca, took a cash cab from Soho to a block down the street."

"Excellent."

"Is the penthouse secure?"

"Yes. I have a crew up there, and they just swept the place."

"Good." I lean in and whisper, "I still have a job to do. Rand's not going to be happy but put him in that elevator and keep him in the penthouse until I get back."

If he even lets me back in the building after this.

Edgerton pulls back, his serious face shadowed with concern. "Take Hopper with you."

I snort and go to say something sarcastic, but Edgerton cuts me off. "I don't want to know the details, but if you're going where I think you're going, you'll need him."

"Is he going to eat my liver with some fava beans?"

"Eh. Liver's too gamey for me."

I have to lock down my startle response because Hopper is hovering, his face about two inches from mine. For a complete psycho, he's surprisingly stealthy. And kind of a smoke show if you don't mind all the crazy.

Fuck it.

"You're driving."

He lifts his fists like little pom-poms, and his eyes light up like someone's shoved a sparkler up his ass. "Yay! I'll go get the car."

"What? Where are you going?" Rand asks, watching Hopper as he skips out the door. "Who is that?"

Edgerton latches on to one of Rand's arms while another security guy grabs the other. He looks back at me as they drag him into the elevator.

"Joe—?" He's cut off as the elevator doors close.

Guilt gets added to the slurry of emotions I'm not acknowledging right now.

I head back through the lobby, hitting the door just as Hopper pulls up in a black crossover-type car. I get in and put on my seat belt as he tears down the street. Unlike the jokester in the lobby, this version of Hopper is serious, locked in.

Good. I'd hate to have to rip out his larynx with my bare fucking hands.

I look behind me and discover that the middle seats have been taken out and the interior is coated in some kind of rubber. That's…perfect.

"You know where we're going?"

"Already in the GPS."

"Won't it track us?"

Hopper taps the rearview mirror. Oh. Looks like we're already being tracked.

"That your RICO agent behind us?"

His eyes flick to the mirror, then back to the road, a small smile playing on his lips. By the time we cross Brooklyn Bridge, he's shaken his tail, and I wonder if that agent knows he has a fan.

Traffic is a little crazy, but Hopper navigates it with ease, and before I know it, we've pulled up in front of my father's massive brownstone, which is three stories high and takes up half a block.

As I'm checking the gun I took off one of the guys I already killed tonight, I realize it still has his blood on it. And I suddenly feel very tired.

We step up to the door, and it's opened by one of my father's goons before I have the chance to knock. Hopper gives the guy a brilliant smile, and the man's lip curls in recognition seconds before he falls to the ground.

I barely hear the silenced gun.

Hopper takes out two more guards in the hallway and one in the living room, his grin broadening with each kill. When we enter the old-school Italian kitchen with the table in the middle, my father is seated, facing us with his back to the sink, wearing only boxers and a white tank top.

He looks small as he blinks up at me from his seated position. There's a cup of milk and a handful of Nilla wafers on a small, white plate in front of him, one of them bitten and crumbly.

He looks nothing like the Viper of Brooklyn, who always loomed large and just outside my periphery when I was a kid.

Hopper shifts next to me.

My father's voice is weathered, tired as he barks out, "Who's this asshole?"

Hopper answers, his voice soothing and resonant. "I'm the right hand to Mr. Luciano Stefano. He asked me to accompany Mr. Portelli here."

Gooseflesh pops up along my arms at the ease with which Hopper transitions into this persona. I think about Rand and wonder if I'll ever make it back to him.

My father bobs his head. "Thank you for completing the extradition. I'm glad your boss could see his way to reason."

Hopper broadens his shoulders, and we exchange confused glances. "Sir, this is not the extradition. Mr. Portelli is under the protection of the Stefano family now. My purpose here is to ensure his safe return to Manhattan."

I tilt my head at Hopper. *First, I'm under their jurisdiction, and now, I'm under their protection?*

He winks at me.

"That was not the deal," my father says, dunking the half-eaten wafer before pushing it into his mouth. The move seems slow and soggy crumbs stick to his finger as he removes it from his mouth.

And then it hits me. It's been years since I've seen my father in person, and he's different. Aged, yes, but this is...he's *affected*. I wonder who sent the goons to Manhattan. Maybe Sal Jr.? I don't give a fuck. He'll be dead by morning too.

I glance at Hopper as something like disappointment crosses his face. I think he was looking forward to squaring up against a worthy foe.

This'll be like taking out someone's nonna.

"There is no deal, Father."

He lets out a breath, shaking his head. Grabbing a napkin, he's unbearably slow as he wipes off his hands and mouth, then pushes himself back from the table. He sways as he rises, and I stifle the urge to reach out and steady him on his feet.

Seeming to find solid ground, my father crosses his arms. I hold my breath, half-expecting Hopper to take him out, but he's just as gravely fascinated as I am. I'm almost relieved when cold steel is jammed against the base of my skull.

My father's narrow eyes finally meet mine, fixing me with bitter judgment as his body shifts, revealing the familiar power. Every bit the viper he always was.

"I told you not to call me that," he grits through his teeth. "You're no son of mine."

"Oh, thank God," Hopper whispers under his breath.

I turn, and Sally's got a gun to Hopper's head, but he's nearly bouncing with excitement. He turns to me, eyes sparking with joy. "I thought he'd had a stroke or something."

Sally's dumb grin stirs the anger in my belly. "Fuck off with you. A stroke? Ha." Nodding at me, he continues, "My father's always had this one by the balls—"

A wisp of air brushes my cheek as Sally falls to the floor, a stiletto knife embedded in his temple. I turn at the dull shaking thump behind me and see my uncle with a hole in his cheek, the back of his head splattered across my nonna's china cabinet, a gun in his lifeless hand. I kick it away out of habit, but he's well past gone.

Hopper holsters his gun and pulls the knife from my half-brother's skull, wiping the blood on Sally's shirt before turning to my father.

Pointing at him with the knife, he effuses, "Sir, you are brilliant. That thing with the cookie? Really fucking convincing. Ten out of ten would recommend you in the next Scorsese film." Gesturing to the dead men on the floor, he tsks. "But you're only as good as your underbosses, you know? And these guys? Ugh. They got the drop on us fair and square—mostly due to your *brilliant* performance—but then they didn't disarm us. That'll get you killed."

"Why would you send for Zio?" I ask, my voice finally coming back to me.

Tapping the blade to his teeth, Hopper doesn't wait for my father's response. "*Oh*. Did you send your best men to kidnap Mr. Wolfe? Is that why you've got family running back up? That's... why would you do that?"

My father's voice is steady, even as his eyes are locked on Sally's body. "I know Joseph. He thinks he's so different from us. Like he's this All-American hero. But I knew he'd defend Mr. Wolfe. Violently, even if he finds violence so disdainful."

"But why Zio?" I ask, unable to keep the plaintive cry from my voice.

My father's face reddens, anger pulsing just under the calm voice. "Because you needed to see. Our family puts loyalty above all else."

My lip snarls at the jab. "Where was my loyalty?"

His voice loses some of its refined edge. "You went to the city. I give you my name and you still leave us? No. That's not loyalty."

This motherfucker right here. I jab my finger at him, letting him have it. "You left me first. I got dumped at Nonna's, and then you forgot about me until I could be your errand boy on the docks. And I never once said anything to anyone."

"You coulda worked your way up!" he shouts, his face hardening into a sneer. "The docks were your *in*, and you acted like you were better than the rest of us. Going to college—for *what*?"

"Nonna made me promise! I was keeping my promise to *her*."

Hopper grins at my father as he gestures to me. "See! You were right about him wanting to be a hero. Not only did he graduate Magna Cum Laude, he killed all your men at the museum tonight. Even the one who was acting like a bodyguard." He turns to me, his eyes sincere. "I know you made your nonna proud. She boasted about you all the time in her bridge group. Also, I saw pictures of the one you gutted from stem to stern tonight. That was some beautiful work right there. No hesitation marks, just plunge and rip."

"Thanks, I think."

The vein on my father's head bulges and his arms shake as he tightens his hands into fists. Hopper returns his attention to the vibrating bit of rage that is Salvatore Portelli and lets out a happy sigh. "You know, I really thought I would have to kill some doddering old man. But the reveal? The possessed eyes? The guns at the back of the head? Chef's kiss, boss. A complete masterstroke."

My father finally loses it, launching himself across the table at Hopper, bellowing in rage and pain. "You motherfucker! You killed my only son!"

And as fast as he's moving, my brain slows everything down. My father's rage, his hurtful words, my hand still holding the gun. For a split-second, I'm hit with the irony of my uncle, now dead at my feet, teaching me how to handle a weapon.

"You've got to get comfortable with a gun, Joey. It's gotta be automatic, so's if you find yourself in a bad spot, you're not hesitating. Hesitation is what gets you killed, mark my words."

He was right, of course. I haven't picked up a gun since I started college, but muscle memory is a powerful thing. I didn't hesitate earlier this evening, and I don't hesitate now. I only know that I pulled the trigger because the cannon sound of the large caliber weapon shakes my soul, as does the way my father's body lands on the table. Broken and unmoving.

Hopper pulls his knife from my father's chest.

Surreally, Hopper is quiet, almost respectful. Like maybe he's giving me a moment of silence. I don't know what to make of that either. He turns to me, finally, and pats my shoulder, eyes glistening in the bright kitchen lights.

"Luca didn't want you to have to kill your father, but that you were willing to do it to save my life? He'll remember that. And I know you've got a body count going tonight, but if it'll make things better, this one's on my tally."

Weirdly enough, that does make it better. And I don't know if I pulled the trigger to save his life or end my suffering, but I'll take it either way.

"Thanks."

He pulls me into a powerful half-hug. "Us bastards hafta stick together, huh?"

I lift my shoulder, needing to get out of this house. Hopper sends off a quick text, then gestures to the front door.

Nudging Sally's body with his boot, Hopper tsks again. "It's too bad his *real* son was so dumb. Like, who knew that the kid he pawned off on his mother would be a true badass, huh?"

"Yeah, Hopper. That's a real head-scratcher."

26

JOE

EDGERTON'S GUYS from the lobby surround us and usher Hopper and me into Rand's private elevator. The one with the constipated look on his face hits a series of buttons, and the car ascends quickly. Much faster than is typical.

The doors open, and we're greeted by Edgerton and a very worried-looking Rand. I'm half-convinced that he's about to kick me out, but then he pulls me into a strong hug, burying his face in my neck. I barely choke back a sob of relief.

"You have no idea how scared I've been. I didn't know if I would see you again," he whispers into my ear.

"I'm here, my love. I ain't going nowhere."

He pulls back and kisses me, no fucks given about who sees what.

"Everything secure?" Edgerton asks the constipated one.

"Yes. Nothing going on downstairs. Not even a RICO crew or nothin'."

I glance at Hopper at the mention of a RICO crew. He seems disappointed, and I briefly wonder about this agent he's so gone over. A stone-faced Edgerton dismisses the crew then leads us into the living room.

As grateful as I am to have Rand in my arms, that doesn't mean I forgot what happened. "What the hell went wrong tonight?" I ask, not bothering to keep the anger out of my voice. "Where the fuck was your team?"

Edgerton holds up a finger to me as he brings the phone to his ear. Rand squeezes my hand, and it is only through sheer force of will that I don't attack Edgerton where he stands.

There's a lot of head-nodding, yesses, and nos, and his face is like granite. His eyes snap to mine for a brief second, then he refocuses on the conversation in his ear. "I understand," he says, ending the call.

Taking a beat, he taps his forehead before squaring up to me. "What can you tell me about tonight?" he asks with no emotion at all.

"They nearly took Rand, you motherfucker. Where. Was. Your. Team?"

Edgerton's granite expression finally cracks. "We were attacked on two fronts. My men by the loading dock were ambushed after giving James the *all-clear*. By the time you and Rand arrived, they were dead, their bodies tossed in the dumpster you passed."

Something about seeing the cold fury and pain under that fucking mask of his makes me feel better somehow. Like maybe this night took as much from him as it did from me.

"How many of your men?" I ask, uncertain about the last man I killed at the museum. "Any museum security?"

Edgerton's jaw tenses as he shakes his head. "Three. And no museum security."

Rand looks at me, eyes popping out of his head. "You killed the guys who killed his team?"

I run the backs of my fingers across his cheek. "They were dead the second they put their filthy hands on you."

He leans in for a soft kiss, and I nearly lose myself in it, even with anger warring in my chest. I turn back to Edgerton, needing more answers. "You said you were attacked on two fronts?"

He nods. "Our surveillance team came under attack, but I don't think they were expecting us to be prepared. We quickly neutralized them."

I notice, belatedly, the deep scratch on his neck. And I wonder how many people he killed personally.

Edgerton clears his throat. "What about your father?"

"Dead."

Rand swallows and tightens his grip on my arm. I don't know why, but that breaks through the numbness even more effectively than the anger. There's not a chance in hell I'll shed tears in front of Edgerton and this crazy bastard Hopper, but it's close.

I lean in for a fast, hard kiss, and he kisses me back, just as hard.

I push down the grief and need, turning to Edgerton. "The only warning I got was from Luca Fucking Stefano and this serial killer motherfucker right here." I turn to Hopper. "No offense."

He grins, rocking on his toes. "None taken."

Edgerton looks at his phone, shaking his head. "When did you speak to Luca tonight?"

"Right before my speech. He told me it's becoming increasingly obvious that Rand and I are an item, which meant leverage for my father. The Stefano and Portelli families have their own extradition agreement."

Edgerton nods. "I'm aware."

"My father asked Stefano to turn me in to him."

Edgerton's lips thin, and his eyes darken. "And Luca refused."

A statement, not a question.

I tilt my head, adding two and two and coming up with five. "How did you know that?"

He gestures the length of me. "You're still here. Tell me more about your father. What was his play?"

I fist my hands, squeezing so tight my knuckles crack. Raking my hand through my hair, I lock down my focus and let the scenarios spin. "Stefano refused to send me back to Brooklyn, so my father went after Rand to force my hand. Which was where he fucked up." Thinking back to Luca's threat, I continue, "If this mess puts Rand on Luca's radar, so help me God, he better not lay a hand on him. I don't want to have to fucking kill everybody."

Who am I kidding? I *did* fucking kill everybody.

Edgerton holds up his hand. "Luca will not lay a finger on Mr. Wolfe. Of that, you can be certain."

More bad math. "What the fuck, Edgerton? You're first-naming the head of one of the most powerful mob families in Manhattan like he's your bar buddy. Who the fuck are you?"

He shakes his head. "That's immaterial."

Oh, I doubt that. The elevator dings and I turn to see who or what this could be now. The doors open on a smiling Luca Stefano.

"Taking out the garbage, I see," he says, making his way to me.

Clenching my teeth, I stick out my hand. "Stefano."

He grabs it in a too-firm shake, a hint of annoyance crossing his handsome features. "I've already said it a couple of times, Joe. Call me Luca. You keep calling me by my last name, and I'm gonna take offense."

I shrug, the only gesture I can manage without giving away how much his being here in Rand's space makes my neck ache. "You make the rules, boss."

He cocks his head, smiling. "I'm not your boss, Joe. But maybe after lending you my pitbull for the night, we're something closer to friends, no?"

Fucking out of the frying pan straight into the fire. I set my jaw, dread filling my guts as a life not of my own making is laid out before me. I look to Rand, who's confused and worried, and I know I'll never drag him into this life.

Maybe a night like tonight burned out my remaining fucks, but I make no attempt at hiding my surprise. "Friends? If all your friends live in your pocket..."

Luca shakes his head, holding up his hands. "What just went through your head right now? Whatever it is, you haven't been listening very carefully. If you want in on the Stefano family, I'll take you in a heartbeat. But I don't force people, Joe. I already said that."

"Then, respectfully, why are you here?"

"I'm here to thank the guy who just made my life so much easier. "

"I suppose destroying everything my family stood for does ease the way for you in Brooklyn."

He shakes his head. "I don't give a shit about Brooklyn. Never did. Your father started a war that you ended. Me and Anthony, we lost some good men, to be sure, but it could have been so much worse."

"What does that mean, *we* lost some men? Who's Anthony?"

Edgerton opens his mouth, but Luca talks over him. "Did Anthony not explain things to you?"

"Who *the fuck* is Anthony?"

Should I be talking like this to Luca with a gun in my front pocket? No. But I'm about to put a fucking bullet in his head if he doesn't start making some goddamn sense.

"That's me," Edgerton says, raising his hand like I just called roll. "I have an agreement with Luca. He's a silent partner in my security operation."

I pinch the bridge of my nose. "You mean to tell me that the people in charge of keeping my man safe are mobbed-up?"

Luca laughs softly while Edgerton looks like I've called his mother a *whore*. "I am *not*. This is a legal enterprise that has to operate in reality. Luca lives in this building. It made sense to reach out."

"So when my father's team killed yours..."

Luca finishes the sentence. "He started a war with the Stefano family. Which you finished." He smiles broadly, despite the disrespect I've shown. "Why do you think I'm so happy?"

"Okay, but the first fucking thing I'm going to do is memorize who your people are, so I know if I'm fucking looking at an enemy or a friend, 'cause one of those guys I didn't recognize, and I still don't know if I fuckin' killed an innocent man or not."

The thought that I maybe killed someone innocent makes me want to throw up. But I couldn't chance it with Rand in the car.

"No, I saw the museum's security footage before I deleted it. He was a sleeper for a different family. Is there anyone else who could be used as leverage against you?"

I shake my head, secretly so fucking relieved and gutted I don't know what to do with myself. "I ain't got no one else."

Luca's expression reads like empathy, something I didn't know a mob boss could be capable of. "That's not true, Joe. Not after what you did tonight. Anthony's team is top-notch, but we had no indication that your father would break the treaty after thirty years. By cutting off the head of the viper, you've prevented further violence."

"Probably wishing you'd just handed me over."

Luca shakes his head. "A deal is a deal. Your father made a promise to my family, and he didn't abide by his own words."

Never make a promise to Luca you don't intend to keep. Got it.

Rand tightens his grip on the back of my neck and addresses the men in his home. "If you have what you need for now, I'll ask that you let us recover from tonight. We can regroup tomorrow when we've all had the rest we need."

Luca smiles and shakes Rand's hand. "That's about the nicest way to ask someone to get the hell out that I've ever heard." Rand seems slightly horrified, but Luca holds up his hand. "We need to give you two some space. You take care of Joe, okay? He's good people to have around."

Rand nods. "Yes, he is."

Luca shakes my hand with both of his, warmly smiling. Hopper gives me a short hug, which I appreciate both for its sentiment and brevity. Edgerton, who hasn't said much, gives me his customary nod and follows them to the elevator.

No sooner have the doors closed than I turn my face into Rand's chest and let out a long breath, my shoulders slumping. Rand gathers me in his arms and holds me for several moments.

I continue to suck in unsteady breaths, the buttery sound of the knife sliding through muscle and bone so fucking loud in my ears. The first splash of blood on the ground, the awful sound of a silenced weapon whispering through the night air.

Breathe, Joe. Just breathe.

Rand tightens our embrace, and I'm grateful to have his bare chest against mine. His scent is familiar and comforting. I inhale him by the lungful and my heart rate slows, bit by bit.

I think about Luca Stefano's advice to listen to Hopper's warning. It's the only reason I bothered to drag my besotted attention from Rand enough to focus on our surroundings. And it saved our lives.

But the price was high.

I feel so fucking dirty that I want to stand under a shower until my skin is scrubbed raw. A vision of Rand standing in the spray with me, washing me, cleansing me of my sins...

Rand holds steady, breathing in and out. Fuck, I need him tonight. I don't know if I can even ask it of him, but I—

Breaking through my overwhelming thoughts with words both elegant and coarse, Rand nuzzles against my ear and whispers,

"Watching you kill those men to defend me was the sexiest thing I've ever seen in my life. It's probably fucked up, but I've been hard as a rock since the museum." Gripping the back of my neck, he touches his forehead to mine, focusing me with his intense gaze. "Unless you have any objections, I'm going to clean their filth off you, and then I'm going to take you the fuck apart."

I let out a ragged breath, and a tear tracks down my cheek. Nodding, I lift my head for a kiss.

27

RAND

WHEN WE WERE WALKING from Tribeca and Soho tonight, I picked up on the fact that Joe was in a spin. He's better now, but I know he hates the bloodshed as much as I know he did not and will never hesitate to save my life.

It's one thing to know and another entirely to witness it first-hand. When he handed me off to security, I thought I'd never see him again. I knew he was going after his father, not because of what was done to him, but because of what was done to me.

The relief on his face when I kiss him tells me he's worried he broke us, but nothing could be further from the truth. I've had plenty of protection in the form of security guards, but I've never had someone protect me because they love me. Ever.

I don't know what will happen with the Portelli crime family now that the leadership structure is dead, but that's a problem for another night. Right now, I need to show Joe that I've got his back. That I know he did what he had to do.

If I thought letting him rail me would do the trick, I'd totally be up for it, but that's not what he needs. I'm more of a soft top when the occasion calls for it, and I just hope that I'm enough for him.

Placing my hand on his lower back, I maneuver him through the living room, then into my bedroom and the ensuite. Wordlessly, I strip him bare, rough with the execution so he knows who's in charge.

Turning on the water, I set it to the perfect temperature before grabbing Joe's hand and walking us into the large shower stall. The first time we did this, I used carefully angled spray jets to get him there, but this time he needs me.

Blood-stained water circles the drain as I rinse him down with the handheld sprayer, then use charcoal soap and a loofah to scrub him raw, ridding his body of any remaining evidence of tonight's violence. I use a softer pouf and a moisturizing wash to clean him again, more gently this time.

He stands under the many showerheads, head bowed and cock soft as I wash and manipulate his body. Once we're both clean, I lead him by the hand out of the shower and dry him carefully with luxurious towels, making sure to run the soft material over every crease and crevice.

I kneel before him and take him into my mouth, with comfort as my only purpose. His hands grip my head as I gently suck and tongue him until he begins to plump. His demeanor remains subdued, but his cock is long and hard when I pull off.

Leading him to the bed with a firm grip, I pull back the duvet. "Lie face up, head on the pillows."

He does as I ask, but his eyes don't meet mine.

"Look at me, Joe. Eyes on me."

His brows stitch together and his chin wobbles, but eventually, he does as he's told. The broken look he gives me just about takes my knees out from under me. Hovering, I place a series of soft kisses on his brows, nose, lips.

"Don't think. Let your mind go. Let me take care of you."

He takes a deep breath and blinks away a few tears. Seeing how profoundly this affects him, I understand more clearly how important I am to him. Lowering my body to his, I kiss him as we connect from head to toe, our hard cocks sliding next to each other.

I trail open-mouth kisses down his neck and across his collarbones, stopping to suck gently on each nipple. He moans, and I grin against the heated skin before moving down to kiss and suck at his belly.

Rolling his sensitive nipples between two fingers, I dive my tongue into his belly button, soft-fucking it until his hips arch off the bed.

I kiss the crease between his hip and thigh, bypassing his dick despite his many protests. Angling his thighs up and back, I spit on his hole, then drag my tongue past his balls and up his length before swirling it around his cockhead.

I do this again and again, stopping at various points along the way to nip and suck at the sensitive skin. I'm careful not to repeat the pattern, keeping him on his toes.

The gentle scrape of my teeth along his skin makes his cock jump. I squeeze his head, licking up the clear pearl of precum. Threading our fingers together, I hold his hand as I pull moan after moan from him, knowing exactly what he needs, what grounds him.

His muscles tense and relax under my teasing pressure, and I continue until he begins to whimper.

"Please," he chokes out, tears building once again. "Please let me come."

He's overstimulated and desperate for more, too far into what we're doing to think about tonight. I flick his nipple, then stop to slick myself up. Flattening my palm against his undercarriage, I smear the leftover lube across his hole.

"Please," he begs in a voice I don't recognize.

"Shh, baby. I've got you. You want to come now?"

"Mm-hmm."

"Want it to hurt a little?"

He swallows thickly and nods.

I shift, hovering over him once again, kissing him feverishly, slipping my tongue into his mouth so he can taste himself.

Palming my cock, I position it, then push hard as the reluctant muscles allow entry. He moans into my mouth as I enjoy the breach and retreat from the taut ring.

He practically sobs as he pleads again, and I smile against his lips. Without warning, I shove my full length inside him, angling up. His voice pitches up and falls low, pain and pleasure as I stroke him mercilessly.

"There you go, baby. Take it." I grunt, fucking into him, consuming him, the strain visible in his jaw and the arch of his back.

I fucking love it, and so does he.

Pushing both legs back until his knees are around his ears, I set a punishing pace, ignoring his pained cries while leaning into his pleasured moans.

I make a point of looking down at his deflating cock, nailing him with an arched brow and a smirk. Grumbling, he squeezes his inner muscles, causing my hips to stutter.

"*Fuck*. You are so fucking *tight*."

He grins as though he's gotten something over me, and I nearly collapse with relief. *There he is.*

I let one of his legs go to reach between us, caressing the ridge of his cockhead with the tips of my fingers. At the same time, I pull all the way out, then ram back into him: caress-thrust, caress-thrust.

After a few rounds of that, he's rock hard and begging me to go harder. I kiss him through his grunts and high-pitched begging, then spit on his cock, taking him in a too-tight grip, rough-stroking over the already sensitive skin.

"*Coming*," he grits out.

I keep my strokes steady, and he comes on a grimace. I angle my hips to thrust up again, sending another spurt of cum through his cock.

When he's finally finished, I grab his shoulders and pull down, thrusting hard through my own intense orgasm, reveling in the tight grip of his body. A few more tears spill down his flushed cheeks as I fill him.

"Thank you, baby," he whispers. "I love you so much. I couldn't bear it if you'd been hurt."

I kiss away his tears. "Let it out, Joe. I'm here. I love you so much."

Rough sex is exchanged for gentle touch, and I pull him into a hug. As he settles down, I part his cheeks and apply gentle pressure to his puffy, abused hole, swirling the puckered skin with my cum while my other hand calms him with gentle circles on his back.

He sniffles as he buries his head in my chest. I stroke his hair and make low, soothing sounds.

"You were so brave tonight, Joe. You saved my life."

He stays silent, letting out a big shuddering breath. I let my hand drift down to spread his cheeks, giving my fingers more room to administer to his hole. "I couldn't tell if I wanted to worship you or fuck you. So I figured that while the adrenaline was high tonight, I'd take this pretty little hole. But tomorrow I'll need you to use me. If that would please you."

He tightens his grip on me and nods against my chest. "I would like that very much." He hesitates, but I don't push, letting him find the words. "I...I don't want to have to do that again. Kill people. I don't—"

I place my fingertips on his lips. "Shh, shh, shh. I don't want you to ever have to do that again either, okay?"

He nods, relief in the slackening of his muscles.

Gently pushing my cum back into his hole, I ask, "Do you want me to clean you up? Or do you want to sleep with my cum inside you?"

I know the answer, but I want him to feel like he has a choice.

Sounding a little floaty, he answers, "Plug me."

I reach into the bedside table and pull out a slim plug, generously slicking it up before carefully inserting it. He winces then relaxes into the sensation of being stuffed.

"Mm, you still have all this delicious cum on your chest. Can't let it go to waste. May I take care of you?"

He nods, leaking a few more tears as I shift him onto his back. I lick the cum spatter pattern across his belly and chest, finishing my clean-up with a few sucks of his soft cock, running my tongue under his foreskin the way he likes it.

The air conditioning clicks on, and he shivers. I cover him with my body and then a blanket, and we fall asleep like that, sated and supported.

28

JOE

"JOE. JOE, BABY. WAKE UP."

I'm drenched in sweat, the smell of blood and gunpowder so far up my nose I can taste it. This area by the loading docks is a terrible place for a pickup. Who set this up? Thank God Rand's in the car. He looks terrified, and there's blood running down his face, but I'm so proud of him. He fought like a beast.

"Joe? Honey, you're having a bad dream."

A warm hand lands on my chest, and I blink awake. Rand is hovering over me, his eyes worried. Relief floods my body, and I grab him, holding him tight.

"Hey there," he says, his voice soft but comforting. "You're all right. You're right here. We're home. We're safe."

I shiver and let him go. "Sorry. Did I...did I hurt you?"

He snuggles into my embrace. "No, baby. You didn't hurt me at all. You were shouting in your sleep." Placing his palm on my chest, his brows stitch together. "Your heart is racing still. Take a few breaths with me."

He takes a deep breath, and I follow suit. Same on the exhale. We do this a few more times, and I feel my heartbeat slow.

"Good job, baby. Let me tend to you, okay?"

I nod, and he goes to the bathroom, coming back with a steaming washcloth. He carefully slips the plug out of my ass, gently cleaning me before running a salve over the irritated tissues. He then follows me to the bathroom and holds my cock as I piss, kissing my shoulders as he does.

Cleaning my cock thoroughly, he warms me with his mouth as I brush my teeth. I have to warn him a few times when he tries to sneak in a little bit of sucking, but otherwise, he's perfect.

This isn't something we do every day—I don't think either of us would enjoy that. But this special care with a tiny bite of submission for him feels like a treat after the day we had yesterday.

Grayson knocks on the door and leaves me with a package I've been waiting for. Rand walks over and sticks his face in my neck, hugging me tightly. "What's that?"

"A present for you."

"For me?"

I assume shopping for a billionaire is a nearly impossible task and that his days of receiving gifts, at least meaningful ones, have long since passed.

I nod. "Hands and knees."

His eyes widen, but he does as I ask. I needed him to be in charge last night, but the arrival of his gift is perfectly timed. It allows me to hold the reins once more while we're in this little bubble outside of time.

I open the box, and he angles to see what I've purchased. His face turns a pretty red as his head hangs between his shoulders.

"I can't believe you bought that."

I grin, removing what looks like an old sci-fi movie space gun from the packaging. "I was going to be jealous of anyone else doing this for you." Plugging the contraption into the wall, I grin at him. "Spread your cheeks."

Lowering his forehead to the bed, he complies. The at-home

laser removal tool comes with instructions that I already read online and memorized, and I'm anxious to get started.

I set it to medium strength and touch the gun to a bit of hair regrowth around his sensitive hole.

"Ooh, that smarts," he says, squirming.

I lean in and kiss the tender skin. "Do you need a lower setting?"

He makes a low, disgruntled sound and resets his grip on his ass. I lower the settings, not really wanting him to be in pain, and take aim at the next tiny section down.

"Oh! Ooh," he says, his voice pitching up as his cock hardens.

"You're doing so good, baby. Keep it up." I rub his ass, wishing I could see more of his embarrassment. "Actually, turn face up. Knees to your shoulders."

He shoots a glare in my direction but doesn't hesitate to shift to his back, reaching forward to spread his cheeks wide for me.

"A little wider, baby."

He's awkward as his abdominal muscles tense to keep his legs in place while he does as I ask. I thrill at the uncertainty in his eyes, knowing he needs this morning as much as I needed last night.

I press and hold the laser on the next section down, and my cock leaks at the sound of his little whimper. He shivers, struggling to maintain his hold, his belly muscles twitching under the strain.

There's not much to laser, and I quickly work through the rest of the sections, not giving him a single second of peace until I've completed my mission.

"I want your hole smooth and shiny, but it'll take several sessions to achieve that. You willing to commit to that?"

Still in the uncomfortable position, his knees around his ears, his body shaking as he holds his cheeks open for my examination, he nods without hesitation.

I kneel forward and lick the irritated pink skin. He grunts, but his cock twitches.

"Too sensitive?"

He shakes his head, and I attack him with gusto, licking, nipping at him as the muscles loosen. Spearing him with the tip of my tongue, I fuck his hole as deep as I can until I feel him begin to clench around me.

"Joe, yes. Joe. Oh my God. Joe, please." His panting cries, the way his voice squeals up on my name...fuck, that just does it for me.

His position prevents him from stroking himself, so I press harder, going just a little further as he shakes apart, losing his hold on his legs and his cheeks, thrusting up as he comes on a whimper, with simply my tongue in his hole.

I sit back, and he spreads out like a warm glaze, twitching and moaning from aftershocks. I snuggle up against him, letting my fingers drift across his over-sensitized skin, stopping to drag a nail across a peaked nipple. He cries out, punching his hips up, completely out of his mind.

I run my fingers through his cum and feed it to him before licking the remnants off his skin.

"I haven't come yet. What will you give me? Your mouth, your ass, or your hands?" I ask, knowing he'd rather float for a few more minutes.

Rand flops over, grabbing a pillow and shoving it under his hips. "Use my ass, please."

I think about our first encounter and wonder if he could have ever imagined something like this between us.

"I just zapped the hell out of your hole. Are you sure you can handle it?"

He tilts his head to the side, his grin visible from behind. "I can take anything you want to give to me."

I slick myself up and push in carefully, my nipples hardening at the sound of his groan. "God, you're such a slut. I could bring anyone in here and your slutty little ass would take every single one of them and beg for more. You could have cum dripping from your nose, and you still wouldn't be satisfied."

He shakes his head into the mattress. "Just your cock. Just your cum."

I roll my hips, loving his grip on my body. "Mm, that's right, baby."

He lies there, taking it, turning me on with the way he lets me use his body.

"So compliant and willing," I murmur, picking up the pace.

I scooch a little farther up and straddle him, going deeper, taking my pleasure as he zones out. Finally, the way his face never loses its blush and the total submission to my cock have their way with me. I pull out, spilling across his reddened skin.

He whimpers as I lick the cum off him, then flip him over, feeding it to him. Back among the living, he blinks sleepily, avoiding my eyes as he licks his lips.

"You shy around me, baby?"

He nods as his blush spreads down his neck.

"Why?" I ask, damn well knowing the answer.

He hesitates, and I flick his nipple. "Tell me."

"I just...I just worry that you'll think I'm not really man enough for you in daylight hours."

I raise my brow at him. "You see how much reassurance I need after we play. Do you think I worry whether or not you think I'm man enough?"

He scrunches his nose. "No. But you're more dominant, and I don't want it as much. Like with the topping—I'll only ever do it when you need it."

I shrug. "Baby, that's the same thing I'm doing. I'm just giving you what you need. Unless you think I'm going too far."

He shakes his head, embarrassment still lighting his delicate skin.

"So, then...maybe you're exactly the kind of man I need, and I'm exactly the kind of man you need. And who cares about the percentages? If we're both happy with it, who the fuck cares? Is there a man-enough task force gonna come into our bedroom with a clipboard and a calculator?"

He laughs, shaking his head. "I suppose not."

"This was my whole point at that meeting. The weakness is in the rigid rules. We don't have to be fifty-fifty on anything, and as long as we've both got one hundred percent consent, we're golden. We are who we are, and who we are fits pretty damn good if you're asking me."

Rand slots his face against my neck, a now-familiar move that lets me know he needs comfort and praise, not embarrassment. He runs his fingers through my chest hair.

"So, what you're telling me—since we don't need to be fifty-fifty on anything—is that you can unclench when it comes to matters of finance, right? That when I say use your salary to invest and let me worry about the rest that I know what I'm talking about?"

"Rand, that's different. We haven't even known each other that long."

"Mm-hmm. But *tu mi ami*," he says, his Italian adorably stilted. "And if six months down the line we decide we're not compatible after I've spoiled you rotten and taken you on expensive trips and bought you expensive things, I'll still have made more on the dividends of my investments than I could possibly spend on you in six months. The money I make by not doing anything is more than I could spoil you with in a lifetime. So stop worrying about what it looks like to have me pay for things and let me handle it. It's one of the things I like about being filthy rich—I can take care of the people I love."

Fuck. He's got a point. It irks me to my bones, but even with my huge raise, I'm still not in the same universe as his portfolio.

"Fine," I huff. "But you have to help me figure out how to invest."

He sucks on my earlobe. "We'll invite Ford over for some of your pasta, and he'll explain it to you."

Shaking my head, I cup his face and bring him in for a kiss. "I fucking love you."

His soft smile is all I need.

Just as we're beginning to move around, clean up, and get dressed, there's another soft knock at the door.

"My apologies, sirs, a Mr. Hopper is here to see you."

Rand looks at me, silently asking if I know the purpose of his visit. I shake my head. Kissing him softly, I whisper, "Thank you for last night and this morning. It was perfect. Now, let's see what this nut job has to say."

29

RAND

JOE PLACES his hand on my back, warm and supportive as we make our way through the penthouse and into the foyer. Hopper stands in my entryway looking like a man who means to do harm.

According to Joe, I'm supposed to take solace in the fact that he means no harm to either of *us*, but it's a struggle. And when Hopper's inscrutable eyes land on Joe's hand still resting on my lower back, I brace, no clue what might come out of his mouth. He looks at us for half a beat, tilting his head to the side, then shrugs, holding up a white bag.

"I brought donuts."

I stifle a laugh, and Joe covers his smile with his hand.

"Hey, Hopper," Joe says, his eyes bright with laughter. "Would you like that with some coffee? Perhaps a cappuccino?"

The neutral look on his face breaks, and he smiles. I can't tell if I'm disturbed or enchanted. Most people look a little goofy when they smile, but not Hopper. He looks even more handsome and a lot more deadly.

Joe growls a little in my ear and turns me toward the kitchen, and I surreptitiously elbow him in the side. "Jealous?" I whisper out of the side of my mouth.

"No."

I love his disgruntled face.

We make it into the kitchen, and I set up espresso shots while Grayson puts the donuts on a platter, which he sets out on the bar. We each grab a barstool, but before we can choose our first donut of the morning, Hopper pushes the platter toward Grayson. "Dealer's choice."

Grayson looks pleased, if a little wary. "Why, thank you, Mr. Hopper."

"It's just Hopper. No Mr."

"Then, thank you, Hopper," Grayson says, selecting an apple fritter.

That squared, Hopper tugs the platter back in front of the three of us, and we go to town on the delicious pastries. I'm about to make fun of the fact that one of his choices is a cronut, but then I taste it and decide to keep my mouth shut.

As we're winding down our carb and caffeine fueled breakfast, Joe knocks on the bar surface and asks, "All right, we've eaten. What's going on?"

Hopper smiles again, but this is not the happy smile from the foyer. It is a much more calculated thing, and it sends a shiver down my spine.

"Luca's busy today but wanted me to let you know that the bodies from the museum have all been taken care of, real discreetlike. Nary a cop in sight, and we aim to keep it that way."

"Any loose ends from my father's side of things?" Joe asks, his lips in a thin line.

"A few. But I spent most of my morning tying them up, and I'll be done by this afternoon."

"No police involvement?"

Hopper tilts his hand side to side. "Eh. The right kind of police involvement if you catch my drift."

Joe nods, then knits his brows together. "I catch your drift. That all the updates you got for me?"

Hopper nods. "Yep."

"Excellent. Then I'm gonna ask you—politely—to take a hike."

Hopper laughs. "Of course. Would be rude of me to get in the way of all the fucking."

I go bright red, but Joe is laughing with Hopper, so...yay? I guess they won't find me chopped up into bits and thrown into the Hudson. I let out a breath, which causes him to chuckle as he makes his way back to the elevator. Throwing us a backward wave, he disappears into the elevator car, and I realize Grayson wouldn't have let him up without checking with me first.

Which means the man I'm assuming makes Ted Bundy look like a kitten has easy access to my space.

Joe cups my jaw. "Don't worry, doll. I'll ask Luca to rescind Hopper's access. Nobody wants that scary-ass dude having free rein over things."

"Thank you."

Kissing me softly, he lightly drags his nails down my neck and across my collarbones. "Now, regarding the other part—"

"The part about the fucking?" I pop my brows, grinning.

"Yeah, that. I doubt either of us is recovered enough for more ass play, but I thought maybe we could get a little sun on the patio, slip into your heated pool and make out like teenagers. Might be fun."

"Hmm. Might be," I say, running my fingers across his bulging crotch.

We grin, and I give Grayson the rest of the day off. Not bothering with swim trunks, we make our way out to the heavily treed balcony and strip. We don't have higher buildings in the direct vicinity, and it's as private as you can get on a New York rooftop.

I slip into the warm water, and he follows, pulling me to him in a passionate kiss. I float up and wrap my legs around him, returning his affection, leaning back to take the hickeys he wants to give me, knowing he'll limit it to areas Armani covers.

After a moment, he holds up a finger and swims to the storage trunk at the side of the pool, pulling out a quilted float. Gently, he tugs it under my body, and I luxuriate in the freedom of floating while stark naked.

Joe runs his hands over my sensitive skin, leaning over to suck me into his mouth. He teases me a little, then drags me over to the water feature, a continuous arc of water splashing down into the pool. My nipples bead up when he pulls me into its path.

The water pressure is smooth and broad. I hiss as the stream makes contact with my balls, then arch into it as he floats me back and forth, letting the forceful water spill up the length of me and back down again.

Grabbing my cock, he stills the movement, aiming the head right where the water arcs down to the pool's surface, holding it steady as it pounds away at me. After a few minutes, I realize that while it feels spine-archingly good, it's not the kind of pressure to make me come.

And I have a feeling he knows that.

"You're giving me blue balls," I whine. "Please, Joe. I need a hand, a mouth, something."

He grunts. "Mmph. You're right. Wanna lie out on one of these obscenely large loungers and see where it gets us?"

I roll over into the water and start swimming. "Race ya!"

"No fair!" he shouts good-naturedly.

He quickly overtakes me, grabbing me from behind, then slinging me over his shoulder like Tarzan. He sucks what promises to be a huge hickey on my hip, then carefully sets me down on one of the covered loungers. I shiver in the shade and reach out with shaky fingers to crank it back just a bit.

Crawling in next to me, Joe angles his body over mine. Taking our dicks in hand, he drips spit onto us and begins to stroke.

"Relax, baby," he says, his rough voice like velvet on the skin.

I lie back and let the sensations take over, the pressure of his grip, the heat of his hand, the way his quiet grunts sound like satisfaction. That goes on for a little while, then he pulls back, stroking his cock, stretching his foreskin out, lewd and grinning.

Silently, he grabs for my cock and spits on it, then slips his foreskin over the sensitive head.

"Oh. Jesus. Christ. I've always—"

I lose the ability to talk, turning into a panting, blubbering mess in an instant.

His voice is deep and gritty as he whispers into my ear. "That feel good for you, baby?"

I can only nod and breathe because my skin, my spine, my balls are electrified. I moan as the pleasure peaks and intensifies, then—*fuck, fuck, fuck*—I come my goddamn brains out. I nearly sob from the release, then almost shoot all over again when Joe tightens his grip on us, trapping the cum beneath his skin.

Grabbing my arm with his free hand, he bucks up, his hot cum flooding the trapped space. I'll be sporting a ring of bruises around my upper arm, and the thought makes my dick twitch.

Careful to not let up on his tight grip, he pulls away from me, managing to capture most of our shared cum under his bulging foreskin. I lick my lips and angle under him, opening my mouth wide and sticking out my tongue.

He lets out a satisfied growl and pushes past my lips. He releases his grip, and the gush of cum fills my mouth. I continue swallowing until he's fed me every last drop.

His eyes rove over my body, sparking with lust. "You're still so hard," he says, running his teeth over his bottom lip.

I nod since words aren't happening just yet. Without warning, he dips down and takes my cock into his mouth. I pull forward, whining. "Too sensitive. Too much."

He pulls back, smirking. "Yeah? It's a little too intense for you?"

I nod, and he grips my hips, sucking me down again. I make a honking sound like a goddamn goose, flapping my arms. He pulls back again with a wet slurp and an imperiously arched brow.

"Do you really want me to stop?"

Shivering, I shake my head, and he goes after me again. I whine and punch the cushions. I try to pull my hips away, only to have him chase the movement, increasing the suction as he rolls my balls in his hand.

Fuck, I feel like he's going to burn out the nerve endings with too much pleasure, and I can't tell if I like it or hate it. Crawling between my legs, he pushes my legs up and back, exposing me because he knows it embarrasses me.

He grins and dives below, licking my sensitive, overused hole. I shout out, then moan again when he traps my head in a tight grip, killing me with teasing strokes as he swirls fingers around my hole. My oversensitive skin is begging for mercy, but my cock wants more pressure, and I'm ninety percent certain I'm about to short circuit.

Squirming, I try to push against his fingers, and he obliges, pressing a finger past the overworked furl of skin.

Pleasure-pain-pain-pleasure-pain-pleasure.

He spits on my cock again and takes it in hand, stroking me with unbelievable pressure. I'm practically sobbing from the too-much of it all, and then I orgasm dry, a shivering drop in my slit the only indication.

"Good boy," he says, dipping down to tongue the slight ejaculate.

I shiver and roll away from him. "Please, no more."

"Okay, baby. You did so good today," he says, his voice soothing my overworked nerves as he hands me a bottle of water.

Still facing away from him, I prop myself up and drink it quickly, relaxing into the chilly sensation making its way down my throat. I take another sip and set the bottle off to the side, curling back into a fetal position.

"Do you want space, or do you want me to hold you?" he asks gently. "I promise not to touch your pretty cock."

Looking over my shoulder, I snarl at him, my emotions all over the place. His smile is warm, and I roll back into his embrace, smashing the side of my face against his pecs.

"Shut up."

"Okay."

"Just hold me tight. Don't stroke my skin. Or anything else," I grumble.

He kisses the top of my head and winds his leg over mine, cocooning me from the rest of the world. He takes a few deep breaths, and I follow his rhythm, slipping into drowsiness and deep relaxation.

How does he know what I need when I need it?

I don't know how long we're in this perfect position, but it's not long enough.

Grayson, looking horrified, bursts onto the balcony, bearing two robes. "Put these on! Get back inside. There are pictures of you two."

My stomach clenches. "What pictures?"

Grayson remains tight-lipped as Joe grabs the robes, helping me into mine before sliding into his. "Grayson, what pictures? Where are they posted?" Joe demands, putting his arm around me.

Grayson—ever unflappable—swallows, looking nervous. My head starts to throb as he answers. "They were taken within the last hour from a camera-mounted drone, and they're everywhere. Page Six, all social media platforms, a byline in the Times."

I lean over, my stomach clenching. Joe puts his hand on my back, and I blindly let him lead me inside. Once the curtains are drawn, Joe pulls up his phone. His phone's notifications start to go off, and I wonder where the hell I left my own phone. He taps a message, and his fingers tighten, all but crushing the phone in his grip.

I think of everything we did in the last hour, and a chill runs straight through me. The life he and I are starting to build together after years of feeling so fucking alone...my throat closes when I think about losing the one thing in my life I never knew I needed.

"Edgerton's on his way up," Joe says, flat rage at the edge of his voice.

I look up at Joe, pressure rising behind my eyes. "I can't—*no*. I can't face him. I can't—I *can't*."

He curves an arm around me. "Shh, shh, shh. It's okay. I've got it from here," he says, leading me back to our bedroom. Looking over his shoulder at Grayson, he says in a low voice, "I'll take care of him. Have Edgerton hold off. He's already chasing this down. Tell him to keep at it."

"Yes, sir." Grayson's quiet demeanor—usually adorned with the tiniest edge of smartass—is uncharacteristically grave.

We make it through the bedroom door, and the second Joe closes it, I collapse into him. Words are a jumble in my brain, and all I can do is picture losing everything—the company that I care about more than I thought I ever would, the friendships I'm beginning to build, Joe—*everything*. Only this time, it's because of who I am. Because people will have seen the real me.

"Baby. *Rand*," he says, command in his tone. I look at him through teary eyes, and he places his hands on my shoulders. "I promise you. The pictures out there right now aren't that bad."

"But we...and then we..." I choke out, still unable to speak.

He smooths a hand down my back. "Look," he says, pulling up his phone. "It's just me holding you. They caught us after."

I grab the phone from his hand and zoom in. It's a beautiful picture of us. I look so safe in his arms, and he looks like a guardian, a warrior protecting his love.

And I immediately feel terrible for even thinking that. This isn't what Joe signed up for, and beyond that, this is all my fault. One hundred percent completely and totally my fault. The only pictures they have are the ones of us on the lounger. Had I simply kept the shade up, they wouldn't have anything. Maybe our tangled legs, but nothing identifiable.

Worse, with this, it's clear I am not the one in charge. That Joe is soothing and comforting me. I try not to think about my father's sneering disapproval, but somehow, that's all I see.

"Hey," he says, cupping my hot face in the chilly room. "Rand, look at me."

My eyes flick to his even though my insides are burning up.

"I didn't have anything to do with this. Nothing about today was about how we play. I promise."

The sincerity in his eyes is unassailable. "I know," I answer with a shaky breath. "I *know*. I just...my father will be furious. And he's going to be so fucking ugly about it." I flap my hands, struggling to take a breath. "And then everyone will see that I'm not an alpha. That I've been hiding behind a façade this whole time. They'll see me, Joe. And they'll know *everything*."

Joe's face softens. "Will they really? Will they really know everything?"

My face burns with shame. "I know...I know that none of it is wrong. Like, in my head, I know I'm not less of a man. But the feeling part of me hasn't caught up. I just...I'm so..."

A sob wrenches its way out of my chest. Fuck, I wanted to be so much better for Joe. For us. I shouldn't care if people see me vulnerable. I shouldn't care if they guess that the powerful CEO who spent years spewing nonsense about alpha this, alpha that is a big ol' bottom most of the time.

His large hand clamps down on the back of my neck, and I lift my eyes, sniffing hard as I try not to cry. His eyes are as serious as I've ever seen them.

"Down on your knees."

"Wh-what?" I ask, running the back of my hand across my nose.

Joe raises a single brow and points to the ground, his eyes dark. My brain blinks a few times, but his expression doesn't change. What we do is less about scenes and more about intertwining kink with a few aspects of our relationship, so this is not quite...*oh.*

Shit. *Stop thinking, Wolfe.*

Just do it.

I swipe at my nose again, sniffling as I go to my knees. Wordlessly, he opens his robe and lifts his chin at me. My mouth falls open, and he pushes the head of his cock between my lips.

My body tenses, my mind protests, and I can hear my heart pounding in my ears.

"Suck. Gently."

My brain's been put in a blender, but I obey.

"*Gently.* Like you're sucking your thumb," he commands, his voice low and dark.

Hornets are buzzing about in my chest, but I comply, giving him the lightest suction possible.

"Good boy. Continue."

His praise is a break in the madness. A fracture in the wall of reaction and emotion. A cool trickle for my bone-dry throat.

His cock stays soft as he strokes my hair, murmuring sweet praises. Relief cascades down my neck and shoulders. My lungs start to regulate, my stomach settles, and my brain goes from a dull roar to a whisper to silence.

I look up at him, my lashes wet.

He winks, and it's like the sun parting dark skies. "Hey, baby. You okay?"

I nod and wrap my arms around him, hugging his legs as I take a few more delicate sucks. There's that tiny prick of embarrassment that is so weirdly effective, but it feels too good to be a dick about it to myself. It's as if the storm brewing inside me has moved off the coast and into another territory.

Releasing his legs, I grasp his cock and pull back to kiss the head. Letting out a steady stream of air, I look up at him with a sheepish grin. He smiles back, even as worry crinkles at the edges of his eyes.

"Better?"

I nod and start to get up. He takes my hand and helps steady me on my feet. We hug for a few seconds, and I let out another long even breath, resting my forehead on his shoulder. "What do we do, Joe?" I know even before I ask that he'll have an answer.

"I've got it covered. But I want to check-in. What's your biggest fear right now?"

My mouth hooks up into a slight grimace. "That you'll decide it isn't worth it. That I'm not worth any of this. That I'm too...*needy*. And that *everyone* will know that I'm needy and not worth it."

He grabs both of my hands and leans in for a kiss. "And how do you feel now?"

"Grateful that you knew what to do to calm me down. Even if it is silly that you had to."

He shakes his head. "Not silly. Do you know how good it makes me feel, how ridiculously big my head gets when I see how my cock can calm and soothe you? Like my big, swinging dick can make your eyes roll to the back of your head *and* stop your tears. I got your fucking SuperCock right here," he jokes, leaning into his Brooklyn accent as he points lewdly at his crotch with both hands.

I snort-chuckle. "It's a Swiss Army cock."

He throws his head back, his hand to his belly as he laughs. "Damn right."

He gathers me in his arms, kissing me deeply. When he pulls back, his expression is serious. "Please know that was just a shortcut because a lot of things are about to happen all at once, and I can't take care of things if I'm worried about you. I'm not trying to collar you or be your Dom twenty-four seven."

I roll my eyes, smacking his arm. "*I know that.* You were just getting me back to good really fast." I dart a look at his phone, still in his hand. "There's more though. Isn't there?"

He holds up a text from Edgerton. "That was a still from a video. They have everything, and they're threatening to show it if we don't pay up."

Before I can go back into full meltdown, he raises his hand. "But that won't happen."

"How can you...?"

"Do you trust me?"

I nod. "Implicitly."

"Then I need you to trust that I will do whatever it takes to protect you."

My stomach clenches, but I breathe through it. "I do."

I'm calmer as he walks out of the room, even if I can't quite settle the feeling of dread in the pit of my stomach.

30

JOE

I TAKE the elevator five floors down and knock on one of the four available doors.

Even more surprising than Luca's location is that he opens the door himself, wearing lounge pants and an open silk robe.

"What? No butler?"

He laughs and lets me in. Where Rand's place is all open space and comfortable, light furnishings, Luca prefers a darker, more elegant style, complemented by the same kind of floor-to-ceiling windows and a smaller, equally lush balcony that brightens and enriches the space.

"You really are old-school, aren't you?"

Luca shrugs, inviting me into his living room. A younger man, mid-twenties or so, joins us. Luca cups his face and brings him in for a kiss.

"Thank you for a lovely morning. You can see your way out?"

He nods and kisses Luca's cheek before shyly leaving the condo.

I keep my face neutral and my tongue silent. I have no judgment for where a man finds his pleasure.

Luca must see something in my expression because he gestures at me. "Go ahead, say it."

I think to check myself because he *is* a mob boss. That is true. But never once have our interactions felt like that. And it occurs to me that despite being surrounded by people willing to say *yes* to him—not counting Hopper, I assume—he might be lonely. He might actually want friends.

So I decide to be a friend.

"I would normally say it's a bad idea to get high on your own supply, but if he's one of your boys, well done."

Luca laughs. "Hooking up is hard when you're me. Using professionals keeps it cleaner."

"Oh, poor rich mobster. I'm sure it's very hard for you," I say, risking life and limb to make this guy feel like he's got someone he can talk to.

His chuckle is genuine, and I decide it's not a precursor to a chalk outline.

"I like you, Joe. You never fail to bust my balls. No one ever does that anymore, and I kind of miss it."

"Well, it's good if you've got a crew that respects you."

"Which is why I was glad you didn't ask to be on my crew, if I'm honest. I'd have to take you because you'd be excellent at most things, but I'd rather us be friends."

I dip my chin. "I could use a friend."

"Excellent. To what do I owe the pleasure?"

"Check out Page Six."

He pulls his phone from the pocket of his robe, his fingers deftly flying across the screen. He lets out a low whistle.

"*A Wolfe in Sheep's Clothing*? What kind of headline is that?"

"They sent a blackmail request to Edgerton. They've got a video. And I know he's going to go through legal channels, and I'm happy to let him do that. But I get a sense he's not comfortable with the mob way of doing things."

"He isn't. We grew up in the same neighborhood, he and I. Did we ever tell you that?"

I shake my head. "No."

"Yeah. We both wanted to do better than our fathers. He follows the law judiciously. He's a good man, but he lets it hamper his business. I don't have such considerations."

"Not a big fan of the law?"

"I appreciate a well-ordered society, but that's not what this is. They got laws out there that help rich people and fuck over everyone else. I don't have nothing to do with those laws."

"So if I asked you, as a friend, to make sure that the folks trying to blackmail my man get the message that it's not appreciated, would that be crossing a line?"

Lucas shakes his head. "Not at all. I like taking care of my friends. I might have a favor to ask of you though."

A part of me wants to restate my limitations, but Luca doesn't strike me as a man who forgets things. "Of course."

"I don't have a lot of friends, and as you so eloquently put it, CEOs and mobsters have a lot in common. I'm thinking of starting a poker night, maybe once a month. Thought maybe you could use some of your newfound fame to invite some executive types."

"Can I assume that one of those executives wears glasses and enjoys brightly colored perfectly tailored suits?"

Lucas shrugs, but I know his tells by now. "If a beautiful, fashionable man should so happen to find his way into my poker night, I'm not gonna complain."

I wink at my new friend. "You got it. I'm sure you've already got my phone number. Send me the date and time, and I'll make it happen."

"It's a deal."

We shake hands, and I make my way back to the penthouse.

Rand is there to greet me. "That didn't take long."

"This building is a one-stop shop for executives and mobsters. Pretty convenient if you ask me."

"What did you find?"

"Oh, nothing. But I can pretty much bet that nothing will come of the video, and the blackmail request will simply disappear."

Rand's eyebrows meet in the middle. "Do I want to know?"

I shake my head. "It's not that bad, really. Just turns out that Luca Stefano needs a friend, and I think I can be that friend. In a real way. And sometime in the next month, we're going to a poker game at Luca's place. He wants me to invite some executive types."

"So...Ford?"

I grin. "Yep."

"I'm going to invite Sherry too."

"Yeah? Maybe you should put her on the board too."

"Not a bad idea." Rand chuckles to himself. "My life is very strange. I got taken down by a mobster, and now I'm friends with them."

"Not much of a difference from the CEO crowd, is it?"

"That's not true. Most CEOs are assholes."

31

RAND

IT'S BEEN two days since the pictures came out, and I'm waiting in the foyer, pacing anxiously. After a small eternity, the doors open and Joe steps into the space.

"Well?" I ask, terrified of his answer.

"Luca and his guys took care of it. There's no more video, and all future threats have been squashed."

"Are you kidding? Oh my God," I say, wrapping my arms around him. "That is such a fucking relief. I still have to handle the company, but at least we won't have this hanging over our heads anymore."

He kisses my forehead. "The company will probably be less of a problem than you think. I know you're worried about how the employees are taking it, but I think we forgot that we've just been ourselves this whole time. A lot of people had already figured it out, and since we're gay, they don't want to be seen as bigoted. So... yay for progress?"

I let out a long breath. "I'll take it. But I still want to address the company at some point."

"Of course. But I don't think we have to approach it like an apology. I think we get to approach it the way we wanted to. This is who we are. We love each other. And we want to make the company better together."

I smile and kiss him. "But that's not it, though, is it?"

Joe shakes his head, his face grave. "I didn't just ask Luca to find out who took the pictures. I needed him to find out who footed the bill. It took a while to get through the layers of obfuscation between the guy who flew the drone and the one who paid for it."

"But they know?"

I nod. "It's preliminary, but Luca is confident in his sources. And you're not going to like it."

My heart sinks in my chest. I know the answer before he gives it.

"My father."

He nods.

I knew there would be a price to pay for turning the board against him.

More than that, I did what Joe suggested and started hanging out with my mom. I quickly realized I didn't really know her at all, including the fact that she is deeply unhappy and my father has been essentially blackmailing her to stay in the marriage.

She had an affair, and he had her followed. There are pictures and videos, and if she divorces him, he will release them.

So, yeah. It's not a surprise at all.

"I'm so sorry, baby. Guys this rich, you gotta go over after their source of power. So, once he's got everything, I've asked Luca to relay a message to your father."

"And that was...?"

"Retire or else."

"Do I want to know what the '*or else*' is?"

"It'd be better if you didn't. I asked Luca to look into your mom's situation as well, and that's been handled too."

I lean into him. He's so protective of everyone in our small circle of friends and family, and it surprises me even less that he's taken care of my mom. "Wow," I joke, "I'm beginning to think that having a mob friend is almost as helpful as having a billionaire boyfriend."

Joe shrugs, smiling as he holds me. "I've got both, and I gotta say, it's a nice balance."

"Yeah, but you like your boyfriend better, don't you?"

"Only because you won't put a bullet in my head if I command you to lick my toes."

"True."

Joe cups my face, still looking concerned. "I know we're joking around now, but this was really serious. How are you doing?"

"Honestly, it feels like I'll finally be able to cut out the last of the necrotic tissue from Wolfe Athletics. My father has only been a hindrance these last several weeks. He's not about actually winning anything or making anything better. He just wants other people to lose, and I don't have any use for that kind of small-mindedness. Not anymore."

"You do have use for me though, right?" Joe asks, grinning as he takes my hand.

I thread my fingers through his, loving the way this small gesture makes my heart speed up. "You, Joe, are my most valuable asset. I could lose every penny, but if I still had you, I'd be the richest man in the world."

32

JOE

RAND SHIFTS uncomfortably right outside of Luca's door. "Should it freak me out that I'm a thirty-second elevator ride from Manhattan's most dangerous mobster?"

I scrunch my nose. "He's a kitten. Don't worry about it."

"Sure. I dare you to call him a kitten to his face."

"Somebody calling me a kitten?" Luca asks, opening the door with a broad grin.

"Well, not Joe, that's for sure," Rand jokes.

I raise my brow at my sweet, clueless boyfriend. "Did you just joke around with Manhattan's most dangerous mobster?"

Rand shrugs. "I'm not the one who called him a kitten."

Luca laughs, and it's genuine. "You two crack me up. Come on in," he says, guiding us through to his stylish living room.

Rand makes a beeline for his friend, Mads, who's already sitting on the couch, looking fascinated and shy. He hops up and gives Rand a hug, then smiles up at me. Sherry is also already here, and she's standing with Hopper, laughing like they're old friends as she smacks his arm.

Oh God. That's...fuck, those two are a dangerous combination.

Luca taps my shoulder, and I follow him into the kitchen.

"You have an update for me?" I ask, eyeballing his pasta maker. Mobsters have the best toys.

"He's tricky, that Wolfe Sr., but we finally got everything. He still dragging his feet on the retirement?"

I shake my head. "No. His retirement and divorce documents were filed on the same day. And hey, Rand's already cut his father off, so I'd rather not bring it up tonight."

"Agreed. You know, it's nice that you protect your man like that. You've got a good relationship."

"I do. I'm a lucky man."

Luca's smile is wistful. "You're both lucky. And tell you what, I'll keep the files, and if you need them at any point, let me know."

"Will do. Thanks for taking care of that, Luca. Means a lot."

He shrugs and gives me a quick hug. "Happy to take care of a friend."

We exit the kitchen, and I immediately run into Rand and his friend, who seems to be eyeballing Edgerton. Barely able to rip his attention from the stern man, he holds out his hand to me. "I don't think we've ever officially met. I'm Mads."

"Joe. It's wonderful to meet you. Rand says a lot of good things."

"Lies," he jokes. Turning to Rand, Mads half-whispers, "So, the guy at the bar—that's Edgerton?"

We follow his line of sight and nod. Mads' sparkling brown eyes widen appreciatively. "He's quite *something*, isn't he?"

"Wait, you haven't met him yet?" Rand asks, concerned.

Mads grimaces. "Haven't had the time."

Rand clears his throat and loudly asks, "But what about your *stalker*?"

Mads smacks his arm as Edgerton approaches us. "Rand, did you just say that you have a stalker?"

Rand shakes his head and points at Mads. "He was supposed to call you weeks ago."

Mads glares at Rand then turns to Edgerton. "He's being dramatic. It's mostly online harassment with some light, probably imagined real-world stalking."

Edgerton goes to open his mouth, but Mads holds up his hands. "I'm here to play poker, and I'd rather not talk about it. No stalkers, no technology, no TrackerTech, just me wiping the floor with you guys as I flex my mad poker skills."

Luca and Edgerton share a look. "You're with TrackerTech?"

Mads sticks out his hand. "CEO and founder."

Luca shakes it and sends Edgerton another look. "We'll enjoy poker tonight, but I'm going to need your card. I've got a business proposition for you."

Mads swallows and proffers his card. Edgerton steps in and takes it from him, tucking it away in his wallet.

Rand leans in. "Did you just see what I saw?"

I shrug, laughing to myself. "I don't know. But I think that stalker guy is about to have a real bad day."

"*Good.*"

We all top off our adult beverages and join Luca in the surprisingly opulent library, just off the living room. He scans the room and checks his watch, looking disappointed.

I nudge him, hoping to get him back to the loose version we saw earlier.

"I think Ford had a thing. He's just running late."

He chuckles, some of the disappointment fading from his expression. "I'm sure you're right."

Hopper appears next to us out of thin air. "Ford's calendar indicates that he's not prone to backing out of commitments. I think Joe's right on this one," he says, popping a crab fritter in his mouth.

Luca smacks his arm. "Jesus, Hopper. What did I say about sidling up next to me like that?"

Hopper looks contrite, and I'll be honest...it's scary as fuck.

"Sorry, brother. Just wanted to let you know that I'm heading out."

Luca rolls his eyes and hugs Hopper with a kiss to his temple. "Playing cat and mouse with your RICO agent tonight?"

Hopper rocks back, grinning from ear to ear.

Scratch what I said earlier. *This* is way more horrifying than his contrition face.

"I'm still trying to figure out if I'm going to let him see me or not. Might flip a coin."

"Brother, please remember our deal. You can have your plaything, but you cannot compromise yourself. I don't want to go after an officer of the law, but if he tries to arrest you, I will kill him. Okay?"

Hopper gives Luca a crisp salute and sends Sherry a funny little wave before leaving the party to the rest of us.

Luca turns to me, shaking his head. "I love my brother to death, but that man ain't right."

A laugh escapes my lips. "Wait, he's actually your brother?"

Luca shrugs. "One of many, I'm sure. My father was indiscriminate that way."

"Did you two grow up together?"

"No. About ten years ago, I started snooping through my father's finances. In addition to his illegal enterprises, I found some old child support payments and had Anthony follow up on them. He found Hopper in a halfway house."

Anthony—Edgerton—shifts. I'm guessing it wasn't a good situation.

"And you just brought him home?"

Luca's brow is quizzical. "Why wouldn't I? He's family. Why should I get the good life while he gets the short end of the stick?"

I think to my family, my brother, who hated me regardless. And to the countless other half-siblings I don't know at all. "You're a good man, Luca Stefano."

"Yeah, keep that under your hat, okay? I have a reputation to maintain."

"Noted."

We get started on the first round of poker, and Mads does, in fact, wipe the floor with us, though Sherry wins some kind of side bet with Luca. The conversation is flowing and we're topping off our beverages when there's a knock at the door.

Luca gets up to answer it, and Edgerton's jaw tenses. I'm guessing he'd rather be the one to open the door, but I doubt that's an argument he'd win.

"Ford," Luca says. We don't have a clear view of the front door, but the smile in his voice is unmissable. "I'm so glad you made it."

"Oh, uh, me too. I got waylaid in a meeting but didn't want to miss the game. And the company. Of course."

They join us in the library, and Ford startles when he sees the participants. He comes right up to Sherry, Rand, and me. "It's nice to see familiar faces here. And Mads! What're you doing here?"

"I'm cleaning up like a mobster in here." He grimaces and looks around the room, sheepish. "Uh...no offense."

Luca's quiet for a second, his eyes glinting with amusement. Mads looks like he's about to stroke out, and Ford is eyeballing the exit. I catch Edgerton's expression, and he seems like he's just about to break.

Mads' voice shakes as he continues, "No, really, guys. I'm cool. I didn't mean anything by it. Please don't, like, fit me with concrete shoes and throw me in the river or anything."

Luca tosses his head back, laughing from deep within his belly, then Edgerton, of all people, joins him. I follow suit because that shit is funny and because I don't know if anyone's ever seen

Edgerton laugh. Eventually, the billionaires unclench and join in, with Mads pretending to pass out on Edgerton's shoulder.

"It's a good thing I'm late then," Ford says, grinning widely. "Mads, buddy, you're about to lose, big time."

"Whatever, Crypto King. I'm the poker night champ."

"Yeah, well, I made half a billion dollars last year running the numbers. And cards are all about the numbers." Ford cracks his knuckles. "Prepare to have your asses handed to you."

The threat is somewhat diminished by his magenta skinny jeans, bright-green argyle sweater, and black horn-rimmed Ray-Bans, but I'm pretty sure everyone at this table likes a challenge. Luca, especially.

He and Edgerton exchange another look, and Rand leans into me again. "I don't know what's going on, babe, but I think our friend group just got really, really interesting."

I kiss his forehead, watching it all play out. No way in hell could I have guessed this is where we'd end up, but I wouldn't change it for the world.

EPILOGUE

JOE - SIX MONTHS LATER

I WALK IN JUST before Rand starts off the weekly board meeting.

Catching my eye, he glares at me, shifting uncomfortably. I've got him fitted with a plug, and he's had a hint of a blush all day long. God, he's never more beautiful than when he's blushing for me.

He joins me at the coffee station, gritting through his teeth, "You didn't tell me I would be fighting a hard-on all day."

I glance down at his stupidly expensive blue jeans. There's a little fluffing there, to be sure, but nothing obscene. "Consider yourself lucky that I left the remote control at home."

He snarls a little and pulls his T-shirt down over his crotch. He acts like he hates these little minor humiliations, but I know he loves them. In fact, he started liking the brief shock of the laser treatments so much that we started adding a little electro-stimulation into our play.

The plug he's wearing has a port that I can snap a little TENS unit into. This morning, I woke him up with a slimmer version, ensuring it was right up against his prostate before turning it on. I made him keep his hands to his sides as I turned up the power. Using a little wand, I zapped at his nipples mercilessly. He protested mightily, but then came buckets just a few moments later, hands-free.

Refocusing on the room, I'm filled with pride at what we've done here. After Wolfe Sr. retired, three more resigned in protest. We replaced them with four employees—Sherry, a marketing team lead, the director of product manufacturing, and a whip-smart employee from the customer service division.

Our conversations haven't always been easy, but it's educational to watch as people begin to understand how their decisions impact profitability and how prioritizing profitability over people impacts quality of life. We rarely totally agree on any one thing, but the choices we're making have made Wolfe Athletics one of the best places to work.

And today I have a surprise for Rand.

When we take a five-minute break at the top of the hour, Sherry sneaks in the surprise. Rand comes back from the restroom and stops in the doorway. Our customer support wunderkind accidentally runs into the back of him, and it's a bit of a comedy of errors for a few seconds while they untangle.

"Weston?" Rand asks, his face lighting up. Weston Eanes, world-class footballer and genuine good guy, is in our boardroom.

"I've been talking with Joe here, and if the board is amenable, I would love to represent Wolfe Athletics again. I love what you've done, and I love that you started listening to employees instead of doubling down. That's what we need. Not perfect leadership, but leadership willing to listen and have vision."

Rand, who isn't one for public displays of affection, looks at me, and I know I'm going to be getting some tonight. He shakes his head, reading me like a book, then leans in and plants a big kiss on my cheek.

"Keep it in your pants, you two," Sherry says, laughter in her eyes.

Weston turns to Sherry. "Are they always like this?"

She rolls her eyes and links arms with him. "You have no idea."

RAND

Standing on a brightly lit stage, I take a moment to look out over the hundreds of professionals, all of whom are trying to do leadership right. It's the Manhattan Ted X conference, and I'm the keynote.

The name of the talk is *Going from Alpha to a True Leader*, and the auditorium is packed with all kinds of familiar faces from business, entertainment, and sports.

Most importantly are Joe, my mom, and Mads, sitting in the front row. Edgerton sits directly behind Mads, but he's not here to listen to me. The stalker has escalated, and while Mads looks awfully proud of me, new worry creases his eyes. Worry that's never been there before.

I'm also surprised to spy Luca and Hopper near the back. As it happens, Luca is a good neighbor. We love our poker nights at his place and, in turn, we've invited him to pasta and pool time on several occasions. He even bought us a thoughtful anniversary gift, a fancy pasta maker like the one in his kitchen.

Now that I understand a bit more about how he operates business, I'm far less nervous around him. Sometimes Ford will join us, but only as a friend, despite Luca's continued interest. He keeps a respectful distance, and Ford keeps nibbling around the edges.

Refocusing on the audience, who've been rapt as I went through the same five bullet points that Joe presented to the board a year ago, I put the final words on my keynote speech.

"I think the biggest surprise in this whole experience is how much I was holding myself back. Now, I'm a billionaire, so there's no need to feel sorry for me in the slightest. But when I look back on that man who thought there was only one way to be, I feel sad for him.

"I mean, what a small box to fit oneself into. One of the things I learned from Joe, my beloved, sitting in the front row"—I pause, letting the audience clap for him—"is that he always had a true north inside of him and, despite the odds, he followed that call. When something didn't resonate, he put up both middle fingers and walked right out the door."

"It was just the one middle finger," Joe shouts. "Don't be dramatic."

The audience laughs, everyone well familiar with our infamous video.

I pause. "He's right, of course, but most of the people in this audience are of significant means. And yet, if I were to ask for a show of hands for everyone who's *genuinely* happy, I wouldn't get very many hands, now would I?"

The shaking heads in the audience tell me I'm on the right track. "What's interesting about your reaction is that a *mobster* once told me that keeping his employees happy and safe meant he had better eyes on his holdings. And I want you to imagine that a sex worker in this man's employ is more satisfied and fulfilled than most of you in this room. And that her employer is more profitable and less, you know, dead, because of it."

Despite a few titters, there's an uncomfortable silence that fills the room. I quiet my voice, and people start leaning forward.

"I've seen the online forums leading up to the conference, and most of you are here because of how quickly Wolfe Athletics recovered from our sharp dive. But I don't think we ever recovered."

The hushed sound of surprise makes me smile. "We didn't *recover*. We started *thriving*. Wolfe Athletics is hitting heights and reaching numbers that we could have never imagined had we stayed inside that narrow-minded box, and taking care of the employees responsible for our wild success is how we did it.

"So I invite you to join me out here. Because the view is spectacular."

There's a half-second of silence before the audience rises, clapping and cheering. Once again, I'm struck by that solid wall of emotion. I look over at Joe, and he's clapping and whistling, pride shining in his face.

"Thank you so much, everyone. I know we have a limited time with these talks, but I did set aside a few minutes for the man himself to come up so we can give credit where credit is due. Joe, you have a few words for us?"

Joe grins and jogs up on the stage, looking beautiful and dangerous in a suit, as always.

"You know, the first thing we did when we really began to implement a new way of doing things was stop wearing suits, so it's weird to wear one now."

"But you look so handsome in a suit," I say, kissing his cheek in front of everyone, enjoying the *awws* and laughter.

He pops his lapels. "I do look good in a suit. And you know what? I enjoy my jeans and T-shirt lifestyle, but there are times when only a bespoke tailored suit will do."

"That's true."

He grins, a dangerous glint in his eye. "For instance, if I've been given a second chance to teach you about the structure of a wolf pack in front of a large group of people, I need to look sharp while doing it."

"Not this again," I say, dramatically touching my wrist to my forehead as the audience laughs.

"Oh, absolutely this again." Joe takes my hand, kissing my knuckles. We get a little lost staring into each other's eyes until a new set of *awws* shakes us from our reverie. Winking at me, he asks the audience, "Do you wanna know what my favorite wolf fact is?"

The audience claps, and Joe turns to me, his eyes shiny. "Wolves mate for life."

THE AUDIENCE GASPS, picking up more quickly than I do on what's happening. Suddenly, Joe is on one knee, and there's a ring in his hand.

"We still disagree on how much you spoil me, but I think we'll always agree on how much we love each other. And God, I'd love it if you gave me one more chance to wear a suit for you. Will you marry me?"

Pretending that my heart isn't about to gallop out of my chest, I tap my chin and face the audience. "What do you think?"

The result is laughter and shouts of "Say yes!" and "I'll marry him if you don't!"

I glare at the guy who said that last one, then look down on my man, on this ex-mobster with a heart of gold, and wonder how I ever got so lucky.

"Of course I'll marry you," I say, reaching into my breast pocket to withdraw a ring of my own. "That was my plan the entire time."

Joe stands, his laughter a joyful sound throughout the auditorium, and we exchange rings, kissing and hugging each other, crying like idiots. We face the audience with both rings on our hands, each of us giving an uncoordinated bow.

I can pick out Mads' whistle from the crowd, and when I look up to our friends in the back, Luca catches my eye and taps his chest. Joe laughs as Hopper bounces on his heels, grinning from ear to ear as he raises his hands in triumph.

When he catches us looking, Hopper points just over his

shoulder to a man who, from this distance, looks to be in sharp glasses and a cheap suit.

"Oh my God, is that the RICO agent?" I hiss-whisper into Joe's ear.

Joe's chuckle is deep and resonant. "Yep."

Hopper looks back and excitedly waves to the harried-looking man, whose shoulders drop. Shaking his head, he makes his way out of the auditorium. Hopper turns back around and beams at us across the space, giving us one of his double-fisted cheers.

Laughing, Joe turns to me and gives me a proper kiss. I lose myself in it until the shouts and cheers from the audience bring me back to the present. After basking in the celebration for another moment, Joe turns to me, hand outstretched.

Smiling, I take his hand, and we walk offstage together.

Time to begin the rest of our lives.

THANK YOU FOR READING EXTRADITION!

Next up: Edgerton and Mads' story, Protection!

Enjoying the #murderswoon? Check out my Wrecked Guardians series!

ACKNOWLEDGMENTS

To Abbie: This is a scary thing, writing a book based on a TikTok plot bunny, and you jumped off the cliff right alongside me. Your confidence never wavered, even as this grew into a whole-ass series. I'm so grateful for your input and support, always.

To Drew: I enjoyed the hell out of your notes. They brought the sex scenes to a whole new level. *chef's kiss*

To Janine and Charity: Thank you for letting me give y'all the slightly underbaked cookie version of this book. I knew I had something special, and your direct, kind feedback helped me make this into the book I knew it could be. <3

To Courtney S.: Thank you so much for teaching me to believe in this dream I'm following.

ABOUT THE AUTHOR

Hi there! I write contemporary gay romance, which is to say I curse way too much, drink exactly the right amount of red wine, and sleep far too little. I'm also lucky enough to live in Central Texas with my wife and our dogs, where the astonishing diversity of humans and landscapes and tattoo shops serve as my muse.

Check out my Facebook reader group, <u>The Fox Den</u>, for giveaways, first-look cover reveals, and more, and follow me on Amazon to be notified of new releases by email.

ALSO BY KELLY FOX

SERIES

Wrecked

Guardians

Rebel Sky Ranch

Mobsters+Billionaires

Wild Heart Ranch

Orpheum Avenue

STAND-ALONE NOVELLAS

Summer Makeover

Bee Cave Magic

Texas Detour

Roots and Sky

Liar's Gambit

-

FREEBIES

https://www.authorkellyfox.com/freebies

Printed in Great Britain
by Amazon

38063864R00175